Lost Eden

G.P. Ching

Carpe Luna Publishing

Lost Eden: The Soulkeepers Series, Book 5
Copyright © G.P. Ching 2013
Published by Carpe Luna, Ltd., P.O. Box 5932, Bloomington, IL 61701
www.carpeluna.com

ISBN: 978-1-940675-09-1

Cover art by Steven Novak.
www.novakillustration.com

Formatting by Polgarus Studio.
www.polgarusstudio.com

v.3.5

*Dedicated to those who do what's right
when no one is watching.*

Books by G.P. Ching

The Soulkeepers Series

The Soulkeepers, Book 1
Weaving Destiny, Book 2
Return to Eden, Book 3
Soul Catcher, Book 4
Lost Eden, Book 5
The Last Soulkeeper, Book 6

The Grounded Trilogy

Grounded, Book 1
Charged, Book 2 (Coming Soon)
Wired, Book 3 (Coming Soon)

Contents

Chapter 1
Consequences

Balance. All life, the world's very existence, hinged on perfect balance. Rain and drought, work and play, love and hate, good and evil, each in measured quantities, rising and falling in a constant struggle for equilibrium. Balance bolstered the natural order of things, and Fatima's job was to record it all. Record, but not change.

As Fatima, or Fate to those who would call her by her title, stood barefoot on packed dirt, her eight arms weaving the fabric of human destiny, she carried a heavy weight within her bosom. She bent her knees to counteract the encumbrance of the yards of shimmering cloth made by her hand, but the heavy burden of a secret bothered her most. Fatima had broken the rules—rules put in place to maintain balance. She'd taken an action, saved a boy named Dane from certain death by giving him a sip of water. A simple, compassionate gesture meant only to counteract the devil's unjust deeds.

But small deeds could have big consequences.

In the process of saving Dane, she'd made him a Soulkeeper. Fate understood the implications all too well. You did not drop a pebble into a sacred pool without causing ripples. All she had to do was read this particular stretch of fabric emerging from her hands—red, pink, and yellow threads, bright and hot colors—that spoke of increased metaphysical activity on Earth. It stung her fingers. Things were heating up down below. How much had her crime cost humanity? She crumpled her forehead and wove faster to alleviate the burn.

Movement caught her eye near the bolts behind her. Without pausing her work, she twisted her neck and shuffled her feet to see who it was. Perhaps Malini was back from Nod with news of the Soulkeepers' latest mission. For a moment, she was blinded by the sparkle from the fabric, the woven destinies of billions of souls, their light seeming to collect at the center of the room. Like a mirror, it reflected her image back at her, sleek black hair, smooth russet skin, graceful limbs, and eyes…

Fate halted her weaving. Her lips parted. Her reflection did not share her black eyes or the dancing lights of souls within them. The reflection's eyes were hazel, as Fatima's had been when she was human. Other differences prevailed. The image did not bear the burden of her weaving or the frown that Fatima was sure she wore now. This reflection was a perfect Fate.

Light. Warmth. Joy. Fatima's doppelganger exuded peace and love. When she realized who had come to see her, she put aside her work and dropped to her knees, both honored and terrified by the presence before her. As a kindness, God always took the form of the person present, a concession meant to keep the soul from going mad.

"M-my lord, to what do I owe the honor of your visit?" Fatima stuttered.

"Rise. We have only moments. I've come to warn you."

Fatima scrambled to her feet, unable to take her eyes off the beauty of the being in her own image who floated to her side.

"There is sin between us, Fatima. I feel a blockage, an invisible wall, keeping me from connecting with you. Tell me so we can move beyond it." God moved closer and met her eyes.

"When Lucifer freed Dane from Hell, he left him for dead. Abigail delivered his body to the gate of Eden. She didn't know any better. In her fallen condition, she'd never been allowed close enough to learn he'd be cast out. The injustice of it all would have tipped the balance in Lucifer's favor. I had to do something. I visited the boat and gave the boy the living water to drink."

"You took his destiny into your own hands." God widened her eyes.

"Yes."

"And your actions produced greater consequences than his admission to Eden."

"He became a Soulkeeper."

God turned away then, clasping her hands behind her back. Fatima shuddered at the elimination of the light and warmth of her attention. "Not just a Soulkeeper, Fatima. Dane's power, along with his personal characteristics, allowed him to slay over a thousand Watchers in Nod. He broke the terms of my compact with Lucifer."

"I don't understand."

"Nod is off-limits to Soulkeepers as the In Between is off-limits to Watchers. He will demand a consequence for the infraction."

"But ... but ... he broke the compact first! Watchers live among men even now, permanently! They taint the water. He'd planned to use Cheveyo to destroy Eden. Not to mention, Auriel took Malini and Dane to Nod in the first place. The two Soulkeepers simply fought their way out."

God's still, small voice was in direct contrast to Fate's panicked one. "All valid points, Fatima, but you must see how your actions have forced my hand."

Fatima did see. The rules existed for a reason. Even though other immortals had taken similar actions to keep Lucifer at bay, it didn't excuse her. She'd given the devil an opening, and surely it was just a matter of time before he took full advantage. She fell on her knees again, tears forming in her black eyes. "Please forgive me. Tell me what I can do to make this right."

With a smile that spread a tangible joy across the villa, God turned back to Fate and motioned for her to rise. "All is forgiven, Dear One, but now we must manage the consequences, and unfortunately the cure for the world's ills will be more than either you or any of the immortals can achieve."

As Fatima rose from the dirt, she noticed a patch of black mold where the ceiling met the front wall in the upper corner of her stucco manse. Her home was a product of her consciousness, constructed of her thoughts and will, but this was not hers. She did not invite the darkness. This was something other, something dangerous. The black mold spread down the corner of the wall to the floor, and then mushroomed, reproducing to the size of a grapefruit, a bowling ball, a bush. Fatima backed away, taking her place behind God, who held Her ground faithfully.

With a final sprout of growth, the black fuzz paled and hardened, and a man in a shiny gray business suit stepped from the darkness. His blond curls set off his lapis eyes, and the perfect smile he flashed took Fatima's breath away. But his expression was icy and his posture arrogant. *Lucifer.*

"I see you are expecting me," he rasped. His voice held the sizzle of Hell and his breath the hint of brimstone. Fatima covered her mouth and nose with her hand.

"Say what you came to say," God said. Her glow increased, pressing his darkness back toward the wall.

He blinked rapidly, and then shifted his eyes downward, smoothing his perfectly tailored suit. "I demand a consequence."

"State your reasoning."

"Your immortal has broken the law. She has created a Soulkeeper of her own will, and disrupted the balance by sending that soul to attack me in my own dominion."

"Were you not also to blame, Lucifer? Did you not break our agreement first? Even now, I sense your minions on Earth, in clear violation."

He gave a half smile and slid his hands into his pockets, pacing toward the archway to the veranda. "No. I did nothing of the sort."

"You lie."

"Yes, I do. It is my nature, and as such, it should be expected. I am entitled to a consequence, and I will not back down until I have my just due."

God approached him, the air crackling with her presence. The back of Lucifer's head glowed brassy in her light. "Very well. What is your suggested price?"

"My price is Fate. She has been in her position far too long. I will choose her replacement, and she will step down."

"No!" Fatima yelled, her hands flying to cover her foolhardy mouth. Why had she allowed her true feelings to show? Now he'd be even more likely to use those feelings against her.

He turned the force of his stare on her, laughing through a toothy half smile. "Oh yes, Fatima. Perhaps, I will not only choose your replacement but take your soul as my own." In a blink, he was in her face, his hand on the small of her back. Her skin squirmed beneath his touch. "You are a beautiful sinner. Hell could use an ornament such as you."

"Let her go." A wash of cool light poured through the room, and Lucifer retreated, joints folding unnaturally in his haste for the shadows. "The Watchers who reside on Earth negate your ability to make such a demand. You are in breach of the law, Lucifer. You must return your minions to Nod or Hell."

"Or what?" Lucifer carefully slithered into the shadow of a bolt of fabric where his eyes could open fully.

"Or the compact is rendered null and void."

"War." The word rolled off his tongue, smooth as melted butter.

God rubbed her chin. "As ever, you are cunning, Lucifer, and perhaps it is time that your superior intelligence is rewarded." She circled right, eyeing him from head to toe as she passed the upright bolts of woven human history. "Instead of exacting your revenge on a peasant girl turned Fate, would you consider a wager for something more?"

"More?" Lucifer narrowed his eyes and licked his lips. His Adam's apple bobbed as he swallowed again and again, salivating at the thought of *more*.

"Our covenant is ancient and worthless, but human hearts must be ruled. Do you agree it is time for a new covenant?"

Lucifer rubbed his hands together. "How will the terms be decided?"

"By human hearts." God snapped her fingers. "If you will follow me outside, I will propose a change."

Fatima and Lucifer trailed the supreme deity out onto the veranda and then into Fate's yard. Above the swell of a grassy green knoll at the back of her territory, an angel descended from the heavens. A blinding aura surrounded the winged woman, her dark hair rippling against her white toga-like dress. When her toes touched down, her flesh hardened from the feet up, white marble swallowing her to the tips of her outstretched wings. The angel looked familiar to Fate, like Themis, a human depiction of justice embodied, only this living statue had wings. Blindfolded, the angel held scales in one hand and a crystal model of Earth in the other.

"We need witnesses." Another snap of God's fingers and Henry and Mara appeared beside Fate, flustered and confused. When they saw the second Fatima, realization dawned slowly, confusion followed by terror. They fell to their knees in the grass.

"Rise, Mara. Rise, Henry. We need your help."

Henry nodded, staggering to his feet. Mara reached for his hand, and he helped her stand.

"Lucifer," God said, turning her full attention on the walking stain on the countryside that was the devil. "This scorekeeper holds in her hand a model of the world. Stare into the depths of this crystal, and tell me what you see."

Lucifer approached cautiously and stared into the translucent orb. "Pinpoints of light and darkness."

"You see human hearts. Some are aligned with me, appearing as points of light, and some are aligned with you, appearing as points of darkness. As you can see, at the moment, the scales are slightly tipped in your favor." God flourished her hand in front of the dark plate of the left side of the scale.

"They appear to be. Get to the point, Oppressor. What is your wager?"

"First, we abolish the compact."

Fate, Time, and Death gasped at the thought. Fatima reached for Mara's free hand, her other firmly in Henry's grip. All three immortals stood connected in their horror. Fatima trusted God, but this was terrifying. None of them had lived in a world without an agreement between good and evil. Her stomach twisted. Lucifer already had the advantage. The scales tipped in his favor. Without the compact, what would keep him at bay?

"And then?" Lucifer prompted.

"We compete for the hearts of men," God said.

Lucifer narrowed his eyes against her light. "Compete how?"

"You release six temptations unto the world, and I release six gifts." She held out her hand toward the statue. "The scorekeeper will record human alignment with good or evil. When the last gift or temptation has come to pass, the challenge will be over and whomever has won the most souls will rule Earth."

"And the other?"

"Banished from contact with humanity for one thousand years. Hark, Lucifer, there will be no cheating this banishment. Should you lose, you will be sealed within Hell for the entire epoch."

Lucifer began to pace in front of the scorekeeper, checked her crystal, and then checked again. "It's a trick. You would not risk so many souls."

"No trick. Six temptations verses six gifts. You have the advantage. A few of your minions are already living among men, men they've influenced to do your will."

"If the compact is dissolved, all of my Watchers can remain above ground?"

"Of course! If the compact is no more, they can journey wherever they wish."

Lucifer tilted his chin up and smiled viciously. "What's the catch?"

"No catch. But the Watchers are still bound by the natural order of things. The sun will dull their powers. The night will strengthen them."

"They will kill to remain strong."

"No compact. No rules."

"Besides the natural laws," Lucifer lamented.

"Yes. All humans have free will. Earth's natural resources have limits. Sunlight gives my souls an advantage, darkness, yours. I can be everywhere at once; you can only be in one place at a time. This is how it has always been and always will be."

Lucifer gave a small, almost imperceptible nod of agreement.

"And one more thing, humans must choose you of their free will. I know you've poisoned the water. Influenced humans are incapable of choosing. They are merely your puppets. If we are to do this, any souls you or your Watchers influence will be deemed neutral."

Lucifer scowled. "Only six temptations and no influencing free will? *Bah.*"

"Only six gifts and you already have the advantage."

While Fatima held her breath, Lucifer stared at the scales, slightly tipped in his favor. She couldn't decide which was worse, a Fate chosen by Lucifer or the potential to have a world ruled by him. The devil seemed to be weighing his options.

"Are you afraid, Lucifer? Should I take your hesitation as an admission of my greater power?" God's voice echoed with a deep hollow tenor that didn't fit her current appearance.

Lucifer growled, his face reddened with anger. "I am the more powerful! I accept your challenge and claim the right to go first. Do you agree?"

God beamed, flooding the hillside with light. "I do agree." She offered her right hand. "In the presence of these three witnesses, the challenge for human souls begins now. Winner take all for one thousand years."

"Agreed." Lucifer slapped his hand into God's. The connection created a sonic boom that flattened Fatima and the other immortals to the grass. The sound rippled outward, visible in the blue sky of the In Between, and a shockwave plowed through the cells of her body. *No*, she thought, *not just my body but also my weaving.* The future had changed. The universe had changed. She was witness to an agreement that might end life as she knew it.

God retracted her hand. She turned toward the crystal Earth in the scorekeeper's grip. "The world awaits you, Lucifer."

He backed up a few steps, a wicked laugh bubbling from deep within. "This is going to be fun." He came apart in a rush of black fog that passed over them and straight into the villa. *Where is he going?*

Fatima jolted at a strange and painful sensation in her abdomen. A thread had been plucked from her body and her weaving. Frantically, she patted her stomach, retrieving her work from deep within. He'd taken something from her. When he'd blown out of the In Between, he'd taken *someone.* Yes, that was it. A soul was missing. But who? What human being was important enough to steal from the fabric of history?

"You know who," God said as she broke apart and blended into the light.

Fatima scrambled to her feet, Mara and Henry cursing at her side in their own pursuit of vertical. One by one they stepped to the scorekeeper and watched the light and the dark dance within the globe.

"Who did he take, Fatima?" Henry asked.

"I can't be certain. There are so many souls."

"You know," Mara said. "She said you know."

Fatima swallowed and raised a hand to the base of her neck. "There is only one person I can think of who is a constant reminder of Lucifer's failures. She is the only one who has denied him time and time again. Her life is a testament to God's grace and mercy."

Henry glanced at Mara, who looked off into space as if reading the stars. The immortals said the name together, in perfect unison. "Abigail."

Chapter 2
Abigail

D r. Abigail Silva-Newman tried to be careful. After all, the people of Paris believed her to be in California, not emerging from a trapdoor in the back room of the Laudners' flower shop. She listened for any sign of activity above her before turning the crank to open the passageway and slipping silently onto the marble floor. As she resealed the entryway to Eden, she heard voices out front, John Laudner and Stephanie Westcott, something about flowers for a barn dance.

Hastily, she tiptoed to the delivery entrance, peering out the small square window in the door to check that the alley was clear. With no one in sight, she cracked the door and stealthily crept behind the delivery van and then the dumpster. Curse this human form, so vulnerable. In her days as a fallen angel, she would simply twist into shadow and deliver herself where she wanted to go through a channel of darkness. Getting there one step at a time was nothing short of tedious. Still, she wouldn't have given up her humanity for any price. Not after waiting ten thousand years to obtain it.

But she had to go. Malini needed her. All of the Soulkeepers needed her. When Jacob said Malini and Dane were back from Nod but needed help, she'd assumed the mission to Arizona to bring them home would be quick work. With hardly a word of explanation, all of the Soulkeepers had left Eden to assist. Only, Malini's call to Abigail over Warwick's blue stone seemed desperate. Something had gone horribly wrong with the rescue mission, and Abigail was the only one left to save them. Well, aside from Gideon, and she wasn't about to place her beloved's life at risk.

On her toes, Abigail rounded the corner of the building, and thanked the heavens for what she saw. Parked on the corner of Asher and Main Street, Stephanie Westcott's scooter waited unattended, keys in the ignition. In any other city, the arrangement would have invited a theft, but as far as Abigail was aware, there'd never been a vehicle stolen in Paris despite the population's regular habit of leaving car doors unlocked with the keys inside. Who would steal it? Everyone trusted everyone else. They left the keys on purpose, in case some other citizen might need them in an emergency. Well, as a former citizen of Paris, she accepted Stephanie's hospitality.

Abigail tossed a leg over the seat and turned the key. The small motor revved to life and she pulled away from the curb, heading up Asher in the opposite direction of Main Street, a roundabout detour to Rural Route One.

"Hey!" Stephanie yelled from behind her.

She glanced back to see the girl whose life she once saved standing on the corner, waving her arms. Abigail didn't stop. She prayed that speed and distance would conceal her identity. Certainly, she was dressed differently than Stephanie would remember: blond hair in a ponytail, yoga pants, T-shirt, and an oversized belted sweater-coat that barely defended her against the fall chill. She'd return Stephanie's scooter eventually, but right now Abigail needed it more.

After an uneventful cruise up the rural road she once traveled regularly, Abigail abandoned the scooter at the edge of the maple grove that used to be hers. Across the street, the Laudners' cheery yellow Cape Cod hadn't changed since her days living here, but where her dark Victorian once stood rose a repainted version in pale tones with brightly colored flowers blooming in baskets outside the windows. The house was a bed and breakfast now.

Jogging into the trees, over the gently sloping terrain toward the place her back garden used to be, Abigail had a moment to think. Anxiety over the mission to Nod had left her careless, reactionary. Why had Malini wanted to meet *here* of all places? Surely if the Healer could come this far, she could make it to Eden. Much more likely this was a trap. Perhaps Lucifer had already captured the Soulkeepers and was luring her to her doom.

She halted, placed her hands on her hips, and tipped her face to take in the blazing red of the maple leaves above her. Rushing into this was a mistake. She needed a plan. Bending, she touched the hilt of the knife in her boot, the one weapon she'd brought from Eden. Would she be strong enough, fast enough, to face a Watcher in her human form?

Curse this mortal body, she would not. She should have thought this through before she left Eden, but her desire to help—no, to be *useful*—drove her toward impulsive behavior. Lucky for her, it wasn't too late to err on the side of caution. She turned and strode back toward the road and the scooter. She'd go back to Eden, get Gideon, and make a plan for recovering the Soulkeepers. There had to be a better way.

"Hello, Abigail." The velvet smooth voice lassoed her shoulders, stopping her short.

She turned to face her enemy. At first the man's attire, a double-breasted suit with Italian loafers, threw her. *Very human.* Then she noticed his eyes matched the deep navy blue, almost purple color of his tie. A Watcher, for sure. Human beings didn't have eyes that color or noses that straight. He twisted the gold, lion's head ring on his manicured finger.

Lucifer was the Lord of Illusions, and his followers boasted similar talents, but under it all, Abigail knew the Watcher's skin and blood were black as tar. "How is your illusion so strong during the day?" she spat nervously. Distraction was her only hope.

"Well fed."

"Who are you? I deserve to know who Lucifer sent for me."

"You don't remember me, Abigail? That hurts. We were once very close."

A deadly smile crossed his full lips, and he smoothed a hand over his meticulously styled black hair. Abigail tried to place his voice, but in her human form, all she could sense was the illusion. Worse, the smell of freshly baked cinnamon rolls had filled the maple grove. His sorcery drew her in, a fly to the spider's web. The smell triggered a memory of a long-ago day, before Lucifer had become jealous of God and led the Watchers to fall from grace.

This Watcher had chosen an illusion not far from his appearance as an angel. Abigail shook her head. Lucifer must be serious about her capture to send his right hand man. "Cord."

He took a step closer. "Good girl. I see your senses haven't completely dulled with your humanity. Now come. Lucifer is waiting."

Abigail took a step back, dropping into the fighting stance Lillian had taught her. She wasn't completely defenseless. She'd learned the martial arts basics Lillian insisted all of them learn. Cord took another step toward her, and she whipped her knife from her boot. "I think it's you who have lost your senses, Cord, if you think for a second I'm coming with you willingly."

Straightening his shirt at the cufflinks, he stepped even closer, so that her blade was mere inches from his chest. He arched a brow and looked down at her pitifully. "A knife, Abigail?" He chuckled.

She didn't waste time defending the virtues of the knife. With everything she had, she attempted to use the element of surprise to her advantage and stabbed underhanded at his gut. The knife cut through the suit jacket, but Cord's hand snatched her wrist before the blade could penetrate his flesh. Still, the point smoked ominously against his black skin.

"Ah!" Abigail squirmed under the pressure on her wrist bones. She kicked and clawed, pounded on Cords arms and chest. An attempt to sweep his legs at the knee failed miserably. Recovering, she kicked him as hard as she could in the balls.

He extended his arm. She was a moth dangling from his fingers by the wing. "From Eden I presume," he growled, staring at her useless knife. "This might have done some real damage if you weren't so humanly slow. Is that any way to treat an old friend?"

Harder. Tighter. Abigail was sure he was crushing her bones. She cried out, and the knife tumbled into the fallen leaves at her feet.

"That's better. Looks like our kitten has been declawed." By her aching wrist, he yanked her forward into his chest, gripping the back of her neck and lifting until her feet dangled above the ground.

She whimpered and struggled against him, but understood the effort was in vain. She had no power against Cord. Lucifer set a trap, and she in her haste and frustration walked right into it.

Cord pressed his face close to hers. "I'm supposed to take you straight back to Lucifer. I wonder if he would notice or care if I made a snack of you first." He ran his lips up the length of her neck. "A bite of flesh or two probably wouldn't kill you."

Abigail swallowed. Eyes shut tight, she braced herself for the strike.

With a deep inhale, he paused, fangs pressed against her skin. "Better not. I wouldn't be able to stop. The smell of fear coming off you is"—he sniffed her neck again— "delectable." Abruptly, he glanced at his watch. "Out of time for games." He tangled his arms and legs around her body in a serpentine fashion.

"What are you doing?" Abigail asked.

"Taking you to Lucifer."

Abigail's spine snapped as he twisted into shadow. Her cells yanked apart, swept away by Cord's sorcery. She again traveled by darkness, just as she had before she'd become mortal. Only, this ride would take her to Hell. Between chastising herself for her stupidity and preparing for the worst, she prayed that this trap had been meant for her and

her alone, and that somewhere, somehow, Malini, Jacob, and
the others were safe.

Chapter 3
Eden

Malini Gupta arrived in Eden accompanied by the other Soulkeepers. Fresh from her mission to Nod, she twirled inside the jewel-encrusted foyer walls, relieved to be home safely. An unexpected wave of joy overcame her. Despite the loss of her hair and the fact that she was still dressed in the clothes she borrowed from the Hopi medicine woman, Malini laughed under the mural of Adam and Eve. Truth be known, she never thought she would see it again. Her work with Dane had been a suicide mission. Truly, only by the grace of God or maybe Fate had she survived.

The twins, Samantha and Bonnie, blew into the school after her, all red hair and long limbs, the scent of sunshine and honey following in their wake. All Soulkeepers carried the scent, but it was especially comforting to Malini today. Ghost, never far behind Samantha, snagged her by the waist and twirled her through the atrium. He asked in a not-so-subtle way if he could get her alone. Ethan and Dane entered next, also hand in hand, although they left the dancing to the twins. Cheveyo, Grace, and Jacob paused in the doorway.

"You're beautiful, you know," Jacob said to Malini. "Even freshly removed from Hell."

"That's sweet, but I'd prefer if you didn't have to see me this way. I hate that *he* did this to me." She brushed a hand over her ragged, talon-shorn hair.

"Maybe Abigail can make you an elixir to help you grow it back. There are plants in Eden with all sorts of healing qualities," he said.

"Nothing short of sorcery is going to fix this overnight. I'm going to have to tell my parents I cut it. They never said I couldn't, but my mom will probably cry."

Lillian and Master Lee arrived, prompting Cheveyo to enter the school through the door Jacob still held open. For the first time, the new Soulkeeper saw the foyer through his own eyes. Sure, he'd seen it from inside Dane, but the experience must have felt different inside his own body. With wide eyes, he scanned the jewel-encrusted walls and stared up at the mural of Adam and Eve beneath the apple tree as if he were seeing it for the first time. Lee stepped to his side and began pointing out some of the notable features of the work of art.

Grace approached Malini and motioned toward her chopped hair. "I can even that up for you," she said. "I've cut the twins' hair since they were small."

"Thank you, Grace. Yes, please. But first, we need to convene the council. I have to know what I've missed, besides my birthday. With the mess Dane made of Nod, I'm betting Lucifer will close ranks. We might have a few weeks to train Cheveyo before he retaliates."

Grace shook her head and opened her mouth to respond. She didn't have a chance. Lillian, who'd been eavesdropping, stepped to Grace's side and whispered, "Malini, I know you are the strongest of all of us, but I need to insist that you take a moment to recuperate. Shower, rest, have something to eat. The council can wait. It isn't healthy for anyone to see you lingering like this." She eyed her tattered clothing and raised an eyebrow. "You're their leader."

Malini looked down at herself. She had to admit she didn't look or feel like a leader in her current condition.

"You're right, Lillian. Would you mind sending a gnome up to my room with a plate, and then let Abigail and Gideon know we're back? We'll convene in an hour."

"Excellent."

With a deep breath, she took Jacob's hand. Like always, he'd meandered to her side, a moon sucked into her gravitational pull. No one said a word as she led him down the hall to the west wing of Eden, to the apartments reserved for the girls. Most often, Malini stayed in Paris, in the house with her parents, so the room designated as hers got little use. Still, it was assigned to her for just this type of occasion.

"I'm not allowed," Jacob said, stopping at the door to the west wing stairwell.

"I'm giving you special permission," she said, a small smile bending the corner of her mouth. "I can't be alone right now. You're necessary for my mental health."

He nodded once and opened the door for her. Together, they stepped into a world of words. While the boy's side, the east wing, was covered in murals painted by past Soulkeepers, the girl's contained poetry. Every inch of the walls boasted beautifully rendered letters in multiple languages.

Jacob paused to read one.

"Come for respite
from a world beyond hope
whose death you hold back with shaking hands
and bloodied knuckles.

Come to remember
dreams of becoming wife and mother
or maybe something more.

Come to forget
there is no time for dreaming
until the Earth is healed
or the sword slips from your hand."

"Depressing, huh?" Malini said, staring at the wall.

"Are they all like that?"

"Pretty much."

She gestured with her head for him to follow her to the second floor. Down the hall, hers was the last room on the left, strangely sparse and impersonal for her tastes. She'd have to remember to decorate. She grabbed a change of clothes from the drawer, jeans and a sleeveless white blouse.

"Will this be appropriate for Paris? I wasn't paying attention when we arrived in the alley. We moved inside so quickly. What day did you say it was again?"

"October fifth." Jacob hooked his pinky into hers. "You should borrow a jacket from one of the other girls."

"I'll have to remember to keep one here for emergencies."

"You missed your birthday," he added in a rush.

Malini stared at him for a beat, trying to decide how she should react to that news. She'd heard it before, but it was just now sinking in. "What did you get me?" Malini asked, deciding to focus on the positive.

"Your family took us out to dinner, and I gave you, I mean Bonnie-you, a scarf."

As grateful as she was for Bonnie impersonating her while she was in Nod, the thought gave her the creeps. It wasn't fair to dwell on the awkwardness, considering Bonnie had kept the wheels on her life while she was away, but the thought of the twin using her identity made her shiver. "A scarf?" She giggled. "Did I like it?"

"Very much. It was red."

"Lovely." Malini bobbed her head repeatedly.

"Would you like your real present?"

"Not a scarf?"

"Nope."

She extended one brown hand and flexed her fingers repeatedly. Jacob reached into his pocket and retrieved a small, embroidered silk bag. Dangling it over her palm, he waited until she reached for it, then pulled it away.

"Very funny, Jacob. Give."

Obediently, he dropped it into her hand. She pulled apart the drawstring top and dug her fingers inside until they hooked on a flat, round object. A vintage silver locket—a plain heart on a silver chain.

"It's beautiful."

"To match your bracelet. Plus, look inside."

She cracked open the heart. On one side was a picture of her and Jacob dancing in the dining room.

"Bonnie took it at the party before you left for Nod."

"The other side is blank." Malini ran her fingers over the etching in the silver.

"A space for our future."

A warm smile lit her eyes from within. She tossed her arms around his neck and held him until Sage showed up with a hummus plate and a disapproving eye. Jacob insisted she eat her fill. Then, she grabbed her clothes and headed for the shower, leaving Jacob sitting on her bed.

He didn't have to say a word. She knew he'd wait for her … always.

* * * * *

Malini tried to avoid her reflection in the mirror as Grace snipped the edges of her bangs with the tips of her scissors.

"I think it makes you look irrepressible and chic. This haircut isn't for the cowardly." Grace smiled. The back and sides of Malini's shiny black hair were clipped short and ended in a sharp line at the base of her skull, but the top was longer with spiky bangs that played across her forehead. A perfect pixie cut.

"My parents will hate it," Malini murmured, running her hand through her super-short tresses. She lifted the hair at the roots, as if she could make it longer by force of will and a few good tugs. Although she wasn't the type to get too caught up in her own looks and made it a habit not to judge others on theirs, a confusing concoction of emotions flooded her when she thought about the loss of her hair. The feelings weren't about vanity; they were about anger. Fury. *Rage.* Lucifer and his Watchers had *made* her cut her hair. With evil intent, they'd forced this on her, to humiliate her.

Malini rotated in her chair in front of the mirror, trying to get a good look at the back of her head. The cut was sophisticated, strong. But did she feel that way or was this style simply a disguise? She watched Grace in the mirror.

Always a mother first, Grace dusted pieces of hair from the sheet she'd wrapped around Malini's neck, then removed it altogether. The older woman's red curls bounced on her shoulders as she folded the drape and began to clean up the bathroom. The sweeping sound lulled Malini into a peaceful contemplation.

When the room was spic and span, Grace finally met Malini's eyes in the mirror. She paused. "Hair grows back. What you took from Lucifer is permanent. You and Dane killed hundreds of Watchers in Nod. Your hair will grow, but he can't force more angels to fall."

Malini nodded, but tears pricked the corner of her eyes.

"You're young for this, too young to experience this kind of loss and abuse. Seventeen is brutally young. Grown men come back from less with PTSD."

Blinking rapidly, Malini shifted her gaze to her lap.

"Even a Healer has feelings. It's okay to let them out. No good ever came from keeping them bottled up."

Tears spilled over her lower lids, and Grace pulled her into a tight embrace. Through a torrent of long, gasping sobs, the older woman held her and rubbed large, slow circles over her back. Face buried in Grace's floral cotton shirt, Malini let it all go. The fear. The humiliation. The agony. The hopelessness. Nod had almost destroyed her.

"Lucifer is strong and evil through and through. He can knock you down, but he only wins if you can't get back up again."

Malini stopped crying. Grace was right. Not only was she alive, but she'd dealt the devil a serious blow. She couldn't stop now. She vowed to forget why she'd cut her hair and instead focus on the result. She was stronger. And, in some ways, she was wiser.

A knock drew their attention to the door. "Come in," Malini said.

Lillian entered with Gideon close behind her. Had someone died? Her expression was morose, pale, and Gideon huddled into her side as if they'd been comforting each other. His face was streaked with tears.

Malini popped out of her chair. "What's happened?"

"It's Abigail…" Lillian's voice broke. "She's gone."

Gideon chose that moment to extend his hand. In it was a note with large scrawled writing. "I found this in our room."

For a moment, Malini's mind couldn't process Lillian's words. Gone? Where would she go?

"And this." Gideon held out one of Warwick's blue stones.

Malini took the note from his hand and read it twice, positioning the paper so Grace could do the same over her shoulder.

"She left Eden? To help me? I don't understand." Malini's voice rose in pitch with the panic that seized her heart.

"Archibald said she asked for the boat and definitely left Eden," Lillian said. "I wanted to talk to you first before I sent out a search party."

Turning toward Grace, Malini paced a few steps, gripping the note as she read it again and again. "This doesn't make sense. Why would she leave Eden?"

"She wouldn't have gone unless she thought you were in danger," Gideon said.

"But all of the Soulkeepers were already with me. She knew I was taken care of."

Lillian closed her eyes and pinched the bridge of her nose. "Where is the sister stone?"

"Lucifer took it from me when he stripped me in Nod— Oh no!" Malini crossed her arms and squeezed, fighting the black hole of dread that had formed at the center of her chest.

Gideon glanced at Lillian. "We think Lucifer used your stone to contact Abigail and make her believe you were in trouble. It's the only explanation. Maybe she thought *all* of you were in trouble. Only an urgent plea would have caused her to leave Eden." He slapped the doorframe. "She never even told me goodbye."

"Of course she didn't, Gideon," Lillian retorted. "She knew you'd never let her out of Eden, even to save us. You would have held her down, if that's what it took, and you'd be justified. Abigail *knew* better."

Malini shoved between them and out into the hallway. "It doesn't matter why she left," she snapped. "We have to find her. I'll go myself, with Jacob. Nobody knows her better than we do."

Gideon grabbed her elbow. "I'll go too."

"No, Gideon. You need to stay here. Lucifer will try to use you. I can't have you vulnerable."

He backed away, crossing his muscled arms over his chest as if she'd bruised his ego. Malini didn't have time to comfort him. She moved toward the door, praying they'd find Abigail before it was too late.

Chapter 4
Lost

Traveling by shadow in a human body was a tenuous venture. Abigail was sure Cord would never have risked it with another human being, not one he wanted to keep alive anyway. Her fragile flesh was stretched and flattened. By the time Cord stopped and released her, the pain was almost unbearable, and she was sure important body parts were bruised or broken. She folded in half from the discomfort, catching herself on her knees.

Breathe. Just breathe. Eyes closed, she tried to pull herself together. She had to keep her wits about her if she was going to get herself out of this mess. The air filled her lungs and, as it did, awareness of her surroundings came piece by piece.

She opened her eyes. Beneath her feet was not brimstone but a newly finished hardwood floor, and the smell in her nostrils was not sulfur but the latex odor of fresh paint. Slowly, she straightened her spine. In front of her, a wall of windows gave a spectacular view of a city next to a large body of water. She was in a high-rise, but where? Architecturally diverse buildings rose beyond the glass, familiar buildings. She wasn't in Hell; she was in Chicago. The body of water at the edge of the city was Lake Michigan.

Turning, she had a moment to take in the meticulously designed room before she noticed *him*. All blond curls and gleaming white teeth, the Lord of Illusions draped one arm over the back of the leather sofa he was sitting on, the other rested casually in his lap.

"Welcome, Abigail, so glad you could join us." Lucifer's quiet voice and hint of a smile seemed innocuous enough, but Abigail knew better. A quiet Lucifer was a deadly Lucifer.

"You. You lured me here." She bit her lip to the point of pain.

"Yes. An easy enough illusion."

"Where is Malini?"

"Burnt to a crisp at the center of Nod." He poked his tongue into his cheek. "There's nothing my Watchers like more than a fire pit, especially one fueled by Healer flesh."

Abigail clutched her stomach. "You're lying." Jacob said Malini made it safely to Arizona after her mission to Nod. But what if, this time, Lucifer was telling the truth? What if the phone call to Jacob, just like the projection through the stone, was all an elaborate illusion to lure all of them to their deaths? Lucifer was capable of as much. He was capable of anything.

"Am I?" Lucifer asked by way of response.

"What do you want from me?" No sense playing his game. If she asked him more questions, she couldn't trust his answers.

He crossed the room in a heartbeat, his face reddening with anger. "What do I want? What do I want, Abigail?" The stench of rotting flesh rolled off his breath and filled her nostrils. "I want the Watchers I lost back. I want you back. But since I can't have either of those things, I'm going to take what you won't give. I'm going to steal your soul."

She tried to step away from his tirade, but he wouldn't allow it. He grabbed her elbow and held her firmly.

"You can't have my soul. My soul is God's now." Instinctively, she touched the cross around her neck with her free hand. It was a wedding gift from Malini and Jacob, one she never took off. For her, it was a symbol of her redemption, a promise she had given her life to receive.

Lucifer laughed wickedly, brushing an errant blond curl from his aqua-blue eyes. "Your soul is only God's when you die. I have it until then." He followed up the threat with a toothy grin that made the muscles in his perfect Greco-Roman profile tighten.

"What do you mean? Are you taking me to Hell?"

"Hell? Why would I take you to Hell? No one lives there anymore."

Abigail jerked and shook her head. "You and the Watchers have to go back. You can't stay here," she sputtered.

"Things have changed, Abigail. The Great Oppressor and I have a new agreement, one that allows my Watchers and me to stay here as long as I desire. And now, I have you to keep me company."

"I'm a prisoner here, in this penthouse?"

"The punishment should fit the crime." He yanked her closer, until she turned her face away to avoid touching his chest. "*Prisoner* is too good a title for you. What I have in mind is something altogether more appropriate."

With one hand, he drew a circle over her head, then another and another. Then he backed away. Abigail lurched with his movement. He'd taken something from her, but she wasn't sure what. For a moment, the flesh over her heart burned as if someone had ripped a Band-Aid off. Her skin had wanted to go with it, tipping her on her toes. She couldn't stop her momentum. Tripping forward, she tried to catch herself on Lucifer's chest. But she didn't stop; her body passed through his unhindered. She rushed forward, catching herself on the wall of windows behind him.

"What have you done to me?" she yelled. Her voice came out reedy and hollow.

Lucifer placed his hands in his pockets and stepped toward her. "Your new existence, Abigail, is for my pleasure. I am the only one who can see you or hear you. You will live out your days in this penthouse. I will feed you when it suits me and starve you when it doesn't. I will keep you alive for my own entertainment."

An icy paralysis crept from Abigail's toes to her ears, and then gave way to heart-racing panic. She turned from the windows. "You can't do this. Don't do this!"

He tilted his head. "I can and I have." He paced away from her, toward Cord who waited, watching, near the door.

"The Soulkeepers will come for me," she yelled desperately.

Lucifer stopped. "The Soulkeepers think I'm boohooing in Hell over the Watchers they killed in Nod. They don't even know I'm topside, and I intend to keep it that way." From his pocket, he pulled an iridescent string, holding it taut between his fingers.

Abigail squinted. "What is that?"

"Thanks to this, Malini won't be tracing you back here. Thanks to this, you are mine for good this time."

Her life's thread! He'd stolen it from Fate's weaving. Abigail lost all sense of reason and lunged for him. Attacking Lucifer was suicide, but then death might be better than being his personal ghost for the rest of her natural life. She passed right through him again.

He cleared his throat, straightened his tie, and turned to Cord like he hadn't even noticed. "You're looking a little peaked. Let's go get you someone to eat," he said to the Watcher.

Cord straightened. "As you wish, my lord." His eyes drifted across the room, skipping right over her. "A stunning piece of sorcery. I can't make her out at all."

Lucifer patted Cord on the shoulder. "A stroke of genius on my part, solitary confinement with the added loss of her body. I'll enjoy watching her slowly go mad in this place."

Cord held the door open for Lucifer. "Brilliant. You are, as ever, the master of misery."

As Lucifer led the way into the corridor, he didn't so much as glance in her direction. The door whined as it closed, clicking shut behind them. Inside Abigail's mind, the sound echoed louder than in real life: her coffin lid slamming into place.

* * * * *

"Where should we start?" Jacob asked.

Malini turned a circle in the alley behind Laudner's Flowers and Gifts, trying to think like Lucifer. Where would he ask her to go?

"He'd want to get her alone," Malini thought out loud. "My first instinct is her old home, but she couldn't travel by staff or reveal herself to anyone in the community, and it's too far to walk."

"Maybe Sunrise Park? You can walk there from here."

Malini nodded. "As good a place to start as any."

She took his hand and led the way out of the alley and toward Main Street. They'd just reached the crosswalk when a familiar voice called to them from the direction of Westcott's grocery.

"Jacob? Malini, is that you?" Stephanie Westcott jogged across the street, her dark brown ponytail bouncing behind her. "What did you do to your hair?"

She didn't say it in a hurtful way, but Malini crossed her arms over her chest nonetheless. "Got it cut. Trying something new."

"It's super cute!" Stephanie gave each of them a short hug, then wound a finger around one long, brown tress. "Maybe I should do that. Did you donate it to Locks of Love?"

"Something like that. It's good to see you, Stephanie. I don't want to be rude but we've got to get going." Malini took a step into the street, tugging Jacob behind her.

"Oh. Are you going to meet Dr. Silva, er, I mean, Newman?" Stephanie asked.

Malini halted. "Have you seen her?"

"Yeah, she borrowed my scooter. Well, technically, she kind of stole it. I came out of the flower shop and saw her driving away. I figured she must need it for something important, so I've been hanging out at the store waiting. Was hoping she'd have it back by now."

"Did you notice which direction she was headed?" Jacob asked.

"Ah, sure. That way." Stephanie pointed over her shoulder and behind her.

Malini looked at Jacob. "The garden?"

He nodded.

"Thanks, Stephanie. If we see her, we'll have her return your scooter to Westcott's. I'm sure there is a reasonable explanation for why she took it without asking."

"I didn't even know she was in town. My mom will want to say hello. Is she staying with your family, Jacob?"

"No!" Jacob said, then softened at Stephanie's widened eyes. "Sorry, she wanted us to keep her visit a secret. She's only in town for a few hours, passing through on her way to the university. You know how it can be."

Malini squeezed his hand encouragingly. "Right. She'll be buried in pies and visitors and never make it to her meeting. I bet that's why she borrowed your scooter without asking."

Stephanie pursed her lips. The explanation didn't completely make sense, but she nodded politely anyway. "So that's why your uncle didn't mention she was here. Rude that she didn't make time to visit, but I'll keep my mouth shut. Tell her I said hello." She turned on her heel and headed back toward her family's grocery store.

"She seems upset," Jacob said.

Malini tugged his arm and began walking briskly toward Jacob's truck parked in front of the flower shop. "After all she went through last summer, can you blame her for expecting Abigail to say hello when she's in town? She was compelled to plunge a knife into Abigail's chest. She helped battle our way out of Fermilab. She's seen Watchers. And why wouldn't Abigail use her own car if she was passing through town? Stephanie knew we were lying."

"So she's upset," Jacob said smugly. "Should we be more supportive? I mean, she must be having a hard time with what happened considering she hasn't gone back to college this semester." Jacob climbed behind the wheel and pulled the keys from the visor.

Malini slid in beside him. "I wouldn't be surprised if Fran Westcott wouldn't let her go back." She sighed. "We should reach out more, to Katrina too."

As Jacob pressed the accelerator to the floor, he thought about that. "Maybe, when we're not trying to find our dearest friend or save the world."

Malini's response crept quietly into the cab. "Agreed." She ran her fingers over the glass of the window, watching the trees wiz by in a blur.

When they approached the house that used to be Abigail's, Jacob spotted the scooter first. "There it is!" He parked behind it and jumped out of the cab. Malini followed, searching the woods behind the bike for any sign of her. She hiked into the maple grove, eyes sweeping the fallen leaves of the forest floor while Jacob did the same thing in the opposite direction.

A few yards into the tree line, Jacob called to her. "Hey, look at this." He bent down to retrieve an object from the leaves near his feet.

Malini rushed to his side to see what it was. "A knife. This is from Eden. Abigail wouldn't have dropped this if she could help it."

"Look there." Jacob pointed to a place where the leaves had been disrupted to reveal the mud below. "There was a struggle here."

"A Watcher took her," Malini said, sniffing the air.

He bobbed his head. "Sulfur. I smell it too."

Malini paced in front of the spot, rubbing her chin. Abruptly, she dropped to the forest floor and crisscrossed her legs.

"What are you doing?" Jacob squatted in front of her. "Are you okay?"

"I need to go to the In Between. I'll follow her thread to see where they've taken her. Then you and I are going to get her back."

"She could be in Hell already. He could be holding her like he did Dane." No one could go to Hell without being ushered in by the devil himself. Hell wasn't like Nod. It was Lucifer's domain as Heaven was God's.

She grabbed his face and gave him a peck on the mouth. "Keep watch. I'm going over."

Chapter 5
The Challenge

Malini tumbled into Fate's stucco-walled villa with a painful jolt. She knew better than to make the journey to the In Between in her present emotional state, but time was of the essence. Every moment Abigail was with Lucifer posed a risk, but strong emotions made crossing between worlds uncomfortable. Her hate for Lucifer, the guilt for letting Warwick's stone land in the wrong hands, and her fear for Abigail's safety weighed heavily on her heart. All of that baggage traveled with her through the ether, like trying to swim in a snowsuit.

Eyes closed, she tried to quiet her mind, breathing deeply with her head between her knees. Once she'd composed herself, she walked the rows of fabric, searching for Abigail's thread. Over time, she'd developed a method for finding things in the miles and miles of material. Hands stretched to her sides, she would trail her fingertips over the bolts of fabric, human years passing like Braille beneath her touch. Souls told their stories in every stitch. Abigail was thousands of years old, but she'd only been human a few months. Malini worked her way toward the newer bolts, waiting for the hypodermal tickle that would tell her she was touching the right one.

When she'd first become a Healer, she'd assumed one bolt of fabric must equal one human year, or at a minimum a consistent length of time. She was wrong. Destiny was a fickle fabric. Fate, as measured by the intersection of souls and the choices they made, increased in activity at certain times in history. The years during World War I and II took up an entire row of the warehouse-like space. The newest material wasn't necessarily at the front. The bolts were organized by significance, not time.

She wandered the rows, mind open, allowing the ancient part of herself to take over. A flash ran up the inside of her arm. She stopped, focusing on the roll her sixth sense told her corresponded to the current year. Carefully, she pinched the corners of the fabric, her arms spread-eagle to encompass the width, and unraveled the shimmering blue cloth. Lives blinked up at her. They flashed in and out of their silver-embroidered home like bits of binary code. She coasted her fingertips over the silky material, faces flashing through her mind in fast-forward as she read the world's history.

She sifted through the threads of the last twenty-four hours, seeing Paris, Stephanie, Jacob, and a blur that she understood was herself. (A Healer's fate was never to see her own past, present, or future clearly.) She'd gone too far. She needed to back up to before Abigail was taken. Sliding her fingers a few inches, she looked again for Abigail, concentrating on her friend's image and allowing the deepest manifestation of her power to take control. Nothing. Abigail's thread was nowhere to be found.

"She's not in there." Fatima stood behind her among the bolts, lanky limbs crossed and eyes downcast.

Malini lifted her fingertips from the fabric. "What do you mean, she isn't in here?"

Fatima's expression drooped. Malini had never seen her look so tired. Dark areas under her eyes sagged over tearstained cheeks and sallow skin. "Lucifer stole her thread," she said weakly.

"Stole her thread! How? Why didn't you stop him?"

She forced a chuckle. "Stop Lucifer? Only one stands a chance at such a feat, God, and unfortunately, She was here at the time. Their interaction was not what you might expect."

"What's going on, Fatima? Why were they both here?" A deep sense of dread wormed into Malini's gut. Fatima, normally a tower of immortal strength, hunched before her, countenance a dark omen that permeated every corner of her abode like an icy chill.

"Follow me." Fatima led her out the front archway onto the veranda and then down the stairs to the rolling hillside beyond.

The silhouette of an angel stood on the top of the tallest hill. "Who is that?"

"Not who, what. Allow me to assist with the distance."

A blink later, Malini stood atop the hill. The In Between was a construct of each immortal's consciousness, and Fate had reconstructed her yard to bring them closer without all the walking. A massive statue rose before Malini. Made of white marble and eight feet tall, the angel's wings spread against the ambient light of the sky. The figure was feminine, blindfolded, her face tipped down, lips pressed together in a stern expression ... *judgment*. In her right hand, a set of scales dangled. In her left, a crystal model of the world covered in pinpoints of light and darkness.

"Lady Justice, angel style," Malini said. "What is this?"

"She is the scorekeeper, the guardian of the challenge. Lucifer demanded a consequence for the role I played in making Dane a Soulkeeper. He asked for my soul and to name my replacement—"

"No!"

"God refused but made an alternate proposal. The compact was dissolved."

"What!"

"A challenge is underway for human hearts; the prize, exclusive rule over Earth for one thousand years."

"This can't be true," Malini muttered. "All of our lives—why would God risk all of our lives?"

Fatima continued. "Lucifer will release six temptations, and God will release six gifts. Each is meant to win human souls to their side. This scorekeeper marks the balance and will record the winner."

Malini brought her nose close to the crystal Earth. "Light verses darkness." White and black pinpoints danced over the globe. Her life and all of the lives depicted within were in jeopardy.

"There's so much darkness. The scales are already tipped in Lucifer's favor. Has he issued the first temptation?" Malini asked.

"Unfortunately, no."

"But he already has an advantage!" Malini grimaced when she thought of his advantage. "The water. His Watchers have influenced many of the most powerful people in America. That's why he has the advantage." She pointed her hands at the scales.

"About that, God made it clear that the influenced don't count in this game. Lucifer will be cautious to overuse that card."

Malini huffed. "So the Watchers can influence people but probably won't. Why doesn't that make me feel better? And Abigail! Oh no, Abigail." She pressed both hands into her stomach.

"I'm sorry, Malini. Lucifer knows exactly what he's doing. He took Abigail's thread so that you could not track her. He wants to weaken you, to distract you, and so far he has. You and the other Soulkeepers are the only ones who pose a threat to his Watchers on Earth. You are the only ones who can lessen the impact of his temptations."

"We are God's best weapons aside from the six gifts."

"Exactly."

Her hands balled into fists. "Where is Lucifer?" Malini asked through her teeth.

"I can't follow him or his Watchers. They have no souls and no threads. We know a few Watchers already inhabit Earth. Death's numbers tell the tale. But without the compact, Lucifer and his minions could be anywhere. They can travel anywhere, without a portal."

"Then track the deaths!" she snapped. "I will fry his Watchers one by one until Lucifer gives me Abigail."

"He will never do that, Malini." Fatima lowered her gaze. "You know he'd kill her before he backed down."

Malini tipped her head and narrowed her eyes. "So what you are telling me is that the Watchers can come and go as Lucifer pleases, to Hell, Nod, Earth, and even here in the In Between. Abigail could already be caged inside a ring of fire in Hell, just as Dane was, but I can't know for sure because I can't track her. She has no thread." She groaned. "What *can* we do?"

Fatima folded her arms, all eight of them, across her abdomen. "I will tell you what you must do. Be patient. Don't draw attention to yourself. Wait until Lucifer becomes careless and tips his hand."

"Do you know what he could be doing to Abigail at this very moment? I can't just abandon her."

Fatima sighed. "When Dane was captured, he called your soul to Hell. At that time, he wanted the list of Soulkeepers. Chances are Abigail is the bait for something he wants. Wait for the ransom note. Wait for him to call you to him."

"And what if he doesn't?"

"Attacking Watchers won't save Abigail. If she is in Hell, no one can reach her. Lucifer will expect you to retaliate. Maybe he's even hoping to draw you out of Eden so that he can kill you. Trust me on this, Malini. Keep a low profile. Wait until Lucifer releases the first temptation, and then take advantage of his distraction to exact your revenge."

Her immortal friend was right. As hard as this was going to be for all of them, she had to close ranks and wait. Lucifer expected an immediate response. He'd be counting on a fast, sloppy retaliation. If Abigail *was* the bait, Lucifer might want nothing more than to flush the Soulkeepers from hiding, all for naught. None of them could travel to Hell to save Abigail. Malini needed to act smart not fast. Perfect timing was their only hope of helping God win this challenge.

"Thank you, Fatima." With a hasty goodbye, Malini journeyed back to Earth, making the agonizing fall into her body in the maple grove. Thankfully, Jacob was there to pull her weeping face into his shoulder.

* * * * *

On the second floor of the Eden School for Soulkeepers, Malini stood at the head of the conference table. Gideon Newman, the former angel turned human, sat in the seat to her left, pale and hunched. Lillian Lau, Horseman and leader of field operations, chose the chair next to him, squeezing his hand to offer emotional support. Master Lee, Helper and martial arts expert, found a spot across the table but perched on the side of the chair as if ready for a fight. And Grace Guillian, Helper and mother to twin Horsemen Bonnie and Samantha, fidgeted nervously in the seat to Malini's right.

"Thank you for convening on such short notice," Malini began.

"Did you find her? Can we get her back?" Gideon leaned across the table, jaw clenched. The skin around his green eyes held the worn and bloated look of an overused paper bag.

"I'm sorry. No."

Gideon scrubbed his face with his hands.

Malini glanced around the table. So much pain. So much worry. "Abigail has been taken by Lucifer as we suspected."

"To Hell, like Dane?" Grace asked.

Malini nodded. "It appears so. And worse, I've learned Lucifer and his Watchers can now travel anywhere, without a portal."

A sharp intake of breath came from Lillian's direction. "But he ... can't! He can't *stay* on Earth. There are laws. Ancient, God-made laws. How could the Watchers be here? What about the sun? They can't—"

"Until now," Malini interrupted. "The compact has been nullified."

Grace covered her mouth with her small freckled hands. "Why?"

"Lucifer and his Watchers were granted access to Earth as a consequence of Fate making Dane a Soulkeeper." Malini paused, rubbing her palms together. "According to Fate, God and Lucifer have engaged in a battle for human souls, winner take all for one thousand years. Lucifer will release six temptations, God six gifts. Each is meant to win the hearts of humans. Upon the last gift, the balance of human souls will mark the winner. I saw the scorekeeper myself. The challenge has already begun."

As if she might burst out of her skin if she held still, Grace erupted from her chair and paced the room. "So stupid. So irresponsible. What was she *thinking* making Dane a Soulkeeper?"

Master Lee sighed, rubbing his milky eye, a Soulkeeper's gift that allowed him to see through a Watcher's illusion. "She was thinking, *save a life*. Dane would have died without her intervention. Any of us might have done the same."

"It's not fair, Lee," Grace snapped. "Lucifer forced Fate to break the rules. If he hadn't cheated and targeted Dane in the first place, she wouldn't have had to save him. Lucifer was not supposed to tamper directly with human lives. Dane was human. He tampered. Fate was justified."

"Maybe that's why God posed the challenge," Malini said quietly. The others turned to face her one by one. "For thousands of years, God has kept the compact while Lucifer ignored it. Evil does as it pleases. Perhaps this challenge is a way to end an agreement that wasn't working."

The five stared at each other, a whole lot of blinking and fidgeting in place of any real progress. Malini needed to bring them back to the task at hand, but she couldn't focus. For the first time since becoming the Healer, she was flying blind, working off intuition rather than her power.

Lillian spoke first. "When you were In Between, did you see any hope of getting Abigail back?"

"No. Lucifer stole her life's thread. I can't see her past or her future."

Gideon let out a shaky breath, and Malini put her hand on his shoulder. "Chances are he's using her as bait. If we wait, he'll send me a ransom note like he did with Dane. Remember? He pulled my soul into Hell to demand the list of Soulkeepers. He'll probably do the same with Abigail, and when he does, I'll bargain for her."

"So we wait? We do nothing while Lucifer tortures my wife?" Gideon spat. Despite Malini's healing comfort, Gideon dropped a fist to the table, rattling the wood and the spirits of everyone seated around it.

"We have no other choice. Lucifer is going to expect us to respond immediately. He's counting on it. He wants to flush us out of Eden. That's been his plan all along. When he approached Cheveyo to act as his Trojan horse, he did it because he knows this is the only place we're safe from him."

"This is bullshit," Gideon said, the first curse Malini had ever heard him use. He shrugged from under her hand and stood, knocking back his chair.

"Remember, Gideon, that Lucifer has the list that Abigail conjured. He knows the names of every Soulkeeper on that list. He knows where we live and where we go to school. The only place we are safe is in Eden."

"So?"

"So, he probably took Abigail to smoke us out. Watchers could be anywhere. Too aggressive and we play into his hands. He already knows Jacob, Dane, and I live in Paris. If he suspects the entrance to Eden is here, the town will be crawling with Watchers in no time. He'll pluck us off one by one. Without the Soulkeepers in the way, his chances of winning this challenge are vastly improved. No, we need to be smart about this. Lucifer will get impatient and careless. He'll make a mistake and that's when we'll move in—when he least expects it. I have to believe that our best bet of getting Abigail back from Hell is helping God win this challenge."

"What about the challenge, Malini?" Lee asked. "How do we prepare when we have no idea what the six temptations will be?"

Suddenly, her upper body felt heavy, and she pitched forward, catching herself on the table. Lee's words echoed in her head. Her heart thumped in her throat. How could they prepare? They were all caught up in some giant chess game between God and the devil, pawns in a contest she could barely hope to understand, let alone influence. Sweat gathered at the back of her neck. The room was too hot, closing in.

A soft touch on her back gave her comfort. Grace was at her side, rubbing circles over her spine. "It's okay, Malini," she whispered next to her cheek. "No one could possibly answer that question. Even Soulkeepers are only human."

With her head still spinning, Malini tilted her face up to look at Lee. "I don't know what's coming, but I do know how we should prepare. The same way we always have. We train. We get better at defending ourselves and working together. From now on we train harder and faster than we ever have before."

Lillian rose from her seat, pointing a finger at Malini. "We can and we will. Once we get Cheveyo up to speed, this will be the strongest team you've ever seen."

"Good," Malini said. "Because we can't think of ourselves as observers. We might not have control over the challenge or the form of Lucifer's temptations, but we are part of this war, and I for one intend to be on the winning side."

Chapter 6
The First Curse

One week later...

Abigail paced in front the wall of windows overlooking the city. She'd become all too familiar with the sprawling penthouse. In a space that took up the entire top floor of the building, she'd counted six massive bedrooms, seven bathrooms and two powder rooms, a gourmet kitchen, a great room large enough to double as a ballroom, and a smattering of specialized areas for entertaining. She couldn't enjoy any of them.

One of the rooms was a library, chock-full of leather-bound books in multiple languages. She suspected the previous owner had left the collection, as Lucifer had never shown any interest in reading. Abigail yearned to pass the time by taking one down and curling up in a plush chair to read, but Lucifer's curse made that particular act impossible. Her hand passed through the binding as it did the telephone, the television, and any pen or paper she wished to employ. He'd turned her into a ghost.

The only exception to her plight was when he fed her. Twice a day he'd provide a meal and at that time his sorcery would break, and she could lift the fork and drink from a glass. Enough to keep her alive, yes, but with no human interaction, she could feel herself slipping away. The ghost world she lived in was a torture like no other.

She tried to focus on the certain hope that the Soulkeepers would find her. Even if Malini couldn't follow her thread and predict where she'd be, Gideon would never give up. He'd find a way to track her down. She just needed to be patient. They'd have her out of here in a few days.

The sound of the front door opening sent her scurrying from the library into the great room, fully expecting to see her rescuers. Instead, Lucifer paraded through the front door, Auriel and Cord following on his heels. He did not spare a glance for Abigail. This was part of her torture. The one being who *could* see her refused to look at her.

"Hello, Abigail!" Cord yelled to the opposite corner of the room.

Asshole. She raised her middle finger toward the back of his head. If Lucifer saw her crude gesture, he didn't respond. He approached the wall of windows, clasping his hands behind his back. The city, shrouded in night, provided a spectacle of shimmering lights but somehow seemed dwarfed by the devil's silhouette.

"I've brought you both here tonight because I am prepared to release the first temptation." Lucifer's voice took on the rasp and crackle inherent beneath his illusion. The sound made Abigail's scalp prickle.

Auriel clapped her hands and skipped to his side, smoothing her sweater and short skirt. "Brilliant, my lord. The world will be yours when you say the word. What will you tempt the humans with? Wealth? Power?"

"The obvious choices, but too direct."

"Lust, my lord," Cord offered. "An illusion to entice even the most prudent soul."

"Another excellent suggestion but difficult to deliver discreetly. It is to our advantage to remain insidious. The Great Oppressive Deity will expect us to be careless and out ourselves to the humans and the Soulkeepers."

"How will you win them to you then?" Auriel asked.

"Wealth, power, and lust only appeal to those with dark hearts. What we need is a temptation that wins the hearts of the good. Nothing breeds darkness like snuffing out the light."

Cord straightened his tie. "Tempt the good?"

"By pretending to be the thing we are not. Harrington Enterprises must become a blessing to the cursed." Lucifer turned on his heel and crossed the sprawling living area to the kitchen island, where he shuffled through a wine rack and selected a bottle. Three champagne flutes appeared on the counter, and he filled them halfway with thick red liquid. Abigail could smell the dank copper stench from across the room. Blood—fresh and raw—with a slight bubble she assumed Lucifer added for affect.

"Join me in a drink, and I'll explain." He handed a glass to Cord and another to Auriel, taking up the third himself. "The first temptation will be pestilence, a virus as crippling as the Black Death."

"Pestilence, my lord? To win human hearts?"

Lucifer grinned. "It won't be the disease that wins their hearts, Auriel. It will be the cure."

"A cure for the pestilence we've created?" Cord looked confused.

"Auriel, you will go to Harrington's pharmaceutical division and give them a direct order from their new CEO, Mr. Milton Blake." He placed an open hand on his chest. "All manufacturing facilities are to produce nothing but the cure for a new and dangerous virus." With a wave of his hand, a medication bottle filled with glowing blue pills appeared on the countertop.

Auriel palmed the bottle and gave a slight curtsy. "Will the humans know how to replicate this?"

"Good point, Auriel. Their idiocy is infallible. Best use sorcery to teach them the recipe."

She grinned.

"And now for the disease," Lucifer said. Shaking his right hand, the illusion of humanity fell away, exposing black skin and long, sharp talons. He dug into his own chest, the flesh and bone parting to expose the blackness where his heart should have been. A pinch and tug and a piece of that blackness worked between his talons like rancid bubblegum, pulling and stretching. The opening in his chest stitched closed while the blackness in his hand expanded. When Lucifer's molding was complete, a great winged beast perched on his outstretched arm. Mangy black feathers, a sharp hooked beak, and eyes as red as the blood in the champagne flutes marked the bird's appearance. The animal glared at Abigail and rolled its black tongue.

Lucifer motioned to Cord. "Meet my new pet, Affliction. This bird will fly fast and far. Ensure he is released in a populated area. Anyone who looks upon him will be afflicted with my pestilence."

Cord extended his arm, and the bird hopped to his new perch.

"Genius. The bird doles out the disease. Only Harrington will have the cure and with it the loyalty of the cured." Auriel laughed and raised her glass.

"Exactly." Lucifer followed her lead. "A toast to a new age. Soon the world will be ours and everyone in it our plaything."

Cord lifted his blood cocktail and joined in clinking glasses. The three drained the red liquid in a few gulps. With a loud smack of his lips, Cord moved for the door, making kissing noises toward Affliction. "Come, sweet bird. Let me introduce you to the city."

Auriel opened the door for him and then followed Cord out of it.

Abigail desperately wanted to warn the Soulkeepers, but her desire was useless. Every attempt at communication had failed; her hand slipped right through the phone. As hopeless as she was helpless, she paced in front of the windows.

Lucifer watched her, elbows resting on the kitchen counter. The pads of his fingers tapped together under his chin. "Do you miss it, Abigail, being part of a team? You could have been where Auriel is today."

She stopped and turned to face him, anger warming her ghostly body. What did she have to lose? "I do miss being part of a team, but not yours, Lucifer. I miss being a Soulkeeper. And as for taking Auriel's place, no one deserves what you have to give more than she does."

His face reddened, and his grin morphed into a scowl. Stomping toward the exit, he didn't bother to look in her direction as he crossed the threshold. "No meal tonight," he said, slamming the door behind him.

Utterly and truly alone, Abigail watched Cord and Auriel emerge from the building, two tiny dots on the street below. Cord raised his arm, and Affliction took flight.

Chapter 7
Sick and Tired

Two weeks later...

Within the circle of Jacob's arms, Malini swayed to the ballad the DJ played from the corner of the gym. At times like this, with her head rested on his chest, it was easy to forget their house of cards could tumble at any moment. She expected Lucifer's first temptation to come sooner rather than later. All of the Soulkeepers practiced daily, ready to defend against an onslaught. This waiting promised a more sinister enemy, silent, invisible, deadly. Perhaps already among them. She pressed her eyes closed. She'd promised herself she wouldn't ruin homecoming worrying about the inevitable.

"What's wrong?" Jacob asked. He kissed the top of her head. *How did he know?*

"Thinking about what I promised I wouldn't think about."

"Well, don't think about it."

"I'm trying but now you are talking about it, thereby making me think about it even more."

Jacob pushed her to arm's length and met her eyes. "Okay. Let's talk about something else. How do you like the homecoming decorations?"

Malini raised her chin to take in the gossamer curtains, the flat wooden cutout of a horse-drawn carriage, and the stage-set balcony reused from the school's earlier production of *Romeo and Juliet*. The theme was *Wishes Do Come True*, complete with a shooting star that sparkled from the ceiling. "I love them. Dane did an incredible job, as always. It's too bad so many people missed it because of the bird flu."

"Yeah, Katrina has it too. The symptoms are so bad she came home from college. I guess the entire student health service is overrun. She's spent the week tossing her cookies, and I mean that figuratively because she can't eat anything."

Malini stopped dancing and looked Jacob in the eye. "Is she going to be all right?"

"I think so. Dr. Howard has some new drug to treat it, Elysium. Said she should be fine in a couple days."

"Hey, I thought we weren't going to talk about anything serious," Malini teased.

"You brought it up." Jacob pulled her back into his chest and started to sway. "So, the decorations. Technically, Samantha came up with the idea while she was acting as Dane, but Dane did most of the work. I wish he could enjoy it a bit more."

"Maybe I should ask him to dance." Malini glanced over at the round table where they'd had dinner. Dane, dateless again, was folding origami cranes out of a stack of cocktail napkins.

"Yeah. I need a break anyway." Jacob threaded his fingers into hers and led her to the table. "Hey, Dane, uh, I'm beat. Do you want to take over for a while?" Jacob pointed a finger at Malini.

"Do you want to dance, Dane?" Malini asked.

Dane scowled. "You guys are sweet but unconvincing. I think I'll pass on the pity dance, thank you."

"Dane—"

"It's cool, Mal. I'm fine right where I am."

She sat down on the chair next to him, facing the dance floor. The music picked up, and the other attendees swarmed the floor, gyrating to the rhythm.

"I'm going to get something to drink. You guys want something?" Jacob offered.

Malini nodded. He left for the buffet table.

"You should have brought Ethan." Even as Malini said the words, she understood the situation wasn't as easy as that.

"I haven't come out to my parents yet. The last thing I want is for them to find out from the neighbors."

"How's your dad doing, anyway?"

"Stable. They've started him on a new medication. Something experimental. He was able to move his hand a few days ago."

"Excellent."

"Yeah, another few months and he might be able to come home and completely ruin my life."

Malini placed a hand on his. "Think positively, Dane. It's possible this experience will change his priorities. How is the rest of the family?"

"Keeping up with the farm, thanks to Ethan and the most hired help we've ever used before."

"Well, that's something."

He returned to folding the napkin in front of him. Malini smoothed the royal blue waist of her off-the-shoulder dress.

"How are you holding up?" Dane asked. The napkin he'd been folding, now in the shape of a crane, landed in her lap.

"Fairly paralyzed with guilt over losing Abigail. Three weeks. Can you imagine what he's doing to her?"

Dane scowled. His normally warm composure turned icy and hard. "Yes. I know exactly what Lucifer is doing to her. And so do you. We've both been in her place, remember? But I also know Abigail, like you and I, wouldn't want us to make a hasty but stupid decision to save her. She'd want us to be careful with ourselves, especially now when there's no telling where or when Lucifer will strike."

Malini sighed, then threw her arms around his neck and squeezed. "Thank you, Dane. You're absolutely right. If our roles were reversed, I'd never want Abigail to compromise the Soulkeepers for me. She'd want us to do exactly what we're doing."

"Exactly. So stop the guilt trip," Dane said into her cheek.

"What is going on here?" Jacob asked, setting the drinks on the table.

Malini plopped back into her chair and lifted a glass of the foamy punch. "You caught us. Our tawdry love affair is exposed."

"As long as it's tawdry. Nothing but the best for my girl." Jacob leaned over and gave her a peck on the lips.

"Jacob Lau, I am going to pretend I didn't see that." Principal Bailey marched to their table and placed a hand on Dane's shoulder. "Can I see you for a moment, Mr. Michaels?"

"Um, sure." Dane followed the older man through the gym doors.

"What do you think that was about?" Jacob asked.

"A problem with the dance? Dane organized it, so he's in charge. Someone probably flushed streamers down the toilet or something."

Jacob took a seat next to Malini and crossed his feet at the ankles. She leaned against his shoulder and rested her head, watching her classmates party on the dance floor.

"It's our last homecoming," Malini said sadly.

"Of course it's not," Jacob insisted. "The whole point of homecoming is to welcome back alumni. We'll be back."

"But it won't be the same."

"The theme might be different."

"We might be different."

Less than a song later, Dane came back in. "He's been crying," Malini said, standing from her chair.

"I need to leave. Can you tell Erica West she's in charge? The DJ has already been paid."

"Of course, Dane. Are you all right? What happened?" Malini asked.

Dane searched her eyes, then looked at Jacob. "My dad … he died. He passed away tonight."

Chapter 8
The First Gift

The angel Gabriel looked down from a place of supreme light, warmth, and love, a place humans often called Heaven or Shamayim and other names that meant the same. With wings outstretched and twitching, he watched the darkness spread across the Earth, carried by a bird made from the flesh of evil. *Affliction.*

The light behind him turned in his direction, and Gabriel raised his wing to shield his eyes. All angels knew better than to look directly at God in His native form. He'd heard it said such a look was the cause of the fall. Lucifer had become so arrogant he raised his eyes to God's. The intensity of the power drove him mad, locking him inside a state of narcissism that spread like a cancer. The Archangel Michael, at the Lord's request, battled Lucifer, throwing him and his defenders from the edge of Heaven. Those who avoided the fall said he'd believed he *was* a god. Lucifer? A god? Perhaps of lies, of illusion, of misery. Who would follow such a god?

"Affliction terrorizes the human souls," Gabriel said. "Please, Lord, they need your healing. You must cure them, or we risk losing them forever."

"You would have me wave a hand and cure them all?"

"Oh yes," Gabriel said. "The joy it will bring them to have their health again. We will surely hear choirs singing your praises."

God laughed, a deep, heady sound that tickled Gabriel's heart. "The world isn't what it once was. If I cure them, they will likely thank penicillin, or in this case, Elysium. That's the name of the drug Lucifer created to cure his own disease."

"Elysium? Isn't that a Greek term for a mythical part of the underworld?"

"The irony isn't lost on me." The light dimmed. "Lower your wing. I've made it safe for you."

Gabriel did as he was told. God had transformed into a man with shaggy hair and sandals. He stuck his weathered hands into the pockets of his cargo pants. "As I was saying, although your compassion is admirable, Gabriel, I'm afraid healing will be confused for an act of human doing or of Lucifer's. To win souls, I must give the humans a gift that will allow them to see Lucifer's temptation for what it is. The best cure for darkness is the light."

Terribly confused, Gabriel wrinkled his brow, leaned over the viewing glass, and rested his chin in his hands. "But how will you help them without healing them. How do you combat Lucifer's terrible trickery?"

The Lord sighed, his breath rippling like a warm breeze through Heaven. "Lucifer's Elysium is a lie. His pestilence is a lie. His cure is not health but an illusion. I think our gift needs to nip at the root of his weakness."

"How?" Gabriel asked.

God reached into the wall of Heaven and pulled. A ripping sound tore through the space and then the wet slurp of molding clay. God worked the silvery stuff between his fingers. "We shall fight Lucifer's pet bird with our own animal companion, one I think the humans will prefer to Affliction. Hold out your arm, Gabriel."

The angel straightened and offered his robe-clad arm as requested. A great shriek preceded a set of talons large enough to wrap entirely around his forearm. The bird was parrot red, shaped like an eagle, and had a purposeful black stare. The animal fluffed her wings and nuzzled Gabriel's nose.

"Meet *my* new pet, Wisdom. Crafted from Heaven's own walls, anyone who sees this bird will understand the truth about the source of the disease and Harrington Enterprises. Lucifer expects the humans to be passive, apathetic fools, but I have already given them intelligence to rival his and the fortitude to act on it. This bird will simply accelerate those human traits."

Gabriel beamed. "Perfect, as always."

"Thank you, Gabriel."

"Would you like me to deliver her to the world for you?"

"Yes, please, Gabriel, and stay with her along the way, to defend her against any foul play. I release my gift into your hands."

"As you wish, my lord." Proudly, Gabriel spread his wings, and so did Wisdom, lifting from his arm with two mighty flaps. The angel ran for the edge of Heaven and tossed himself over, wings folding in, body dive-bombing to Earth like a bullet. Wisdom followed his lead. When they breached the atmosphere, Gabriel used his ability to blend into the light, shifting over and between skyscrapers and schools, houses and playgrounds at a speed hardly noticeable by humans but enough to do the trick. With Wisdom at his side, he began his journey to every city in every state and every country in the world.

He couldn't reach everyone, of course. Some were inside and wouldn't see Wisdom, but from the beginning of time, this was the way of good things. Those who did see must tell those who didn't. They always had, and they always would. Because, Gabriel knew, the way of God was stamped upon human hearts.

He flew on, the outskirts of the tiny town of Paris coming into view, where an elderly man with gray hair and square glasses was stringing Christmas lights on the eaves of a cheery yellow Cape Cod. The human male had propped his ladder carelessly with one foot on solid ground, and the other on the loose pebbles of the driveway. Early for Christmas, Gabriel thought, as this part of the world was still firmly entrenched in autumn. He supposed the elderly man meant to avoid having to do the task in icy conditions.

Wisdom passed the man first, close by his head. Gabriel had a moment to observe the wonder and awe on the man's face at seeing the great red bird before the shock straightened his spine with a snap. The man's plaid shirt-covered arms shot out to grab the top of the ladder to steady himself while he searched the sky for the bird. The sharp movement caused the ladder to move away from the roof. Worse, the leg resting on the stones slipped. With a deep, "Whoa!" man and ladder toppled.

Gabriel did not hesitate or consider the consequences. He would not have the man's injury or death on his hands. The angel swooped down and cushioned the old man's fall, careful not to be seen. The act was lightning fast and completely effective.

Alongside Wisdom, Gabriel continued on, leaving the man lying under the oak tree in his front yard, staring up into the heavens.

* * * * *

"Jacob, Jacob! Come quick!" Aunt Carolyn cried.

Inside his bedroom, Jacob dropped the tie he was unsuccessfully trying to knot around his neck and jogged down the hall to the stairwell. Aunt Carolyn's ample body plugged the open front door.

"What's going on?"

"Oh, Jacob, come quick," she whined, flailing her stubby arms at her sides. "John fell off the ladder!" She took a step onto the porch and continued down the three concrete stairs to the lawn. "Check if he's breathing!"

Uncle John was flat on his back, the fallen ladder at on odd angle across the lawn. Jacob rushed past Aunt Carolyn's ambling figure, prepared to perform CPR, but paused when he noticed his uncle was grinning, staring at the sky like he'd simply lain down to watch the clouds. "Uncle John?"

"Is he dead?" Carolyn yelled.

Uncle John's hand shot up toward Jacob who obliged by helping the man up. "I'm not dead, woman. I'm more alive than I've ever been."

Aunt Carolyn's round face puckered. "What are you talking about? I saw you fall off the ladder."

John placed a hand over his heart. "A miracle, Carolyn. Something caught me."

"Caught you?"

"I know it sounds crazy but I felt arms cushion my fall, like my own personal guardian angel was looking out for me."

Carolyn ran a chubby hand over the back of John's head. "Did you bump your noggin, John? You are acting strangely."

With his hands in his pockets, Jacob mulled over the idea of a guardian angel. The way the ladder was strewn across the lawn and his uncle had nary a scrape seemed to indicate divine intervention. Jacob had experience with the divine as a

Soulkeeper. He'd learned never to underestimate even the smallest of events.

"What did the angel look like?" Jacob asked.

Uncle John pushed Carolyn's hands away and turned toward him. "A gigantic red bird."

Jacob's eyebrows shot up. "The angel looked like a red bird?"

The older man nodded slowly.

Aunt Carolyn made a small huffing noise, mouth open and hands on hips. "Guardian angel or not, I think you should have an x-ray, John Laudner. Who knows what kind of damage might have been done."

"I'm fine, Carolyn. Look, don't wrinkle your pretty dress by putting your hands on your hips like that. I'll get changed and we'll go pay our respects at Willow's Bridge as planned."

Willow's Bridge was Paris's only funeral home and the place where Luke Michaels had been cremated. The family had put off the visitation a couple of weeks while they finished the soybean harvest. Jacob was ready to help Dane move on from the loss, but he suspected Aunt Carolyn's attendance had more to do with her interest in the gossip the wake would provide. Everyone in town wanted to know if Mrs. Michaels planned to sell the family farm now that its patriarch was deceased.

"Promise me you won't say anything about the bird, John. Clare Barger will never let me live it down."

John waved her away, scowling, and strode toward the house. Jacob followed, picking up his tie from his chest and starting the knot again. As he entered the house, Katrina descended the stairs, adjusting her long-sleeved blue dress. The glimpse of her shoulder blade jarred Jacob into dropping his tie again. She was thin, no—skeletal. Her skin stretched across the sharp contour of bone without the pad of muscle or fat. Before the bird flu, that blue dress seemed clingy. Now the fabric hung on her bones like a coat hanger. Her once shiny brown hair was dull and lifeless, as were her eyes.

"Mom, have you seen my medicine?" Katrina asked.

Carolyn marched toward her. "Haven't you finished your course, yet? You've been taking it for weeks."

"The bottle says to keep taking it until I don't have symptoms when I stop. Every time I stop, I throw up."

Jacob followed the two into the house, noticing how large and hollow Katrina's eyes had become. "Do you need something to eat?"

"No, Jacob, I just need my medicine. Mom!"

The sound of rustling pills came from the kitchen, Carolyn digging through the mass of vitamins and painkillers she kept in a basket on top of the refrigerator. "Ah, here they are. You're almost out."

Katrina met her at the kitchen table, taking the fluorescent blue pill with a shaking hand. Jacob winced. She didn't even use water to wash it down.

"Try to get better, honey. These things are costing us an arm and a leg. Elysium is like gold. Do you know people are getting held up in the city, not for their wallets, but for their Elysium?"

Jacob moved for the stairs, starting again on his tie.

"I guess when you need a pill to feel normal, you'll do anything for it. Thank God Harrington Enterprises found the cure or I'd still be in bed," Katrina said.

Stopping halfway to the second floor, Jacob turned around and returned to Katrina's side. "Harrington Enterprises? Did you say Harrington Enterprises?"

"Yeah, they make Elysium," she said, holding up the bottle. "What's wrong? You look pale."

Jacob shook his head. "No, nothing. Just curious." Harrington had a pharmaceuticals division; it didn't necessarily mean the Watchers were tainting the drugs like they had the bottled water. Then again, with what he'd learned from Malini, it couldn't be a coincidence. Jacob sent a hasty text to Malini, then jogged up the stairs and finished getting ready.

Chapter 9
Willow's Bridge

Malini arrived at the Willow's Bridge Funeral Home, anxious to see Dane. He'd been busy helping his family the last few weeks and missed most of the training sessions in Eden. She worried that when the challenge caught up to them all, Dane would be the most vulnerable. Aside from the advantages all of the Soulkeepers developed over time—above-average speed, agility, and health—Dane didn't have his own inherent powers. Instead, he borrowed other's gifts, which had come in damn useful during their last mission but could be a detriment if a legion of Watchers marched up the street.

Not to mention, she wanted to know he was okay, personally. Dane thought his dad was getting better. No one in the family expected him to die when he did. But for Dane, his relationship with his father was a story without an ending. He'd never had the opportunity to come out to his dad. What did it do to someone to know that the person who raised them never understood who they really were?

"Thanks for waiting for me." Jacob touched the elbow of her black suit. "Have you seen him yet?"

"No. My parents and I came separately. They've already gone through without me."

"Are they still angry about your hair?"

Malini smoothed her hand over her ear. "They say they aren't angry, but my mother didn't share our homecoming pictures on Facebook. I'm sure she's hoping it will grow out before any of our extended family sees it. Did you come with the Laudners?"

"Yeah. They parked around back and went in the side door by reception. Aunt Carolyn brought a casserole. Listen, I've got to tell you about something that happened today."

A honk from behind them almost made Malini fall off her high-heeled shoes. She caught herself on Jacob's chest, and shot a dirty look toward the offending vehicle.

Ethan smiled from the driver's side window of Lillian's car. "Ah, sorry. Didn't mean to scare you, Malini ... much. Will you guys wait for us?"

Jacob sighed. "Sure." He gave a small wave to his mother, who was in the passenger's seat. She must've changed at the shop and come straight from work.

Malini watched Ethan maneuver the Volkswagen Beetle into a parking space. "I'm glad your mom convinced Ethan to come with her. I don't care what the family thinks; Dane needs him today. Not to mention that he's put in as many hours as Dane on that farm this fall. I think he's learned as much about soybeans as soulkeeping."

"About that, haven't they ever asked him where he lives? The guy works there every day. Paris is a small town. Aren't any of them curious where he came from?"

With a quiet laugh, Malini threaded her fingers into his. "Grace took care of that months ago. He has an apartment in town. He's a writer; doesn't come out much."

"Oh. People believe that?"

"Seems so."

Lillian jogged to Jacob's side as if her burgundy sheath dress and heels were athletic gear. Ethan followed close behind, keys in hand. "Are you ready to go in?" he asked.

Malini nodded and held open one side of the heavy wooden double doors for the others to walk through. The dark wood foyer was crowded with flowers, all of them supplied by the Laudner's flower shop. She filed in at the back of the line of people waiting to offer their condolences to the family. Jacob grabbed a card from the basket near the entryway and showed it to her, while Lillian and Ethan signed the guestbook. The picture of Luke Michaels was one from years ago with a full head of brown hair and piercing gray eyes exactly like Dane's.

"He looks so young," Malini said.

A stocky redheaded woman in front of them turned around, blotting her eyes with a tissue. "It's just so senseless. I can't believe this happened."

Malini reached out to comfort the woman, resting her hand on her ample shoulder. "I'm sorry for your loss. Are you family?" She didn't recognize the woman from town. Maybe a cousin?

"Oh no. I was his nurse at Terre Haute Hospital. You just get to know the families working with patients the way I do. It sticks with you when things like this happen. Just not right. I wanted to pay my respects."

Lillian nodded empathetically. "He was too young. Struck down in his prime."

"Yes, of course. But I mean the whole thing with the medication. Atrocious!"

"I'm sorry—What was your name?" Malini asked.

"Patricia. Patty. Very nice to meet you." She extended her hand. Malini accepted her handshake and introduced Jacob, Lillian, and Ethan, who was growing more uncomfortable by the minute. They took a few steps forward with the line.

"So, what were you saying about the medication?" Lillian prompted.

"Didn't you hear?" She lowered her voice. "His medication was discontinued. Harrington Pharmaceuticals stopped production of all medications except Elysium. Luke's condition was rare, as was his prescription therapy. The hospital couldn't find another source in time. If you ask me, that's what killed him."

Malini wanted to continue the conversation, but Jacob was poking her in the side. She tried pushing his hand away but eventually gave into his prodding. "What, Jacob?" she said through a tight smile.

He leaned over and whispered in her ear. "That's what I texted you about. Elysium is made by Harrington."

Malini exchanged glances with Lillian, who fidgeted as if she were covered in ants. "Thank you, Patty. We didn't know. I'm sure the family will find comfort in your presence."

Patty nodded, dabbing her eyes again, and turned back into line.

They'd reached the front of the funeral parlor where an urn containing Mr. Michaels's remains was surrounded by more flowers and plants. While the family visited with Patty, Malini said a prayer for Luke Michaels. She couldn't get her head around how a fully grown man could fit in the small metal container. Life was fleeting and fragile. He'd spent his life building the largest farm in Paris to end up here.

"Thanks for coming, Mal," Dane said, calling her over. He wrapped his arms around her for a quick hug.

"Hey, man." Jacob extended his hand while Lillian and Ethan hung back. "Sorry, again, about your dad."

"Thank you."

"Ethan!" Mrs. Michaels called. Dane turned toward his mother, eyebrows raised, then exchanged glances with Ethan. The gray-haired woman budged between them and hooked her hand inside Ethan's elbow. "There you are! I thought

Dane would have invited you to stand with us. You're practically family." She pulled him by her side in line.

Ethan's mouth fell open, and Dane stared at his mother as if she'd grown a second head.

Mary Michaels lowered her voice. "There's no reason for us to keep pretending this isn't what it is. Today, we are a family grieving. All of us. We all need each other."

Next to Ethan, who took his position in the receiving line with equal measure of shock and aplomb, Dane nodded, eyes misting. He turned to shake Lillian's hand and accept her condolences. Pulling Mrs. Michaels into a tight hug, Malini was speechless with admiration. Finally, Ethan and Dane got what they deserved. Acceptance.

When Lillian and Jacob had finished with the line, Malini followed the others to the reception room, where they joined the Laudner family at one of several folding tables set up for guests.

"You should try Carolyn's casserole," John Laudner said to Malini. "Jacob will tell ya how good it is. Best Bacon Cheeseburger Breakfast casserole in town."

Jacob glanced at her, then flashed Carolyn a practiced smile. "Uh, yeah. Real cheesy," he said, bobbing his head.

In the chair beside John, an exhausted-looking Katrina rested her head in her palm. She snorted at the exchange. "Yeah, it's delicious, and contains your entire daily requirement of calories per serving." She giggled and Carolyn slapped her on the shoulder.

"Katrina!"

"Oh, come on, Mom. You use an entire stick of butter in that thing."

Carolyn pointed a chubby finger in Malini's direction. "It's a treat, for special occasions."

"I'll be sure to try some," Malini said. "Katrina, you look like you need more than a day's worth of calories, care to join me?" Malini's comment landed on the table between her and Katrina like a thrown brick.

Elbows anchored on the table, Jacob's cousin extended her hands, fingers knotted in front of her. "I'm not hungry."

Uncle John rubbed his short gray hair with his palm. "You need to eat, darling," he said softly.

Pulling out a chair across from him, Lillian agreed. "I haven't seen you eat a full meal since you've been better."

Jacob stepped closer and slightly in front of Malini, as if protecting her from the inevitable onslaught. "Here it comes," he whispered.

"I'm not better. That's the problem. People don't get better without medicine. If Dad would let me take mine, I might be able to keep something down."

John groaned but answered her with an element of control Katrina didn't share. "You've been on Elysium for weeks. The doctor said it was supposed to cure you in two. You've got no fever anymore. You know what I think, Katrina? I think you're addicted to the Elysium."

Katrina grimaced. "Addicted? I'm not addicted. Do you say a diabetic is addicted to insulin? I feel sick to my stomach when I don't take it. I can't eat if I don't take it." She slapped the table. The other wake-goers filing into the reception room glanced toward her table.

"Withdrawal symptoms. I bet you get a headache too," John whispered. "You know, when I was in the military we had some guys addicted to opium. Same thing. Elysium is addictive; mark my words." He sat up straighter in his chair and turned to look Malini directly in the eye. "You know, the way the world is today, it would not surprise me if the company purposefully made Elysium to be addicting. They must be making a mint."

Malini raised her eyebrows. "It's possible." More than possible, actually. A tingle traveled up Malini's spine to her scalp.

John turned back to Katrina. "I'm gonna help you quit. You'll feel so much better when you do."

With a burst of energy that seemed to come out of nowhere, Katrina stood up and grabbed her purse. "You are not a doctor, Dad, and you have no idea how I feel or why. Half the globe is on Elysium trying to fight this crazy virus. How do you know I don't need to be on it longer? At least let me talk to Dr. Howard."

Aunt Carolyn tugged on the side of her floral dress. "Katrina, sit down. You are making a scene," she said in a loud stage whisper. Her brown eyes darted around to the other guests in the reception area. Everyone had stopped what they were doing and stared in their direction. "Sit down and we'll talk about this like adults."

"Oh, for Christ's sake, Mother!" Katrina shouted. "Am I embarrassing you? Am I marring your precious perfect family image? Give me a break." She stomped out the side door, slamming it behind her.

"That was awful," Jacob said flatly. Lillian and Malini nodded in agreement.

"It's the Elysium," John said, rubbing his upper lip. "And I'll tell you something else. The thought occurred to me today that Harrington Enterprises created the virus so that they could cure it."

Aunt Carolyn rolled her eyes. "Oh, John, now you're sounding crazy."

"I'm not crazy. Do you know how much money Harrington is making off Elysium? I read that one in every thousand people is on it now. It's suspicious, too, how they stopped producing all other medications before the outbreak. It's like they knew it was coming."

Lillian made a small coughing noise. "Will you excuse me? I need to get some air." She caught Malini's eye and gestured with her head toward the door.

"See, John. You are scaring people away with this mumbo jumbo," Caroline chided.

Malini tipped her head. "No, I want to hear this. John, why do you believe Harrington created the virus?"

"I was stringing lights today and fell off the ladder. Someone ... something broke my fall." Uncle John paused when Aunt Carolyn gave him a death stare. He cleared his throat. "Afterward, lying there staring up at the sky, it occurred to me out of the blue that no one has ever died from this bird flu. Doctors say it's fatal, and they are prescribing Elysium to anyone who will take it. The stuff's like gold, too. Hundreds of dollars for a month's supply. But I haven't heard of any actual deaths. Hell, they've had the cure from the very beginning. I'm telling you, it's Harrington. They developed this virus, then cured it for the sake of profit, and they're greasing all of these doctors' pockets to get everyone hooked on it. How is it that Harrington was so far ahead of the curve on this? When did they do the R&D? I'll tell you when, before anyone knew about the virus. A bit too convenient, don't you think? Well, I'll tell you one thing, if I catch this from Katrina, I'm not taking Elysium. No way."

At this, Carolyn Laudner stood up with a huff and headed toward the bathroom. John gaped at her back. The other attendees slowly returned to their casseroles.

"I believe you, Mr. Laudner," Malini said. "I don't think Harrington Pharmaceuticals can be trusted. When this is all over, Katrina will thank you for taking care of her."

"I appreciate that, Ms. Gupta. You are as smart as Jacob says you are."

Malini squeezed Jacob's hand. He smiled. "I'm going to go check on Mom." He led Malini through the side door where Lillian waited.

"Are you thinking what I'm thinking?" Lillian asked.

Malini nodded. "All this time we've been waiting for Watchers to march up the street. The first temptation has been here for weeks. We're not just dealing with infected water; they're using Harrington to infect people with a virus and addict them to their *cure.*"

"How do you think John knew?" Lillian asked. "He's a smart guy, but this would be a leap for anyone."

"Don't know," Malini said.

"When he fell off the ladder today, he said an angel caught him, in the form of a red bird," Jacob said.

"Hmm," Malini pondered, "maybe God has sent His first gift after all."

The Westcotts exited the reception area then, parting the group. When they came back together, Jacob whispered, "So how do we stop Harrington?"

"I'm not sure," Malini said. "But I think it's time we paid another visit to Harrington Enterprises."

Chapter 10
The Mission

Malini suspected her idea would be controversial, but the vehemence in the room surprised even her. While she didn't think the council would come to blows, the tension was palpable. Each of them had a personal interest in this, and none of them knew what to expect.

"It's too dangerous," Grace said.

Gideon stood, knocking his chair back. "Too dangerous? It's not aggressive enough! We've waited too long. It's time we engaged in the challenge." He paced the conference room.

"Gideon's right," Lillian said. "We've suspected Harrington for long enough. It's time to find out exactly what we are dealing with."

"The twins are the natural choice," Malini said. "They can pose as insiders and find out how much control the Watchers have over Harrington. It's possible we only need to take out one or two influenced leaders to stop the production of Elysium."

Master Lee stroked the short stubble of his chin. "Grace, it is understandable that you would fear sending your daughters, but they are more than ready. I've never trained stronger warriors, mentally or physically."

"Hey!" Lillian said.

"Except you, Lillian, of course." Lee coughed behind his hand.

Lillian shook her head. "Actually, after seeing them fight, you are probably correct. They are stronger than I am. And they're ready for a mission."

Grace threaded her fingers. "So, I'm in the minority."

Malini shook her head. "No one blames you, Grace. Bonnie and Samantha are your daughters and the only family you have."

Grace nodded, a tear breaking free from the corner of her eye.

"But they are also Soulkeepers with a unique and useful ability to be human chameleons. We need them."

Pale and agitated, Grace rubbed under her eyes. A heavy weight settled over the room. The members of the Soulkeepers' Council knew that she'd be outvoted if it came to that, but they wanted her to make the decision on her own.

"I want Jesse to go with them," Grace said, straightening. "He can act as mission control and provide backup."

Malini nodded. "Agreed. But I think we should keep the team small. Lucifer has the list Abigail conjured of Soulkeepers. Outside of Eden, he can detect our souls if he wants to. Jacob, Dane, and I need to continue attending Paris High School. He knows we go there, and it's possible our absence could raise suspicion. Cheveyo isn't ready for a mission."

"And Ethan?" Gideon asked.

"Our second line of defense should the twins fail," Malini said grimly. "He'll hang back in Paris and use a staff to blink out there if Jesse calls for help. That way we'll have a single point of contact for communication purposes."

Gideon placed his hands on the windowsill and leaned out over Eden's vast jungle. The school didn't need glass windows. By some unexplainable phenomenon, the birds and insects chose not to come inside. Same for the gentle sweeping rain that kept the jungle bright and lush.

Malini looked at Grace, Lillian, and Lee. "If we've come to an agreement, would you mind excusing yourselves so that Gideon and I can talk?"

Grace nodded, blinking her eyes slowly and pursing her lips. Standing, she headed for the door. "I'll tell my girls. Why do I feel like they'll be more excited about this than I am?"

"Because they will be," Lillian said. "They've been begging for a mission since Arizona."

Lee freed himself from his chair in one lithe move and followed Lillian and Grace from the room. Malini closed the door behind them, and then returned to Gideon's side. She placed her hand on his shoulder, so that her fingers grazed the bare skin of his neck. The flesh-to-flesh contact pumped healing energy into him.

"I know what you're doing, Malini. It's not working."

"No?"

"I feel the warmth and the calm. I am touched by your kindness. But this hurt in me does not need healing. It is not an injury. This is my body telling me I need to do more. This pain is my warning that something's wrong, that I need the other half of me back. This is love, Malini. You can't heal this because it is as whole as it has ever been."

She swallowed the lump in her throat and rubbed his back through his shirt. "I know it's been hard for you. I know you've wanted to leave Eden to try to rescue her. But no mortal comes back from Hell, Gideon, without divine intervention. There's nothing you can do."

He straightened. "You're right. It has been hard for me, but not unproductive. I have something for you." From the table, he retrieved a file folder and handed it to her. "An updated organizational chart for Harrington Enterprises along with a diagram of its offices. You'll notice a new CEO has recently been named. A Mr. M. Blake."

"What happened to Mr. Harrington?"

"No one knows. It's not public knowledge. He simply resigned, and he and his family disappeared."

"Hmm. Suspicious. Influenced, likely." She followed the lines of the chart to boxes containing the last names of various vice presidents and directors. She didn't recognize any of them, but then she didn't spend her days watching CNBC. "I'll share this with the twins. Thank you."

He met her eyes. "Do you think, if we help win the challenge, God will bring Abigail back?"

"Yes, I do. Have faith." As Malini pulled him into her embrace, she hoped and prayed she could do the same.

* * * * *

After the conversation she'd just had with her mother, Bonnie Guillian desperately needed to blow off steam. A mission, finally. But the task before her couldn't be more dangerous. Best-case scenario, she'd be sniffing out a major nest of Watcher activity. And it didn't help that her sister and loverboy were on the same team. Talk about a distraction.

Bonnie swept her long red hair up into a ponytail, tying it back with a black elastic. When it was as tight and smooth as possible, she squatted down to readjust her running shoes. Master Lee had shown her a special way to tie them, tighter at her instep and looser at the toes, to make for a more comfortable run.

"How do you get there again?" she asked Dane. She'd bumped into him in the foyer down the hall from the conference room where Samantha and Ghost remained. Those two were grilling her mother for information. Only, no one knew anything. That's why they were going on this mission, to answer the questions.

"It's hard to give you specific directions. There are no street signs," Dane said.

"I know, but 'wander aimlessly through the jungle' doesn't help me much." She wanted to find the ocean. She wanted to be alone. Rumor was that Dane had been there.

"I followed Archie back. All I can tell you is to head left into the jungle and follow the trail to the end, then keep going."

She stood and nodded. "Got it." Plugging her ears with her headphones, she set her favorite playlist, and then walked briskly toward the giant front doors.

"Bonnie, wait!" Sam called from behind her.

Bonnie pretended not to hear her. For maybe the first time in a decade, she didn't want to see her sister. Bonnie loved Samantha. Always would. Only she was sick of her incessant whining about Jesse, or Ghost as everyone else called him, that she thought she might hurl. If the two weren't tongue wrestling around every corner, there was some sort of drama that required Sam's full attention. Bonnie couldn't remember the last time she and Sam had shared a conversation that wasn't about Ghost. Oh, wait. Yes, she could—in Nebraska, before they'd moved here. She pulled open the door.

"Wait!" Samantha's hand closed around Bonnie's bicep.

Bonnie stopped and pulled her earbuds out. "Yeah?"

"I'm going to go running with you."

A frown crawled across Bonnie's face. "Wouldn't you rather hang out with Jesse? We're done with training for the day. You guys could be *alone* until dinner." She made the word alone sound illicit.

Sam straightened her ponytail. "I thought I'd spend some time with you."

Bonnie rolled her green eyes and jogged out the door.

"Hey, what's with the attitude, Bon-bell? If you don't want me running with you just say so." Samantha synced into step beside her, matching her gait exactly with clockwork precision.

"Maybe I just wanted to be alone," Bonnie whispered. She tried to pick up the pace, but Samantha matched it. Her sister laughed at the comment.

"Oh. Oh! You're serious. You want to be alone? After Mom tells us we're assigned one of the most dangerous missions ever? After we find out we could die?"

Bonnie didn't reply. She could hear the hurt in her sister's voice and wasn't proud to be the one who caused it.

"Why, Bonnie? What did I do?" Samantha begged.

Deep within the jungle now, the cries of monkeys and birds overhead could not drown out the pain in her sister's words, and Bonnie felt compelled to answer. "I'm just sick of everything always having to do with Jesse. Even this mission includes Jesse! If you must know, I wanted one Jesse-free hour."

Samantha gave an exaggerated gasp. "You're jealous! You're jealous that I have a boyfriend and you don't because the boy you thought you liked turned out to be gay."

"I'm not jealous. Yes, I was disappointed to find out about Dane, but there are other fish in the sea. I'm not going to say I'm happy about being a perpetual third wheel, but I'm happy for you. I really am."

"Then what's the problem?"

"The problem is, I don't know you anymore without him. He's invaded every crevice of your life. It's like you've become one of those celebrity hybrids, Jemantha."

Samantha jogged quietly by her side, weaving between trees until the path became so narrow that she had to follow behind. She became so quiet for so long that Bonnie slowed to check that she was still there. She was, her footsteps slowing to match Bonnie's. Sam didn't say anything but hit her with a sour stare. Bonnie accelerated again.

"We both knew this would happen eventually," Samantha finally said.

"What would happen?"

"One of us would have to break away."

This brought Bonnie up short. She turned in the shelter of the trees, feeling the humidity press against her, suffocating her. Hands on her hips, she willed Samantha to elaborate, and of course she did. They'd been reading each other their entire lives.

"Bonnie, we've spent every minute of seventeen years together. We share flesh for heaven's sake. When we do what we do, we literally become one person sometimes. But we aren't one person. We are two women who, I think, have dreams of marriage and babies and futures. You must have thought about what would happen if one of us married before the other?"

"What are you saying?"

"I'm saying we can't always live together. Things are going to change. They have to. We each have to come to terms with the reality that someday we will have separate lives."

Bonnie pushed a clump of ferns with her toes and watched the leaves curl in on their stems. "No, Sam, I haven't thought about that, and I certainly don't consider it reality. Here's my reality. We are Soulkeepers and anyone who loves us, especially another Soulkeeper like Jesse, is going to know that we can't be separated. Doing so would render us powerless. And if that person loves, truly loves, either one of us, they will work to find a way to keep us together. I don't know, maybe we each own a side of the same duplex. But honestly it sounds like you're ready to make a clean break. Maybe it's you that hopes we won't always be together."

"That's not true." Samantha glanced toward her toes.

"We're twins. You can't lie to me." Bonnie continued down the trail.

"So I want my own life! Is that a crime? I want a husband and babies and to pick out my own carpeting without having to ask my sister's opinion."

"You know we'd always pick the same thing."

"That's not the point. The point is ... The point..." Samantha stopped, and Bonnie, who'd been intermittently looking over her shoulder at her sister, did too. Bonnie followed Samantha's stare to the opening between two fat palm trees that looked a lot like pineapples.

"It's beautiful," Bonnie said.

The ocean rolled in, washing up a white sand beach with fat liquid fingers that left trails as they receded. Instinctively, she took off her shoes and socks and stepped onto the soft shoreline, moving toward the line of sea foam.

She sensed Samantha do the same at her side. The sea called to her, and she stepped closer until the water just barely washed across the tops of her feet and the sand squished between her toes.

"Look who's here?" Samantha said.

Bonnie looked where her sister pointed. Down the beach a ways, Malini sat on a piece of driftwood, enchanted staff in hand. "Looks like she wants to talk."

"Nothing more anxiety producing than a talk with the Healer."

"Maybe it's girl talk. She wants to tell us how Jacob isn't paying her enough attention."

Samantha laughed at the absurdity.

At a stroll, Bonnie approached the driftwood, shoes in hand.

"Hi, you guys," Malini said. "I suppose you suspect I'm not here for the view."

"What's going on?" Bonnie asked.

"Did your mom tell you about the mission?"

"Yeah, we leave for Chicago after Thanksgiving. Lillian is hoping the crowds of shoppers will give us some cover." Bonnie popped her knee up and leaned against the driftwood, half sitting.

"Lillian knows what she's doing. Before you go, I wanted to give you this." Malini pulled a necklace from her pocket. Bonnie had seen the red stone before, most recently on Dane. The disc-shaped gem was set in a black leather cord. Very masculine. "I can re-set it for you if you would like. I have a gold chain with a mount that fits the stone."

"No, it's beautiful," Sam said.

"Only…" Bonnie began. "There's only one stone but two of us."

Malini dangled it from her fingertips and smiled ruefully. "But you're always together."

Bonnie frowned and crossed her arms over her chest.

"It will work for either of you, Bonnie, or both of you if you are touching," Malini explained.

"What do we need it for anyway?" Sam asked.

"Use it when you are in need of guidance, when you are confused or in danger. Relax, look deep into the stone, and you will have access to the oldest, wisest part of myself, the part of the Healer that is eternal."

"I want Bonnie to wear it," Samantha blurted.

"What? Why?" Bonnie argued. She hated that her voice sounded defensive.

"Because I'll have—" Sam stopped short.

Bonnie's shoulders slumped. "You'll have Jesse to protect you. The stone is my consolation prize."

Bonnie snatched the necklace from Malini's hand and yanked it over her head. The cord got stuck on her ponytail. She wrestled it free, face heating with embarrassment, then succeeded in putting it on, adjusting the cord so the stone rested at the base of her neck.

"I didn't mean it like that, Bonnie," Samantha snapped.

"Thank you, Malini. I hope I won't need to use this, but it comforts me to have it." Bonnie gave a small wave in Malini's direction then took off running, shoes in hand. She broke into a jog, heading for the path that would take her to the school.

For once, Samantha didn't follow her.

Chapter 11
Forever Darkness

A bigail pressed her hands against the glass and looked out over the city of Chicago from her penthouse prison. It must be close to Christmas. The buildings were decorated in gaudy baubles of red and gold with swags of evergreen in the windows and balconies. Tiny people walked the sidewalks below, arms laden with packages, joyfully choosing the perfect gifts for loved ones. A constant flow of traffic carried folks on their way to making happy holiday memories. At least that's what she imagined. She couldn't say for sure due to the distance.

She wondered what Gideon was doing. No doubt the gnomes had decorated Eden for Christmas and perhaps the Soulkeepers would have a party to celebrate. Her heart sank thinking about the Soulkeepers. She'd assumed they would have rescued her by now. Then again, Lucifer did not want her found. And when Lucifer set his mind to something, he usually got what he wanted. The reality was this: if the Soulkeepers hadn't found her by now, they likely never would. Her heavy sigh wasn't even enough to fog the window. Ghost breath.

He was torturing her. For the last two weeks, he'd fed her the same thing. One meal a day. A pasty dish from a Korean restaurant in the city—some type of porridge. It wasn't the food she detested; it was the hunger. One meal a day was barely enough calories to keep her alive, and always on his schedule, when he chose to feed her. She rested her forehead against the glass, giving herself over to the heaviness that followed her everywhere. She couldn't do this much longer. Her mind, once strong and self-assured, was cracking from the solitary confinement.

But she had a plan. The only part of this apartment she could touch was the walls. Lucifer must have walls for his cage, or his pet ghost would pass through and escape. Every Thursday at two thirty, the cleaning lady would come, a Polish woman in a babushka that put too much care into the devil's abode. Care that included vacuuming. She'd watched the woman plug in the machine time and time again, saw the small spark as the prongs met the outlet, and formed a plan of escape. This time when the housekeeper came, Abigail would lower her hand to cover the outlet. If her presumption was correct, the electricity would travel through whatever she was made of, conducted by the prongs and the solid magic of the wall, and hopefully stop her heart.

Sad that it should come to suicide. Better to take herself out than to allow Lucifer to use her as ransom against the Soulkeepers. Suicide meant no one would be tempted to risk their lives for her anymore.

Right on schedule, the front door opened and the bent figure of the cleaning woman backed into the room, pulling her cart of tools and supplies along with her. As usual, her head was wrapped in a red scarf, tied under her chin, that hid her face, and her body was covered in a loose-fitting, long-sleeved dress that gave her a billowing, round appearance.

The woman closed the door, positioned her bucket and mop in the kitchen near the sink, and then busied herself unloading the vacuum cleaner. Abigail moved closer, silent as a draft, and readied herself. The woman reached for the cord, and Abigail lowered her hand, feeling the hard, smooth expanse of the wall. She took pleasure in the cool paint, perhaps the last thing she would ever touch. She stopped her hand's descent just above the outlet cover.

The housekeeper unwound the cord and lowered the prongs to plug it in. This was it. All Abigail had to do was slide her hand down to block the outlet, make the woman stab through her enchanted flesh and electrocute her. She stopped short of her goal. Could she do this? After all she'd gone through to become human, could she throw it all away? Ten thousand years she'd waited. What was a few more?

She pulled her hand away and began to weep silently. No, she would not take the easy way out. Starving or not, she'd accept her fate. Somewhere, deep inside, she hoped her suffering had purpose. In the past, her pain always had, even the self-sacrifice that made her human. Funny, she'd needed to die then. Now, her intuition told her she must live. There was a difference between self-sacrifice and personal escape.

Crumpling into a ball, she sat down and leaned against the wall.

"I knew you wouldn't do it," a soft voice said. "You're stronger than that. Always have been."

Abigail glanced up in surprise to find her reflection looking down at her from under the babushka. The housekeeper untied the headscarf and cast it aside, freeing a cascade of honey-blond waves. Abigail looked at herself—the best version of herself—and her mouth dropped open.

"It's you!" Abigail beamed. God came for her! She hoped desperately that the Lord wasn't a figment of her imagination or her injured psyche.

"Yes. It is I." God opened her arms. "I'm here for you Abigail."

Abigail pushed herself from the floor and tossed her arms around her salvation's neck, and for the first time in weeks could feel the result. She did not pass through. The warmth of the hug infused her, and bright light lifted her soul. But the best part was the love. Abigail lost herself in the all-encompassing love.

Too soon, God pulled away. "I'm sorry, I can't stay long."

Abigail sputtered, "You-you're not taking me with you?"

"No. It's not your time, and I need you here."

A violent tremor rocked Abigail's body. "No. Don't leave me here."

"I know this is difficult for you, but you have been chosen for this role because you are the strongest. The world needs you, Abigail. This trial you are suffering will come and go, but the gift you will give to the world will be eternal."

Lowering her eyes, Abigail wept in earnest again. "I'm not strong enough," she squeaked. "I can't do this any longer."

"You can. I know you can. Everything you need to survive is already inside of you."

She shook her head. "No. There is nothing strong inside of me."

A bright flash crossed the penthouse like a lightning strike. Abigail forced herself to look up into the light.

"Trust in my plan," God said. "You've always known that life wasn't about living forever. When you became human you accepted your inevitable death to be part of the greater good."

"I did." Abigail crossed her arms over her growling stomach.

"Then trust me. Wait on the plan. Keep your eyes and ears alert. I promise you, this is not your end."

Abigail nodded slowly.

"Now, I have only a moment before the dark one arrives, but I have a gift for you."

"A gift?"

God reached into her cleaning cart and handed her a small snack box.

"Mixed nuts?" Abigail stared at the strange label. "To eat?"

"Yes. But only one per day. Try one now."

God didn't have to ask her twice. Abigail ripped into the box, selected one that reminded her of a walnut, and popped it between her lips. As she chewed, the flavor of roast beef and gravy, mashed potatoes, and fresh asparagus worked through her mouth. When she swallowed, her stomach filled with the contentment of a square meal.

"Place the box in your pocket. He won't see it there."

She did. The same pocket in the same belted sweater-coat she'd worn the day she arrived. "Thank you. Thank you," Abigail whispered.

"I must go. Be patient. I promise you, this is not the end."

Abigail nodded. In the blink of an eye, God was gone, replaced by an old, wrinkled woman who promptly picked up her errant babushka and tied it around her head, then began to vacuum. The housekeeper passed right through her in her pursuit of cleanliness, moving from room to room while Abigail watched in her ghostly form. She finished in the kitchen just as Lucifer walked in the front door, bag in arms.

"Good evening, Mr. Blake. You're home early today."

Mr. Blake? Abigail tucked the name away inside her mind. So Lucifer was posing as a human now. Interesting.

"Not so, Mrs. Bobik. You're late to finish," Lucifer snapped.

The old woman glanced at her watch. "Oh, how the time has flown tonight. I will finish up and get out of your hair."

"Please."

Abigail cringed, hoping Lucifer wouldn't be suspicious of the woman's lateness. But then, the devil was too proud to suspect God could get the best of him. She could always trust in his arrogance.

Mrs. Bobik finished and left in record time.

The old woman was barely out the door when Lucifer fixed his acidic blue eyes on Abigail. "Enjoy your day?"

She didn't justify his greeting with a response but turned toward the window.

He laughed deeply and used the remote control on the wall to fill the room with dark opera music. She didn't have to turn back around to know the *plunk* on the counter was a white, waxed cube half full of Korean porridge. She could smell it.

"Bon appetit!" the devil drawled.

Abigail turned in time to see him disappear into his office, laughing. She approached the carton, determined not to waste food even though she was no longer hungry. But when she looked into the take-out container, her stomach rolled. The contents swarmed with maggots. The food was spoiled.

Gagging, she closed the container and placed it back inside the paper bag. She would have liked to put the whole thing in the garbage under the sink, but Lucifer's enchantment only allowed her to touch the food and packaging. With her hand resting on the box in her pocket, she returned to her place by the window and waited for God's promise to unfold.

Chapter 12
Harrington Enterprises

"The street is blocked. You'll have to go on foot." The cab driver pulled over at the edge of the burgeoning crowd, scratching the stubble on his chin as if the people in front of his cab were a mystery to him.

"There must be a thousand people on this street," Bonnie said, handing the driver a twenty. "What's going on?" She opened the door and let Ghost and Samantha out while the driver made change.

"Are all these people shoppers?" Ghost asked, adjusting the backpack on his shoulder, heavy with weapons from Eden.

"Nah. These guys are picketing that, er, pharma company. All bullshit. These hipster tree huggers think Harrington created that bird flu goin' round in order to sell the cure." He handed her eight dollars change.

Bonnie pocketed the five and handed him back the three singles. "You don't think Harrington's behind the bird flu?"

"Listen, girly, I don't know nothin' about these conspiracy theories but when I got sick, I took the Elysium and now I'm better. Thank you, Harrington." He made a rough salute with his meaty hand.

A sharp tug on her elbow reminded Bonnie they needed to keep moving. "Right," she said to the cabbie. "Glad you're feeling better."

The driver nodded and pulled back into traffic.

"Looks like Harrington is in deep doo-doo over Elysium," Samantha said, eyeing the picketers as she blended into the crowd.

"Well, you heard Mom; that's why we're here," Bonnie whispered. "Malini suspects there are Watchers behind this, and we know Lucifer's behind the Watchers. We gotta try to find the source. If we can kill the Watchers influencing the executives at Harrington, we might get a foothold in this war."

The woman next to her thrust her sign in the air and shouted, "Elysium is poison! Elysium is poison!" Her sign had a giant "E" with a red slash through it and smaller letters that said *Elysium is more addictive than heroin, cocaine, and meth combined.*

Ghost leaned in and whispered into Bonnie's ear. "I'm going to blip to the front and see what I can see. I'll text you."

She nodded, as did her sister on his other side. Then he was gone. The crowd pressed in around them. Slowly, they snaked through the mass of chanting bodies and bouncing signs toward the front of the building.

"I'm scared, Bon." Sam squeezed her hand, muscling her way through the throngs of people. "These people look really angry."

"They're not angry at us," Bonnie said.

Sam paused in the crowd and cocked her head to the side, meeting her sister's gaze.

"I won't let anything happen to you, Sam."

Jolting, Sam fumbled for the phone vibrating in her pocket. "Jesse says there are cops upfront enforcing a barricade so that workers can come and go from the building. They are verifying everyone. The lower levels aren't even Harrington-owned, but everyone who gets in has to show credentials."

"Oh," Bonnie said. "So how do we know who to look like to get in?

Sam shrugged.

They reached Ghost at the front of the crowd and pressed against the barricade. "I could blink inside the building," he murmured.

"Don't be stupid," Bonnie whispered in his ear. "If Sam and I go and get into trouble, you can always blink in to help us. Unfortunately, that scenario doesn't work the other way around. You've got to be our backup, Jesse."

Slap. Sam's hand smacked Bonnie's arm.

"Ow!" Bonnie turned toward her sister, who was sniffing the air like a dog. "What's your problem?"

"Do you smell that?"

All three turned their heads toward the front doors to the Harrington skyscraper. A security guard held the door open for an important-looking man exiting the building. The man paused outside and said, "Thank you, Fredrick," in an entitled and condescending tone that didn't match the words spoken. Bonnie watched his straight white teeth flash with every word. The man smoothed the silky fabric of his double-breasted navy suit arrogantly, and the professional cut of his black hair didn't move, even when the wind came off the lake and blew Bonnie's red locks back. That breeze carried with it what her sister had smelled, the scent of Watcher.

Bonnie locked onto the man, scanning him from head to toe and elbowing Sam to do the same. Six-foot-four, broad shoulders, narrow hips, chiseled jaw. She gagged on the stench of the black-skinned snake underneath and unconsciously toyed with the red stone necklace through the collar of her coat. She noticed Ghost adjust the backpack of weapons on his shoulder and cover his nose with his hand.

The Watcher pulled a pair of sunglasses from his pocket, unfolding them with a quick snap of his wrist. A gold lion's head ring glinted from his right index finger. As he raised the glasses to his face, Bonnie was afforded a straight-on view.

His dark-blue eyes shone almost purple, an impossible color for humans unless they were sporting contacts.

The wind shifted, her long red hair floating forward over her shoulder. Those purple eyes locked onto hers. The smile faded from the man's face, and he slid the sunglasses on. One step, then another. He was coming for her.

"He saw me," Bonnie whispered, but she needn't have said anything. Sam was already pulling her back into the crowd, and Ghost was blinking in and out of sight, searching for a good place to hide and regroup.

"This way," Sam said, eyeing her phone. "Jesse says there's an alley."

Holding hands, Bonnie allowed Sam to pull her through the crowd, snaking in and out of the protesters. Again and again, Bonnie looked over her shoulder, searching for the Watcher, but the mass of people had closed in behind them. The man was gone.

The crowd began to thin as they reached Ghost two blocks from Harrington. Two dumpsters obscured the entrance to the narrow, brick-lined alley where he waited.

"Squeeze through," Ghost said from the other side.

Bonnie looked at Sam, who nodded and checked to make sure no one was watching. Bonnie slipped through first, her mass shifting down her leg until an abnormally large foot landed on the other side. She slimmed her body to slide through the gap, sending her extra inches to her foot, then her leg, her hip, and so on. When she was completely on the other side, she pulled Sam through, incorporating her extra mass so that she could fit.

"That was definitely a Watcher," Sam said when she'd resumed her natural form and shape.

"Definitely. And he saw us. Do you think we lost him?" Bonnie looked through the gap in the dumpsters for any sign of the beast.

"I think so," Ghost replied. "I hate to be the one to state the obvious, but one of you needs to become that guy. That's our way in."

Bonnie widened her eyes at Samantha. It made sense, but the thought was terrifying. They'd have to separate. Only one of them could go because the man's form could not contain both of their mass. But who would go and who would stay? Bonnie watched her sister swallow, her twin's eyes shifting to Ghost, who looked like he might cry.

No words had to be said. And, while she knew that Sam would argue with the notion, her sister needed to stay with Ghost. The two were an item, and separating them could cause a distraction they didn't need.

"I'll go," Bonnie said.

"No," Sam protested. "We should draw straws."

Bonnie rolled her eyes. How predictable. "Sam..." Her sister's eyes darted away. Enough said. "I'll go."

"Hmm, so that's settled, then," Ghost muttered, shaking his head.

Grasping her sister's hand, Bonnie melded with her twin, concentrating on the Watcher's illusion and the sound of his voice. Her body changed, absorbing the parts of her sister she needed, growing taller and more muscular. Her long red hair retracted into her head and her face morphed. When she'd replicated the Watcher she'd seen, Bonnie pulled away, detaching from her sister.

"Is it right?" she asked the now smaller version of Sam. Her sister looked about twelve.

"Perfect. You even remembered the ring," Sam said.

Bonnie looked down at the lion's head ring and nodded. "How's the voice?" she asked.

"Go lower," Sam said.

Bonnie tried again. "Thank you, Frederick." She tried to imitate what she'd heard earlier.

"Perfect," Ghost said.

"Let's do this."

A column of black smoke descended between them, forming into the Watcher with an echoing growl. He landed closest to Sam and blew into her, knocking her to the pavement.

"Jesse! Help!" Bonnie yelled to Ghost, who had the weapons from Eden in his backpack. She didn't wait for him to save her sister. She barreled into the Watcher, fists flying. The creature retaliated, talons swiping toward Bonnie's face. But, before contact, the creature hesitated, confused by her mirror image appearance and his own vanity. It was all the opportunity Ghost needed. From the backpack, he whipped a chain around the Watcher's neck. Blessed with Eden's holy water, it hissed as it touched his skin. The man howled and fell to his knees. In a few brisk moves, Ghost lassoed his wrists.

Standing, Bonnie tugged Samantha up from the pavement.

"You two get out of here. I'll take care of this," Ghost said.

"What about you?" Sam cried.

"I'll kill it and meet you." He hooked his foot in the strap of the backpack.

Bonnie tugged at Sam's elbow.

"Bonnie, here," Ghost said, tossing her a card on a clip that he'd wrestled from the Watcher's lapel.

Bonnie caught the item. The Watcher's picture stared back at her from under the Harrington Enterprises logo. This was his identification, and her only way of getting inside. The name on the card read, C. Maxwell.

Ghost retrieved a dagger from the backpack and raised it to the struggling Watcher's neck. Sam watched, shivering.

"Do you need our help?" Bonnie asked.

"No. You're wasting time. It's more dangerous if you're here," Ghost insisted.

"Let's go," Bonnie said, grabbing Sam's hand and forcing her to move. Ghost could take care of himself, and he was probably right. If something went wrong, he could dissolve into thin air. If she stayed, Samantha would be a liability, as small as she was presently.

Bonnie forced Sam between the dumpsters, then back toward the building. Toying with the ID badge, she prayed she could pull this off. This Watcher wasn't just influencing executives; he was employed by the enterprise. Bonnie wondered how deep she was descending into the enemy's lair, and hoped she had what it took to make it out alive.

Chapter 13
The Beast

Bonnie broke from Samantha and approached the security guard in front of the doors, gripping the Harrington Enterprises ID between her sweaty fingers.

"Mr. Maxwell. Back so soon?" the guard said, pulling the door open for her.

Bonnie nodded. Best not to offer an explanation. "Thank you, Fredrick," she said in the voice of the Watcher.

"You're welcome, sir."

As she approached the bank of elevators inside, she raised her knuckle to push the call button and noticed her fingers were white from gripping the ID so tightly. She slipped the square plastic badge into her suit pocket.

"You know better than that, Mr. Maxwell," a female voice said. Bonnie turned toward the click of heels on the marble floor. A gorgeous security guard with a thick braid of long blond hair approached, reached inside Mr. Maxwell's pocket, and clipped the ID to the lapel of his suit. She gestured toward the doors. "With this chaos, everyone has to follow policy. Even you."

Bonnie smiled. "Thank you." The words came out way too high. She cleared her throat. "Thank you."

The blonde giggled and winked. *Oh crap, was she flirting?*

To Bonnie's relief, the elevator doors opened, and she escaped inside the empty compartment. She punched the button for the fourteenth floor, Harrington's front desk per Gideon. The elevator ascended. Hovering above the number pad, Bonnie stared at her hands—man hands. Mr. Maxwell's illusion had well-manicured fingers, long and tapered. These were executive hands, not hard-working hands like her father's. He'd been a cop in Nebraska before he was killed in the line of duty, a beat cop, always willing to lend a helping hand. Bonnie didn't remember much about him; she'd almost entirely forgotten the sound of his voice, but she remembered the feel of his hands—rough, callused, hard-working hands.

The doors opened and Bonnie stepped out into a vast, pale space with floor-to-ceiling windows and sandstone floors. Shiny steel letters on the front desk read *Harrington Enterprises.* Heart racing, she glanced at the mousy secretary behind the desk—short, slightly overweight, emerging pimple over her left eyebrow. Definitely not a Watcher.

"Mr. Maxwell? Back so soon? I thought you were getting lunch?"

"I forgot something in my office," Bonnie said in her practiced baritone.

"If you have a moment, Mr. Blake asked for you. He's meeting with the board in conference room A, but afterward, he requested a meeting with you and Ms. Thomson at his private residence. He said to remind you to allow extra time to get across town due to the picketers."

Bonnie nodded, hoping the woman couldn't see the nerves she kept bottled up inside. She moved to the right. Gideon's map of Harrington showed executive offices down the long hallway. Soon, she came across an office labeled *Cordelius Maxwell, Vice President*. She slipped inside.

The scent of death and blood hit her immediately. "Ugh," she whispered, feeling nauseous. She rerouted her breathing through her mouth. The huge executive office was meticulously clean. Not a grain of dust on the hardwood floor. Not one document on the granite-topped desk. Where was the smell coming from?

She crossed to the desk and moved the mouse in a circle to wake the computer. Password protected. She expected as much. She opened the top drawer. Nothing. No pens, pencils, staples … nothing. She closed it again. Opened the side drawer. Nothing. The file drawer. Nothing.

"What does this guy do all day?" she whispered. Her eyes fell on a credenza against the wall. Slowly, she walked over to it and opened the long, narrow drawer. Fingers. She gagged, bending at the waist and catching herself on her knees. The entire drawer was filled with human fingers. White, black, yellow, brown, some manicured, some with dirt under the fingernails. All lined up and displayed like some grotesque collection.

She closed the drawer and swallowed repeatedly to keep from vomiting. Thank God she hadn't eaten anything since Eden. There was no way she could fight the urge to empty her stomach if there was anything in it. Disgusted, she backed toward the exit.

She pulled up short when the door to the office swung open. A familiar-looking blonde in a black suit poked her head in.

"Cord, I thought you were going to eat?" the woman said.

Bonnie nodded, thinking it safer than testing her impression again.

"Well, get on with it. Lucifer"—she closed her eyes and shook her head—"Mr. Blake wants to meet at the penthouse as soon as he finishes with the board."

Bonnie stiffened. *Lucifer.* She'd said Lucifer. She looked at the woman's badge dangling from her lapel. Auriel Thomson. *Auriel.* She was in the body of Cordelius Maxwell, *Cord.* Cord and Auriel, Lucifer's right and left. He was here. Watchers weren't just influencing Harrington Enterprises, they were *running* it, and the CEO was Lucifer himself!

"What is wrong with you?" Auriel asked.

Bonnie swallowed. "Need to feed," she murmured.

"Well get it done. Blake isn't a patient man. You know that as well as I do." She began to close the door but paused over the threshold. "Do you have a window open in here?"

Bonnie shook her head.

"It stinks. Like sunshine and fresh air."

Shifting her gaze toward the sunny window, Bonnie racked her head for something to say. Auriel could smell her, the scent of the Soulkeeper within filtering out her skin. What could she say? How could she explain?

Don't panic. Think! Bonnie narrowed her eyes, trying to remember her lessons from Eden. A Watcher like Cord wasn't human. He wouldn't offer an explanation.

Bonnie shrugged and flashed Auriel the finger. The blond Watcher peeled her lips back from her teeth and left, allowing the door to close behind her. Bonnie blew out the breath she'd been holding.

The sound of Auriel's heels faded as the Watcher made her way down the hall. Bonnie counted to ten to make sure she wouldn't have to deal with her again, then skated back out, walking quickly the way she'd come. Unfortunately, in that direction, Auriel had stopped at the end of the corridor and was talking to a balding and overweight human in a lab coat.

Bonnie shifted left. If she remembered Gideon's diagram correctly, this hall led past the conference rooms and break area and eventually to the elevators. A burst of laughter came from conference room A, and she picked up the pace. As she rounded past the break room, she heard the door open behind her and glanced over her shoulder. There *he* was, all blond, blue-eyed evil wrapped up in a tailored purple suit. *Lucifer. Lucifer was here in the flesh!*

While shaking hands with the departing board of directors, the devil caught her eye and nodded. Bonnie tried not to react. One mistake and he'd have her soul. She nodded back, skin crawling, and turned the corner for the elevators, thankful for the stretch of hall and distraction of the board members that hopefully hid her scent. The front desk was unattended. Bonnie wondered where the mousy woman had gone, maybe to the bathroom or perhaps a Watcher was having her for lunch. At least, she wouldn't have to make small talk with the secretary while she waited. She punched the button.

The voices from the conference room closed in. The board of directors would need to leave. What if one of them wanted to talk? What if Lucifer showed them out? She pressed the button again, then eyed the door to her left. The stairs.

Ding. The elevator arrived and the thick metal doors slid open, molasses slow. *Cord!* The real Watcher met her eyes through the crack in the opening elevator. Bonnie dodged for the stairs, the real Cord stumbling out behind her. She made it through the door, slamming it behind her in his face. There wasn't a lock. Calling on her Soulkeeper strength, she jumped the railing, falling to the landing below.

The real Cord smashed into the stairwell above her. "You're dead, Soulkeeper!"

Bonnie dropped to the next level, feet flying as she rounded the landing. Heavy footsteps pounded behind her, and a growl echoed through the staircase. Heart hammering against her breastbone, she dropped over the next railing. But he was too quick. He landed next to her. Talons ripped. Blood sprayed the wall. She crumpled to the floor.

In an instant, he flipped her on her back, wrapping a hand around her neck and bringing his face close to her shredded one. "Why do you look like me?"

Bonnie didn't answer. She struggled against his grip, but he pinned her hands under his knees. She didn't stand a chance.

"In a quiet mood, are you?" he hissed. "Lucifer will loosen your lips. Although, your friend has left me in need of feeding, and it might be interesting to try a bite of such attractive flesh." He licked the blood from her face. She moaned, jerking her aching cheek away from his tongue.

Cord plucked Bonnie's right hand out from under his knee and brought her fingers to his mouth. "Maybe just one."

Bonnie began to weep as he inserted her pinky finger between his teeth. He clamped down on the tender flesh below her second knuckle. She screamed, anticipating the bite.

Instead, the Watcher's mouth opened again, an inhuman squeal crossing his lips. Cord dropped her hand and twisted away from her. A chopstick stuck out of the base of his neck. *Wham!* Ghost formed over her, kicking the Watcher in the gut and sending him flying. Blinking forward, Ghost thrust a second chopstick into the Watcher's ear and a third in its upper right side, plunging it deep, under the ribs. Cord dropped like a rock, black blood flowing.

Ghost's hand found hers and yanked her to her feet. "Come on. That's not going to kill him."

He helped her down the stairs, half carrying her—quite the feat considering she weighed two hundred pounds in this form. "I don't understand. Why didn't you kill him before?"

"I tried. A vigilante from the crowd spotted me and rescued *him!*"

"Oh God, Jesse…"

"I was able to blink out of there, but I had to leave the weapons behind. Thank God for the Chinese restaurant on the fifth floor."

"Is Sam okay? Did he come after you?"

"Yeah. I made sure he didn't find her. In fact, I distracted the bastard as long as possible. I think he got sick of chasing me." They reached the bottom level, a landing outside a spa with a waterfall and a rice paper screen. The serenity did not match the panic within her.

"Two doors," she said.

"Better go out the back. That way leads to the lobby and security," Ghost said.

Pounding footsteps began again above them.

"Sounds like Cordelius has healed himself," Bonnie said. She thrust against the bar to the rear exit. Ghost pulled her onto a side street, where a small crowd rushed her.

"What do you know about Elysium?" one man asked, shoving a microphone in her face.

Ghost pushed the man aside and ushered her around the corner, where Sam was waiting. She pulled Bonnie into the closest door, an Irish pub. The place was dark and nearly deserted. *Perfect.* Inside the bathroom, they joined again, quickly shifting back into themselves.

"You need Malini," Sam said, pointing to the part of her face that felt raw and open.

"Yeah, let's go." Bonnie grabbed her sister's hand and raced out of the pub. Ghost hailed a cab, and she pushed Sam through the door he held open for them. Just as she lowered herself to the seat next to her sister, she saw the real Cord emerge from the building. The crowd closed in on him, obviously confused that the same man had exited twice. Those almost purple eyes met hers, and a sneer played across his lips.

She slammed her door.

"Floor it!" Ghost yelled. Thankfully, the cabbie complied.

Chapter 14
The Second Curse

Alone in the devil's abode, Abigail ate another nut from the package God had given her. Today, it tasted of a full Italian dinner: salad, spaghetti, and cannoli for dessert. The box had kept her alive for weeks. Not the same as eating for real though. Her body had changed, her hands bone thin, her skin taking on the gray tinge of death. And there were other changes. Changes she'd rather not think about.

The box was almost empty. Did that mean she'd be rescued soon? Escape? Or maybe, her purpose would be served and she would die. Blind faith was a human condition, a privilege she'd fought for. She'd stopped trying to make sense of her circumstances a long time ago and simply surrendered to them, holding fast to the hope that this too would pass, one way or another.

The door opened and Lucifer stormed in, face red. Auriel was on his heels, followed by a Watcher who could barely hold his illusion together. Flashes of snakeskin broke through spots on his neck and face. He slumped into the nearest chair, and Abigail got a clear view of his indigo eyes. *Cord.* Based on the black blood on his shirt and his struggling illusion, he'd been roughed up by a Soulkeeper. A human couldn't do that kind of damage.

Lucifer rounded on Cord, dark menace filling the room. "Tell me everything. Every detail."

"She was a redhead. Tall, thin. Beautiful by human standards. And a twin."

"A twin?" Auriel repeated, wrinkling her nose. "Twin Soulkeepers?"

"Yes. I smelled them in the crowd, then tracked them down to an alley three blocks east. I saw red hair and attacked. One had transformed into ... me."

"The one who was in Harrington? To think, a filthy Soulkeeper walked through our front door!" Auriel shrieked. "I thought he smelled of sunlight." She lifted the back of her hand to her nose.

Lucifer paced the length of the great room. "There were two on the list that fit this description. I thought we eliminated them." Flames filled his narrowed eyes. "Eden. They've been hiding."

Cord cleared his throat, his skin blackening around the mouth. "The twin, the one who didn't look like me, was smaller. It was as if they worked together to form the illusion."

Lucifer stroked his chin. "Soulkeepers as a group are not like us. They cannot imitate others on a whim. These two must have a gift, a specialized skill. I could not sense her soul. It must be part of her power to mask her humanity." His dark eyes turned toward Abigail. "Explain about these twins, Abigail. What is the nature of their power?"

A sharp tug engaged deep within her chest, Lucifer's sorcery compelling her to speak the truth. She resisted. Centuries living as a Watcher had taught her that Lucifer could not undo her free will, and Abigail refused to help him. She'd die first.

When enough time had passed for him to realize she would not comply, he growled in her direction. "Shouldn't you have starved to death by now?" The dark one glared at her. He knew. He knew she should be dead by now.

Abigail stiffened.

"There was something else, my lord," Cord said, thankfully breaking Lucifer's maleficent stare. "Another Soulkeeper I couldn't see. Invisible. I remember his smell but never saw the one who stabbed me in the neck."

Abigail snorted. She would have loved to see Ghost make a fool of Cord.

A lamp flew from Lucifer's hand and passed through Abigail's chest, exploding against the wall behind her. She drifted toward the window, unharmed. If Lucifer was going to kill her, she'd go out making him as angry as possible. Abigail rested her hand on the box in her pocket. No, God promised this would not be her end.

Auriel paced, ignoring Lucifer's outburst and fixating on Cord. "The Soulkeepers you saw, Cord, were they young ones? Teenagers?"

Cord nodded. "The ones I saw? Yes."

"The Soulkeepers are almost always teenagers," Auriel said, running her finger along her bottom lip.

"It is the Great Oppressor's way to work on the soft hearts of the young," Lucifer said.

Auriel approached him, pressing herself against his chest. She placed her hands on the lapels of his suit and lifted her eyebrows. "Young ones are required to attend schools here, my lord." She grinned wickedly. "All of them. We know three who attend Paris High School."

Lucifer nodded. "We've tried to attack directly before, Auriel, with disastrous results. I'm not ready to expose our cause or risk our numbers. Better to be insidious."

Auriel shook her head. "They have a system. All the young ones are required to learn the same thing. Perhaps *we* should run the schools and ... reeducate them."

Lucifer pinched her chin and shook gently. "You are a genius, my dear. We keep an eye on the Soulkeepers and win the young humans to our side." Lucifer grinned. "We take a page from the Great Oppressors book and strike at the young, reeducate them to see things our way. We win their hearts."

In her ghostly form, Abigail raised a hand to her mouth to cover her gasp. The second temptation. Lucifer was planning to direct it toward *children*. She wanted to do something, to stop him or to alert the Soulkeepers, but she couldn't even help herself. All she could do was watch and listen.

"What is your will?" Auriel asked, showing more teeth than necessary when she smiled.

Lucifer held up his index finger, the nail extending to a sharp point. "You and I, Auriel, are cut from the same cloth." He ran his finger down the center of his chest, slicing it open to reveal a black, swirling mass where his heart should have been. Abigail squinted and thought she could see faces in the darkness, souls forever trapped, powering the ultimate evil. Lucifer used his razor-sharp nail to cut a wedge of darkness from the mass, then stabbed into Auriel's chest.

The blond Watcher yelped in pain, her face twisting as the blackness wormed its way inside her. Black veins tangled under her skin toward her ear. Even through her illusion, Abigail could see her eyes wash red before fading back to blue.

"My second temptation is *ignorance*. Auriel, you are the vessel. Start with the Secretary of Education. Anyone you talk to will adopt your new curriculum: I've made you ultra-persuasive."

"What is the new curriculum?" she asked.

Lucifer shrugged. "No math or science or language. Teach them the virtues of evil. The benefits of war. Greed is good. Prejudice is necessary. Doing evil is their entitlement."

She nodded. "We teach them the truth. We teach them to think like Watchers."

Lucifer grinned. "I want Watchers or the influenced running every school in the country. Go. Get started."

Auriel bowed at the waist and backed from the room, letting herself out the front door. Lucifer waited until she was gone to turn on Cord.

"You failed me, Cord."

"What?"

"You allowed the Soulkeepers access to Harrington. They know! They know now that I'm running the company, and if they know I'm running things topside, soon those imbeciles in the In Between will know. They could make things … difficult. All because you weren't more careful with yourself."

Cord bowed his head. It was useless to argue. Once the devil had your number, he wouldn't stop calling until you picked up. "Yes, my lord."

With a grunt, Lucifer thrust his hand into Cords gut. Abigail had to look away. Cord cried out, a wicked, high-pitched howl that made her cringe. When she glanced back, Cord had lost his illusion entirely, his black scaly skin and leathery wings spasming on the carpet in a puddle of his insides.

"You are not allowed to die, Cord," Lucifer hissed. "You will suffer here until I say you may leave, and then you will pull yourself together, capture the nearest human, and heal yourself. And you will not be detected. Do you understand?"

Cord was unable to speak but gurgled in the course of his torture.

Lucifer blinked slowly and turned toward the window, sliding his hands into his pockets. With a deep sigh, he said, "Looks like it's almost Christmas." He rubbed his hands together.

It was a full hour before Lucifer freed Cord. Somehow, the Watcher, mouth gaping like a fish out of water, restored his insides to his abdominal cavity. He sewed himself up and hobbled toward the door, a weak illusion snapping into place.

Abigail sighed. God help the first human Cord came across in his current state.

* * * * *

Bonnie, Samantha, and Jesse poured into the Eden School for Soulkeepers, desperate to tell Malini what they'd learned. But it was Gideon who met them at the door. She grabbed him by the shoulders, meeting his eyes. "He's here. They are all here!" Bonnie stuttered, panting from the run.

"Who's here?" Gideon asked.

"Not here-here. Not in Eden. He's topside. He's running Harrington!"

At that moment, Grace jogged into the atrium, looking from Bonnie to Samantha. "Who's running Harrington?"

Samantha ran to her mother and hugged her tightly, but Bonnie hung back, trying to slow her racing thoughts. She needed to tell them what she'd learned.

"Lucifer," Bonnie managed. "Watchers aren't just influencing the executives at Harrington. Lucifer *is* Milton Blake. Cord and Auriel are also executives. He's playing the game from Earth and Harrington Enterprises is his headquarters."

Gideon made a sound like a cough and backed up a few steps. Grace's eyes widened. "You're sure? You saw this?"

"Close up. I posed as Cord. I was as close to the devil as I am to you," Bonnie said, suddenly more aware of the wound on her face that kept drawing her mother's eye. The pain had spread from her cheek to her neck and shoulder.

"You need to have that healed," Grace said, releasing Sam from her embrace.

"Where's Malini?" Bonnie asked, swaying on her feet.

"She's upstairs. Stay where you are. You're in no shape to climb the stairs. Archibald," Grace said to the gnome, waiting in the shadows. "Please find the Healer and ask her to come here at once." He blinked out of sight.

"We have to assemble the council," Bonnie insisted. "The Watchers know it was me. Cord almost killed me. If it wasn't for Ghost taking a pair of chopsticks to Cord's jugular just in time, I'd be shredded."

Grace crossed herself and approached Bonnie with arms outstretched, but her daughter wasn't finished.

"And something else," Bonnie said. "I don't think Elysium was just about greed, Mom. I think Malini was right; it was one of the six temptations."

Samantha agreed. "It's the game. You should have seen the picketers."

Gideon exchanged glances with Grace. "Malini and Dane's mission failed. Lucifer didn't retreat, he advanced."

Grace nodded. "All this time, we were waiting for the signs. The signs were all around us."

Abruptly, Ghost blinked into existence next to Gideon. "But think of the implications," Ghost said. "If Lucifer is Milton Blake, he's not living in Hell."

Bonnie pointed a finger at him. "Yes! The secretary made it sound like Cord and Auriel meet him there regularly to talk about highly confidential stuff at his private residence. She said Cord should allow extra time to get across town. He's living somewhere in the city, Gideon. And if I know Lucifer, he'll keep his prize close. Abigail might not be in Hell after all. There's a chance we can rescue her."

Gideon took a step back, as if he'd been pushed. His eyes widened. "We have to go. We have to get her," he murmured.

"We will, Gideon. If you can research Milton Blake's home address in the library, I'll go myself as soon as Malini gives the okay."

Out of the corner of her eye, Bonnie saw her mother cringe. But after surviving today, Bonnie wasn't about to lose her nerve. Abigail had been missing far too long. If she was still alive, they had to do something. It wasn't just about Gideon. They all needed her. Abigail had forgotten more about the Watchers than any of the Soulkeepers had ever known.

"I'll find the address," Gideon said. "And names and pictures of every person in that building, including the doorman."

Bonnie smiled stiffly, feeling woozy. The foyer swam, then tipped. Gideon caught her before her head hit the floor and a wave of pain rocked her body. Luckily, Malini arrived moments later, healing hand at the ready.

Chapter 15
School Days

"Jacob, you're daydreaming again. You'll never pass your physics final if you don't review your notes." Malini pursed her lips and tapped her finger on his notebook.

"Excuse me for being distracted. It's hard to concentrate on physics when you've just learned the devil is CEO of an international conglomerate and in competition for human souls on earthly soil. We shouldn't be here, Malini. We should be killing Watchers."

A calculus textbook hit the table next to Jacob's hand. "You guys might want to keep it down. I think I heard the word 'Watcher' halfway across the cafeteria." Dane plunked in the chair across from Malini, leaned back, and threaded his fingers behind his head. He closed his eyes.

"Not you, too," Malini said. "We've got to study. We get through these winter finals, and then we have all Christmas break to work. Gideon found ten properties owned by Milton Blake in Chicago. Abigail could be in any or none of them. After finals, we can search for her and hunt Watchers all holiday." Malini angrily turned the page in her book.

"Who cares about finals? Abigail could be out there. The world could be ending," Jacob whispered.

Malini huffed. "And what if it doesn't? I've been accepted at the University of Illinois, Jacob. I have goals. If everything works out, I want to be ready for real life."

Dane opened one eye to glare at her. Jacob rested his head on his fist. Neither said a word.

"Okay, that sounded crazy," Malini muttered. "Of course college isn't more important or more real than saving the world or Abigail, but damn it, I want to go. I want what everyone else gets to have. I want to sleep in a dorm and maybe join a sorority. I want to wake up late for class and ace the test anyway. I want to study in a library with more books than people until the wee hours of the morning." She slapped the page of her open book.

Pulling back his chair, Jacob walked around the table and wrapped an arm around her shoulders. She leaned into his side. "You'll have that, Malini. Somehow, when this is all over, we'll have normal again."

Dane cleared his throat. When Malini looked his way, he glowered at her and shook his head. "Don't make promises you can't keep, Jacob," he said. "Malini, you and I have been to Nod. You've seen the enemy. You're the goddamn Healer! Life isn't fair and you might not get any of the things you want. I might not either. All we have is today and knowing we are part of something that could change the world. So study if you want to, or don't. None of us knows what's coming next. Choose and have no regrets."

Stunned, Malini sat up straighter, eyebrows shooting toward the ceiling.

"Hey, back off, Dane," Jacob said.

But Malini grabbed his hand. "No, Jacob. He's right. Life has no guarantees and I've never been promised normal. It's time I get over it."

"Malini—"

"Don't. Sometimes we have choices and sometimes life decides for us," she said bitterly. "Today, I'm choosing to study, because that's how I want to spend my time. It makes me feel good knowing that if I do have a chance at my dream, I'll be prepared. And if I don't, well, I can always take my frustrations out on some Watchers."

Dane leaned over the table to bump her fist. "That's my girl."

Jacob shifted in his chair but didn't say anything.

The bell rang. First period. Malini stood from the cafeteria table and gathered her books. "Good luck, you guys."

* * * * *

With the last oval filled in, Malini hunched over her AP History final, certain she'd aced the exam. A few more hours and she'd be free, if you could call it that. Truth was, outside of school, the answers didn't come multiple choice or in time-boxed essays. Things weren't always right or wrong, or black and white. And there were no holidays from real life.

The door whined open and a tall, lean woman entered the room, wearing a red suit and heels. "Pencils down, everyone," she announced, clapping her hands together.

Malini twitched. The rotting smell of Watcher permeated the classroom. She placed one hand over her mouth and reached for her phone to text Jacob.

"Excuse me," Mr. Anderson said, standing from his desk. "I think you are in the wrong place. This is the advanced placement history exam. The students have thirty minutes left."

"There's been a change to the curriculum," the woman said, tossing her brunette locks over her shoulder and batting her eyelashes.

"Uh, I don't think so, miss." Mr. Anderson bunched his bushy white eyebrows together. "Perhaps you have the wrong room? Can I ask your name?"

"There's no mistake, and my name isn't your business," the woman said. "I'm your replacement. You've been fired."

Mr. Anderson halted, face reddening. He approached the woman and lowered his voice. "Come with me. Let's talk this over with Principal Bailey. I'm sure there's been a mistake."

"Principal Bailey has taken a leave of absence. He's been replaced by Principal Pierce. You can go see her if you'd like." She turned away from him, heels clack-clack-clacking on the linoleum as she paced to the front of the classroom.

Looking more than a little confused, Mr. Anderson pushed through the door, Malini guessed to sort things out with the new principal.

Malini's first instinct was to leap over her desk and kill the Watcher at the front of the room, but that would be a bad idea for a number of reasons. First, even if her class survived the trauma of watching the woman fry beneath her touch, she'd out herself as a Soulkeeper to everyone. Second, if the Watcher had backup, she might be overpowered and taken. She was a Healer, not a Horseman, and was never the first line of offense. And third, Healers were hard to see. While she was incognito, she might learn why the Watcher was here.

"There is no need to complete your exams," the woman in red said, clasping her hands in front of her hips. "Due to recent changes in the state's curriculum, this test will not be graded. You may leave for holiday break early. Reschooling will begin when you return."

"Reschooling?" Amy Barger asked from the front row.

The Watcher smiled. "Yes. The state has determined that there is too much emphasis on learning facts, exercising logic, and creative problem solving in the classroom. The curriculum is being redesigned to better prepare you for life."

"Like what?" Phillip Westcott asked.

"Like ... like..." The Watcher seemed genuinely confused by the question for a moment. "Like how to make people want things and force people to do as you please."

The students glanced around the room. Amy responded, "You mean, like entrepreneurship? Motivating people, marketing and sales."

The woman in red giggled. "Or dictatorship. Maybe the benefits of slave labor. We will explore all of the options. I will expand your minds."

A rumble of voices rose up as her classmates asked each other if this was real. Malini hoped Jacob read her text and was on his way, because she could hold her tongue no longer. "Is this curriculum change only for our school or every school?"

The Watcher's eyes narrowed and focused on her. "Every school. What is your name, student?"

"My name is Malini Gupta, and I do not believe that learning how to control other human beings against their will is a worthwhile educational pursuit."

"No, I don't suppose you would." She bared her teeth. "Would you join me in the hall, Ms. Gupta?"

"Hell yeah." If there was one thing she could always count on from a Watcher, it was arrogance. This snake-skinned POS thought she could take on the Healer single-handedly! Malini smiled as she passed the red suit, never breaking her hate-filled glare as she led the way into the empty hallway.

Red Suit followed her, facing off down the rows of mustard-yellow lockers. The door to the classroom closed behind her.

"A Soulkeeper. What a pleasure it will be to end you."

Malini smiled. So that was it. This egotistical fallen angel didn't recognize she was the Healer. She thought she was enough to take on a Horseman or Helper on her own. Malini would enjoy teaching her a lesson.

As Lillian had shown her, Malini stepped backward into a fighting stance. "What are you waiting for? End me."

The Watcher attacked from straight on. Malini dodged to the right, punching with her left hand, her healing hand. The sizzle, when her knuckles hit the Watcher's cheek, filled the hallway with a sulfur stench. The woman whirled, one hand clutching her burnt face, the other lashing out, talons breaking her illusion. Malini caught her hands, threaded her fingers with the Watcher's. She gave her a focused dose of Healing.

"Who are you?" the Watcher squealed as the burn advanced up her arms, bringing the Watcher to her knees. The red suit faded away, as did the human skin, and the shiny brunette hair. Flames licked up the creature's shoulders, burning higher around its ears, scorching Malini's skin in the process. She didn't let go. She'd burned before, worse than this. She'd enjoy watching this snake fry.

The Watcher's wings unfurled and slapped the tile floor in one last attempt to escape. Black blood sprayed across the lockers, and then the flames engulfed the Watcher.

Malini let go. One step. Two steps back. She watched the incineration, smiling. When she reached the water fountain, she carefully washed away the burn on her arms and splashed water over her face. She used the bottom of her shirt to pat her eyes dry. *Crap*, she'd have some explaining to do when she got home. One sleeve was gone, and scorch marks permanently marred the pattern on the front. She sighed and turned back toward the classroom

The students had moved into the hallway. White-faced and open-mouthed, they stared at her and the pile of ash that smoldered in the middle of the hall.

"It's not what it looks like," she said.

At that moment, Dane and Jacob burst into the hallway. Dane was covered in wounds and soaking wet. Jacob was unharmed but looked as if he might be sick at any moment.

"School's been compromised. We've gotta get out of here," he blurted, then seemed to notice the Watcher-shaped bonfire and the gaping students.

"I know," Malini said sadly. "I'll grab my stuff. There will be more. I'm willing to bet the new principal has scaly skin."

Jacob nodded.

As she passed the group of her peers, packed shoulder to shoulder for safety, and retreated into the classroom, she heard Dane clear his throat behind her. She glanced back to see him addressing the crowd. "Um, you've just witnessed the newest project of the experimental theater group!" he said in a bombastic voice, arms extended to his sides. "If you're interested in joining, we will be meeting every third Wednesday after break."

The crowd broke into whispers.

"How did you do that?" Amy Barger asked.

Dane mumbled something about mirrors.

"I'm in," Phillip Westcott said.

Malini couldn't help but laugh.

Chapter 16
Christmas

Jacob watched the fire lick up the sides of the Laudners'
fireplace Christmas morning, hoping he could get through
to Katrina. She curled like a cat in the sage green recliner on
the other side of the fire. Wearing nothing but a cami and
sleep shorts, the bones of her shoulders poked under her skin,
her knees seemed too large, and her calves were gone,
replaced by skin and bone.

"You're taking it again," Jacob said.

She didn't answer right away. Instead, she rose up on her
knees like a prairie dog to look over the back of the chair, but
the Laudners and Jacob's mom were in the kitchen preparing
breakfast.

"Yes," Katrina said. "I got some from school before break. The new nurse is handing Elysium out like vitamins. Everyone is taking it."

"The pills are killing you, Katrina." Jacob lowered his voice. "I told you before, Watchers are running Harrington. Elysium is purposefully addictive. It's made to keep you weak and under their control."

Katrina shook her limp head of hair. "I know what you said, Jacob, but I've been thinking about it. I've been possessed. This is different. When I take Elysium, I feel really good. It hasn't changed me. If anything, I'm a better person when I take it."

"How do you figure?" Jacob asked incredulously.

"More patient, laid-back."

"You're laid-back because you're high and you don't care about anything but the pills."

"Exactly. So, in a way, it's a good thing. Plus, I finally lost the extra weight."

"Extra weight!" Jacob had to force himself to keep his voice down. "Katrina, you are starving to death. You eat Elysium and nothing else. You look like a skeleton."

"In your opinion."

"In any opinion. I'm surprised the doctor hasn't admitted you for anorexia."

"He tried. I'm over eighteen. I refused."

Jacob buried his face in his hands. "It's killing you."

Katrina stood and walked over to his chair. "I think it's keeping me alive. I only want to die when I don't take it."

Frustrated, Jacob met her eyes. The green was cloudy and dull. From this angle, with the light from the fire burning behind her, she looked like the walking dead, like a zombie. "I can help you. I helped you before when you were possessed. There might be herbs I can bring from Eden to lessen the withdrawal. Malini can heal you again."

"You don't get it," she said through her teeth. "I. Don't. Want. Your. Help."

"Katrina—"

"What's going on here?" Lillian asked from the archway to the kitchen.

Jacob spilled the beans. "Katrina never stopped taking the Elysium. She's got a stash somewhere. She doesn't think she needs to quit."

Uncle John and Aunt Carolyn appeared behind his mom. Aunt Carolyn's festive red-and-gold plaid apron seemed in sharp contrast to the expression on her face, a tearful grimace better suited for a funeral.

"Katrina, is this true?" she asked.

Katrina backed toward the stairs. "Yes, Mother. It is true, and it's my life. I can do what I want. Elysium is perfectly legal."

"And perfectly addictive," John said. He reached for the phone. "I'm calling Doc Howard. If you won't help yourself, maybe we can find someone who will help you."

Uncle John dialed as Katrina bolted up the stairs. Jacob heard her door slam. A few moments later, John hung up the phone.

"I left a message with his answering service. We'll get this under control. Doc Howard told me there are thousands of Elysium addicts. Twelve-step programs popping up everywhere. Should've done this a long time ago."

Aunt Carolyn rubbed John's shoulder and then returned to the kitchen, following a billow of pancake-scented smoke.

A flurry of pounding footsteps turned Jacob's attention toward the stairs. Katrina was back, changed into jeans and a gray sweater and carrying a suitcase.

"What are you doing?" Lillian asked, blocking the door with her body.

"Leaving."

"No," Jacob said. "Come on. You can't leave."

Uncle John returned to the room in a panic. "It's Christmas, Katrina. Stay for breakfast and open presents. Your ma made the pancakes in the shape of reindeer. Your favorite."

With three people blocking the door, Katrina didn't have a choice. She dropped her suitcase and stomped toward the kitchen. Jacob glanced at his mother and then at John, who looked like he might be sick.

"Let's try not to let this ruin our holiday," Uncle John murmured.

The family gathered around the table. Aunt Carolyn bowed her head and said grace, Jacob following along with one eye on Katrina. His cousin stared out the bay window, eyes vacant, an empty shell of a human being. He texted

Malini, who promised to come by as soon as she could break away.

Three pancakes and two sausage links later, Jacob watched Katrina get up from her untouched breakfast and move for the living room. Uncle John stood to follow her.

"Relax, Dad. I'm just going to the bathroom," Katrina said.

Slowly, John sat back down. Katrina slipped through the archway into the family room.

Lillian elbowed Jacob's upper arm. "Go check on her. Pretend you're going upstairs or something," she said.

But it was too late. The front door opened and slammed shut, sending Jacob and his mom racing from the kitchen, Uncle John beside them. By the time they wrestled the door open, Katrina was backing out the driveway, spraying pebbles in her haste. As she shifted from reverse into drive in the street, she met Jacob's eyes. He thought he saw a softness in the empty green, an unspoken apology, but her expression hardened just as quickly, and then she drove away.

Behind him, Aunt Carolyn started to weep.

* * * * *

Jacob popped into existence next to Malini inside a cluster of trees on the edge of the Barger's farm. There'd been a cluster of animal killings since the Watchers took over the school, and based on the pattern, the Barger's herd was the next target. He handed Malini his enchanted staff and readied himself for some good old-fashioned Christmas Watcher slaying.

"Did Katrina ever come back?" she asked.

"No. No one has any idea where she went."

"Maybe back to school?" Malini offered.

"A school that is now run by Watchers who are handing out Elysium like candy. Great."

Malini frowned. "There was nothing you could do, Jacob. She's an adult, and she's not in her right mind."

"Yeah."

The Barger's cattle grazed in the last washes of winter twilight. In the late December chill, Jacob could see the cows' breath.

"Get ready, Jake. The Watcher has to feed before full dark or the cows will go in."

Jacob bent over and uncapped his ankle flask, shaping the water into his favorite broad sword.

"Do you want me to help?" Malini asked.

Jacob kissed her cheek. "Nah, I got this."

As predicted, a ripple flashed on the horizon and then an oily black fog dripped from its center. A man formed next to a Guernsey roughly a hundred yards out. Even if Jacob hadn't seen him arrive, his underwear-model good looks gave him away as a Watcher, as did the fangs he bared aimed at the cow's neck.

With the superhuman speed of a veteran Horseman, Jacob leapt over the fence and crossed the field, feet falling lightly on the frozen ground. The hungry Watcher never saw him coming. Before the creature could break skin, Jacob's sword relieved him of his head. The Watcher's surprised noggin bounced off the side of the cow and rolled down the hill, where it lost its illusion and melted into a puddle of black goo.

Malini clapped as the bubbly black remains hissed into the grass. The cow mooed appreciatively and joined the rest of the herd while Jacob swaggered back to Malini's side.

"I told you, I got this," Jacob said, smiling and pointing his thumb at his chest.

"Nice work."

Jacob willed his sword of ice to melt and bent to return the water to his flask. When he straightened again, his face was grim. "How long can we do this, Malini?"

"Do what? Kill Watchers? Forever."

"No. Live double lives. In a week, we're supposed to go back to school—a school run by *Watchers*. I'm thinking we should avoid that at all costs."

Malini shrugged. "So we won't go. We'll figure something out."

"It's not just that. Look how far Lucifer has come. We haven't found Abigail. Half the world is addicted to Elysium. Paris is crawling with Watchers and we are trying our best just to keep them from eating the farm animals while pretending to be normal teenagers."

Malini stepped closer. "I know. This can't last forever. But my intuition tells me it's too early. A change is coming. I can feel it in the air. But, for now, we have to stay focused and organized."

He sighed.

"And as for Abigail, Gideon found ten properties owned by Milton Blake in the Chicagoland area. The first six were decoys. We're getting close. Abigail *has* to be in one of the last four."

"We hope. Unless he has her in Hell like he had Dane."

Malini blinked slowly, her face twisting at the thought. "When Abigail first went missing, I thought Lucifer would call me to him like before. I thought he was using her as bait against us. After all this time, I think he just wants *her*, Jake. I think he has come to see her as some sort of prize. None of us can go to Hell, but I'll keep sending out teams to Blake's properties until we've searched every one. I'm not giving up on her." She handed him back his staff. "Come on. Let's patrol town."

"Hey, Malini."

"What?"

"You want your Christmas present?"

"Hell yes."

"Well, I don't have it here."

"Tease."

"It's in my room. An early edition of Silas Marner."

"Hello! Way to ruin the surprise."

Jacob spread his hands and laughed.

"Silas Marner. Cool. Leather bound?" Malini asked.

"You bet. You said it was your favorite."

"It is." She pecked him on the cheek. "Thanks. I'll even forgive that you have absolutely no patience."

Jacob held out his hand and made the gimme motion. "What did ya get me?"

Malini pulled a tiny, flat package from her back pocket. Jacob tore the glittery paper off. His lips twitched when he saw what was inside.

"Seeds."

"Cherry seeds."

"You gave me cherry seeds for Christmas."

Malini rolled her eyes. "It's romantic. We can plant them when all this is over, if or when we ever get our own place. You know, Mara told me that Heaven is full of cherry blossoms."

Eyebrows raised, Jacob pulled her into a hug. "Merry Christmas."

"Merry Christmas, Jacob." She laced her fingers into his. "Now come on. Let's go see if any of the Watchers from the school are stupid enough to show their faces in town tonight."

Chapter 17
Winter's Quarry

Four weeks later...

Bonnie tried to remain inconspicuous as she stared across the street at the North Wabash Avenue skyscraper Gideon said contained the devil's penthouse.

"I can't believe I finally get my chance to be useful," Cheveyo said, pulling his coat tighter around his body.

"Don't count your chickens before they've grown up and laid eggs," Bonnie said.

"I don't think that's the expression," Cheveyo said, laughing.

"So then how's this for an expression?" Bonnie stretched her mouth open with her gloved fingers and waggled her tongue.

"Stop messing around," Samantha said. "We need a plan."

Bonnie eyed the door to Lucifer's building through the dark lenses of her sunglasses with apprehension. "Chances are it will be like all of the others, a completely empty decoy."

"I don't like this," Samantha said. "I've had a weird feeling all day. What if Lucifer is inside? Or worse, what if Cord is there?"

"That's why we have Jesse staking the place out," Bonnie said. They'd come at noon on a Wednesday. Across town, Harrington Enterprises was not only open, but an interview with Milton Blake was scheduled for WGN. The public's outcry about Elysium had reached a fevered pitch. Bonnie hoped Lucifer, Cord, and Auriel would be sufficiently distracted with Harrington business that, if this was Milton Blake's actual residence, it would be empty.

Sam crossed her mittened hands over her puffy purple coat. "I wish Jesse would get back soon. I don't like to think of him in there alone."

As if his name was a magic incantation to conjure him to her side, he formed next to her, slipping his arm around her waist. Sam jumped at the contact.

"Your wish is my command." Ghost chuckled.

Sam smacked him on the shoulder, and then yanked him into a quick hug. "So what did you find out?"

"Yeah, Ghost, spit it out. I think my balls are freezing off out here," Cheveyo said. Originally from Arizona, he hadn't ever experienced a Midwestern winter. The puffy coat he'd borrowed from Jacob was warm, but every time the wind blew, he scrunched up his face like it hurt.

Bonnie didn't think the weather was that bad, but then again, she and Sam had grown up in northern Nebraska. Cold, flat, and inhospitable in the winter, Nebraska had toughened her up in more ways than one.

Ghost cleared his throat. "He owns the penthouse, the entire top floor. You need a special key to get up there. The elevator won't even reach that level without it."

Bonnie groaned. "Great. How are we supposed to steal the key from Lucifer?"

Ghost grinned. "I don't know, but you could just use the one I stole from security." He held up a cylindrical silver key.

Seizing Ghost's face between her purple mittens, Samantha kissed his cheek so hard it left a red mark. "You are the best, Jesse Larsen. The absolute best."

"Jesse can slip in undetected, but can we pull off Cord and Auriel?" Bonnie asked Sam.

"They'll have to be smaller versions. It's going to be difficult to replicate the bulky clothing," Sam said.

Their own bulky clothing would add to their mass, but Bonnie was right, Cord's muscled frame topped two hundred pounds and Auriel's tall stature added to her mass.

"I could do Cord and you could do a random woman. Security might go for it. A romantic interlude?"

Sam tipped her head. "Maybe, but what do we do about him?" They all stared at Cheveyo.

"Hey, these guys are Watchers, right?" he asked. "Obviously, the only reason I'd be with them is if I was their food or carrying their bags."

Bonnie's eyebrows shot skyward, and she grabbed her sister's hand. "Brilliant! Let's find a place to change."

"Did I miss something?" Ghost asked.

No one answered. The two redheads were already ducking inside a shop at the end of the street.

* * * * *

"Good afternoon, Mr. Maxwell," the gray-haired woman in the doorman's uniform said to Bonnie as she opened the door for her. She gave a curt nod, avoiding eye contact. Cord wouldn't be the friendly sort. She needed to stay in character.

Behind her, Cheveyo and Samantha entered the building, boxes from the local stores stacked in front of their faces. Sam had changed her appearance to look like an extremely petite Hispanic woman, but Cheveyo had no disguise. They'd have to hope the packages did their duty to block his face; a number of Watchers might recognize Cheveyo from Nod. Of course, if they ran into Watchers, they were doomed anyway. Their smell would give them away.

"That way," Bonnie said in Cord's baritone, pointing in the direction of the elevator.

"Mr. Maxwell," the woman at the front desk called. She waved her hand and smiled.

Bonnie stopped, turned slowly toward her, forcing her face to contort into a busy man's scowl.

"You have a message," she said softly, fear seeping into her voice. "Ms. Thomson left you this envelope." She held up a large manila number.

With measured steps, Bonnie approached the counter, motioning for Cheveyo and Sam to continue toward the elevators. She snatched the envelope from the woman's hands without saying a word.

"Asshole," the woman murmured.

Bonnie pretended not to hear her. Quickly, she slipped past the large security guards outside the elevator. They seemed to recognize Cord and know not to make small talk. She joined her cohorts in the elevator reserved for penthouse residents and slipped her key into the top slot. The doors closed and they began to ascend.

Ghost formed inside the compartment, catching himself on his knees. "Jeez, I can't do that again, guys. I feel like someone is pulling me apart cell by cell."

"You held it for too long, Jesse. You can't do that," Sam said.

He raised an eyebrow. "Should I have formed in front of security? How about the other residents in the lobby?" he snapped. "I'm trying my best here."

Bonnie placed her hand on his shoulder. "We know, Jesse. You've done a great job."

"Not to interrupt, but what is that smell? It reeks like something died in here," Cheveyo said around his stack of packages.

"I smell it too," Samantha said. "This is a five-star complex. You'd think they'd keep it clean."

Bonnie sniffed, then followed the smell back to the envelope. She weighed the package in her hand, pressed her fingers around the object inside. Stupid. Stupid. Why did she accept this from the front desk? Now when it wasn't there for Cord to pick up, he'd ask questions. Likely it wouldn't take long for him to figure out she'd been there.

Her fingers pressed against the fleshy roundness inside the envelope. Realization dawned. "It's a human finger," she said solemnly. "That's what you're smelling."

"Wha—?" Cheveyo squeaked, glancing from face to face as if someone might say it was a sick joke.

But no one was laughing. Bonnie had told everyone in Eden about Cord's drawer full of fingers. Each of them stared at the package with equal parts disgust and dread. Then the doors opened.

A small foyer greeted them with mirrored walls and a potted plant that, upon closer inspection, was artificial. Two sets of double doors formed the ends of the foyer, one to their left and one to their right.

"Which way?" Bonnie asked. She took a step inside and the elevator doors closed behind her. Cheveyo and Sam propped their packages against the wall and looked expectantly at Ghost.

"I don't know," Ghost said, arms wrapped around his abdomen as if he was holding himself together. "I didn't go inside before, and I couldn't possibly now."

Sam hugged his shoulders with one arm. "It's okay, Jesse. Just rest."

"Maybe the door's open?" Cheveyo said optimistically. He looked from one door to the other, shrugged, then headed for the one on the left. He never had a chance to test the knob.

The door opened on its own. A hunched woman in a loose-fitting dress and a babushka that hid her face, backed into the foyer, pulling a cart full of cleaning supplies. Cheveyo lurched forward to hold the door open for her. She muttered her thanks and wrestled her cart over the threshold.

"Good afternoon, Mr. Maxwell," she said to Bonnie before pressing the button to call the elevator.

Samantha, Ghost, and Cheveyo entered the penthouse, but Bonnie lagged behind. Something about the cleaning woman was familiar. She caught herself staring, wondering if they'd met before.

The elevator doors opened, and the old woman backed her cart into the compartment. Their eyes met. The woman looked exactly like Bonnie, down to the mole on the right side of her face! Bonnie's mouth dropped open.

"You'd better hurry, Mr. Maxwell," the woman said with a wink.

"Wait!" But the doors closed, and the doppelganger was gone. Had she just seen God? No. It couldn't be. The resemblance must have been an uncanny coincidence. The more she thought about it, the more she was sure she was mistaken. The scarf hid most of the woman's face. Bonnie shook it off and entered through the open door.

Inside the penthouse, Bonnie paused to take in the heart-sputtering view. Lucifer's abode was massive. A wall of windows bordered an open floor plan, and Bonnie was sure it was more open than most. The sixteen-foot ceilings provided an insane view of the city. Lucifer enjoyed living large, that was for sure. Sleek leather furniture was the focal point of the room, and Ghost had already made himself comfortable, trying to recover from overdoing it earlier.

"Let's split up and search," Bonnie suggested. Ghost looked at her as if she was out of her mind. "Not you, Jesse. We need you to recover in case we need your help getting out of here."

He flopped an elbow over his eyes and stretched out on the couch. "Brilliant minds think alike."

Bonnie surveyed the layout of the penthouse. The glass walls seemed to bend in an arc, following the shape of the building. She guessed the penthouse was a large oval with the elevators at the center. "I think this place is like a giant donut. Sam, could you take the rooms to the left. I'll go right. Cheveyo, can you check out the kitchen and that bathroom?"

"Sure." He looked across the living room, over the counter, and at the refrigerator. "Although I'm pretty sure if Abigail was here, you could see her. Am I looking for her in the cabinets?"

Bonnie shook her head. "Lucifer is the lord of illusions, Cheveyo. She won't be in plain sight. Look for anything that seems strange or out of place. And be careful."

He nodded.

The first room Bonnie entered was a library that looked rarely, if ever, used. Methodically, she jostled each book with no idea what she was looking for. A secret room hiding Abigail? Maybe. A bathroom was next. Then, a sprawling bedroom with its own bath. Another bedroom. Another bath. Bonnie searched each, running her hand along the top of the dressers, digging through the mostly empty drawers. Nothing. Not a clue to Abigail's whereabouts.

A half hour later, she bumped into Samantha outside of a massive bedroom. "This place is huge," she said.

"Fourteen thousand square feet," Bonnie said. "Or so says Gideon. It was originally designed for an oil sheik."

"Shit. Well, I searched like a hound dog. Nothing. Do you think Lucifer has her in Hell after all?"

The sound of falling footsteps drew their attention to the hallway. Cheveyo sprinted toward them, eyes wide and hands shaking.

"What's going on?" Bonnie asked.

Cheveyo rubbed his forehead with the back of his hand. "I think there's a soul in the kitchen!"

Chapter 18
Found

Abigail didn't know much about Cheveyo. She'd never met him in person, except when he was residing inside Dane's body, but she did know that his power had to do with possession. He'd possessed his friend Raine's body and of course Dane. Possession had to do with inhabiting the body, but she'd heard Cheveyo could also sense a person's soul. He'd been able to communicate with the people he'd possessed. Could he sense her soul, even if he couldn't see her?

She approached him in the kitchen, waving her arms and crying out. He stopped, listened for a moment, and took off down the hall. *Crap.* How could she show him and the others she was here? The boy returned with Cord. For a moment,

Abigail recoiled until she realized Cord wasn't really Cord, but one of the twins disguised as the Watcher. Bonnie or Sam?

A petite Hispanic woman jogged to Cheveyo's side, the sweet scent of sunshine and honey wafting in her wake. The scent was a dead giveaway they were all Soulkeepers, no matter how menacing the one disguised as Cord looked.

"I feel her. Right here. I can't see her but my gift knows her," Cheveyo said.

Thank God! He could sense her. But what could they do? They couldn't see, or hear her.

"Can you, like, possess her or something, Chevy?" the Hispanic woman asked. One of the twins, she was sure.

He passed his hand through Abigail's torso. "Not if I can't touch her."

Abigail's heart dropped. So close to salvation and still caught in Lucifer's grip. She pressed the heels of her palms into her eyes, a grown woman, crying like a child.

"Hey, Bonnie, you could use the stone," Cheveyo said, placing his hands on his hips and turning toward the Cord doppelganger.

So it was Bonnie disguised as the Watcher, which meant the other woman was Samantha.

"How can the stone help?" Bonnie asked.

"The red stone around your neck is the same one as Dane used to have, right?"

"Yeah. Malini gave it to me."

"Well, when I was stuck inside Dane's body, and he used the stone, when we got to the other side I was myself. Separate. With physical form. This cowboy guide who was helping us said the In Between was a manifestation of consciousness. Separate consciousness, separate reality, or some shit."

Bonnie unbuttoned the top buttons of the dress shirt she was wearing and pulled the red stone over her head. "What do I do? Abigail's not possessing me. How do I take her with me into the stone?"

Cheveyo rubbed his chin. "I'm not sure."

Samantha chimed in, "Malini said you're supposed to stare into the stone and blank your mind."

"That will get me through, but how do I take Abigail?"

"Just because we can't see her doesn't mean she can't see us," Sam said. "Think about Jesse. He's always there, even when he's not."

"So, you're saying?"

"Let's tell her to stare into the stone while you stare into the stone, and maybe she'll hear us."

Brilliant, brilliant girl, Abigail thought. She approached Bonnie's side.

"Did you feel that?" Bonnie asked.

"Feel what?" Sam said.

"Yeah, I did. A cold breeze passed between us," Chevy said.

"Let's do this. She's here. She has to be." Bonnie plopped down in the middle of the kitchen floor and pulled out the stone, dangling it between her fingers. "Abigail, if you can hear me, look into the stone." She pointed at the gem to reinforce her command.

Abigail positioned herself behind Bonnie's shoulder and stared into the red stone, clearing her mind. The change happened quickly. The red of the stone spread across the room, shingles of red glass tiling the space around her and Bonnie. She heard the girl scream as they began to fall. With a smack that bent her knees, Abigail landed in a dark room, and then the blackness peeled back, revealing a new reality.

The first thing Abigail noticed was the green. Giant trees surrounded her. Pines, redwoods, sequoias. Thick trunks reached for the light above and crowded her shoulders. She was at the center of a dense forest, and by the slope of the terrain and the giant boulders poking out of the forest floor, she would guess on the side of a mountain.

"Abigail?"

She turned around to see redheaded, freckle-faced Bonnie staring at her, full lips slightly parted.

Abigail nodded her head and started to cry, her hello catching in her throat. Bonnie opened her arms, and Abigail ran into them, accepting the younger girl's hug, the first human contact she'd had in months.

"Thank the Lord," Abigail said.

"What's happened? What has Lucifer done to you?"

"I'm a prisoner. No one can see me or hear me aside from him. I've been living like a ghost for months in that place. I can't leave."

"How do we get you out?"

"I don't know."

A tall man in hiking gear rustled from the dense forest. His hand shot up to adjust his *Life is Good* cap over his brown hair, blue eyes flashing to Abigail and then Bonnie. "Welcome, hikers. You three need a guide?"

"Three?" Abigail asked. She glanced behind her, to a petite young woman with long golden-brown hair, somewhat familiar. "Who are you?"

"Hope," she said with a smile.

"Hello, Hope," Abigail said softly. She opened her mouth to say more but the guide cleared his throat.

"I'm sorry to interrupt, but my job is to get you three out of the woods." He laughed heartily. "And I feel we should get started. My instincts tell me we don't have a lot of time."

"You are a part of the Healer?" Bonnie asked.

"Yes. An ancient part." He pointed toward a footpath behind him. "I will lead you on the trail, and you will ask questions about the future. I will answer. Be thee warned, the future is a dangerous thing. Our fates are tangled and constantly changing. I can tell you the future as it stands today, but a single choice could change tomorrow."

Abigail fell into step behind the guide. "Is this it? Is it time for me to be freed?"

"That's a question about the present," the guide said. "I can only answer about the future."

"Oh, I get it," Bonnie said. "It's like Jeopardy. You have to phrase the question in terms of the future. How will I save Abigail?"

"Bonnie," Abigail whispered. "You're assuming you *do* save me. It's an unsure future based on choices you haven't made yet."

"The question is valid," the guide said. "Now let's get you an answer." He stopped, poking the underbrush with his walking stick. A family of fireflies rose from the underbelly of a fern and blinked their posteriors in the shade of the large trees.

"Lucifer's spell is a lie. Bonnie, you will save Abigail by removing her from the space where the spell resides."

Bonnie pressed a finger into her chin. "How will I remove her if I can't see or hear her?"

"By removing her while you can see and hear her."

"You mean, while she's here, in the stone?"

The guide nodded. "Lucifer's spell is an illusion. Abigail has both a body and a soul. You can't see her because of the sorcery attached to the place she's in, but if you remove the stone, while she is here, you will break the spell."

"Thank God. How do I go back?"

"Wait," Abigail protested. "Does Bonnie survive saving me?"

The fireflies circled each other. "Yes, although evil sees her for what she is."

Abigail frowned.

Bonnie shook her head. "If evil hasn't seen me for what I am yet, the revelation is overdue. I'm going to go back and get you out of there." Bonnie sat down on the trail, crisscrossing her legs. "Send me back without Abigail," she demanded of the guide.

"Don't you want to know more about your future?" the guide asked.

"Not really. The future's a scary place. I think I'll rescue Abigail and take my chances."

"Smart girl." The guide placed one boot on her thigh and pushed. Red crystals formed around the twin, swallowing her body beneath the sole of his shoe. A black tear opened in the tree trunk behind her, receiving the falling crystal cocoon. Bonnie toppled into the darkness. The glass shattered. She was gone.

Abigail watched the bark stitch back together and thought of Oswald.

The guide continued down the trail. "What about you, Abigail? Do you have any last questions for me?"

Nervously, Abigail glanced over her shoulder, wondering if Hope had questions too, but the young woman had lagged behind. She cleared her throat, mind racing with questions about her future. Like Bonnie, there were things she didn't care to know. One question popped into her head, one that could help the Soulkeepers more than any other. "What is the next temptation?"

The guide halted. "Good question, Abigail." His walking stick slapped the ground and a swarm of flies tornadoed from the underbrush, black and buzzing. The guide stared at the mass of insects for a long time.

"It is difficult to know the future actions of the evil one. Great evil is a tentacled virus, stirring up trouble in every direction. Nevertheless, there is a pattern to Lucifer's choices. His time on Earth has left a thread, and his future is tangled with the Soulkeepers."

"What do you think it might be?"

"Lucifer began with pestilence, gaining from the resulting addiction to the cure. He followed with ignorance." The guide tapped his chin. "There is only one thing that the devil loves more than keeping someone physically weak and mentally confused."

Abigail thought about that. Hadn't the temptations mirrored what he'd done to her? First he'd made her body not her own, then he'd tortured her psychologically by isolating her. Then he'd threatened her with starvation. "Terror," Abigail said. "Lucifer's next step will be to terrorize humans into allegiance with him."

The guide nodded. "That is what I see. Many will die. No place is safe."

"I'll tell the Soulkeepers. We'll have to rotate in and out of Eden."

"No place is safe, Abigail. Not even Eden."

She shook her head. "Not even Eden?"

The guide met her blue eyes with his. "Not even Eden. Warn them, Abigail. Change is coming. Malini must protect the remnant."

"The remnant? Do we lose someone?"

The guide didn't have a chance to answer. The red came for her like a swarm of bees, aggressive and painful. Tiny red shards of glass swirled in the air around her, flushing her from the forest and into black nothingness. The force swept Abigail out onto a carpeted floor, next to a round table. She gasped and coughed, feeling nauseated from the spinning and the movement.

Hands gripped her shoulders, strong, capable hands that smelled of sunlight and honey, and a brown face appeared in front of hers.

"There you are," Cheveyo said.

Abigail turned her head to see Bonnie, still disguised as Cord, holding the red stone. "It worked, Abigail! You're out."

"Help her up," Samantha said. "Jesse just texted me from out front. He heard security say Mr. Blake was on his way home. Apparently, Lucifer has quite a reputation. The staff is panicked."

"We'd better get out of here," Bonnie said, punching the elevator button with her elbow.

Abigail allowed Bonnie and Sam to help her to her feet. When Cheveyo looked at the whole of her, he gasped and his hand flew to his mouth. She suspected as much.

"What is it?" Bonnie asked, holding Abigail at arm's length to get a better view. She inhaled sharply, glancing from Cheveyo to Samantha who pressed a hand over her heart.

The elevator doors opened and Abigail stepped into the compartment. Lined with mirrors, she saw the first reflection of herself since coming to Lucifer's condo. Cheeks gaunt, the dark circles under her eyes made her look like a skeleton. Her hair was matted, dull, and dirty. But it was the change in her body she would have rather not thought about that stood out. Stretching the fabric of her T-shirt, draped on either side by the oversized sweater coat and poking out above her yoga pants, her abdomen rounded from her bottom rib to her hipbone.

The others stepped into the compartment behind her. Bonnie was the first to say it out loud. "Abigail, you're pregnant."

* * * * *

Bonnie turned the key and hit the button for the atrium. Everyone was staring. You couldn't miss it. On her skeletal frame, the pregnancy looked like she was smuggling a basketball under her shirt.

Abigail ran her hand over the mound. "Yes. I'm pregnant."

The elevator descended into silence.

"W-well, it's not Lucifer's, if that's what you're thinking!" Abigail stammered. "It's Gideon's. I suspected I was pregnant before I left Eden. Lucifer never touched me. No one ever touched me."

Bonnie opened her mouth, closed it again. She glanced at Samantha and Cheveyo. The descending elevator took on the ambiance of a funeral parlor.

"You're afraid he's done something to the baby," Abigail said.

"It's just, you're so thin," Bonnie admitted.

"And malnourished," Samantha added.

Cheveyo shot both of them a harsh look. "Don't you worry, Mrs. Newman, you have a Healer back in Eden that will fix you and the baby up. A few days drinking the water, and you'll be as good as new."

Bonnie rubbed her toe along the shiny floor. How did any of them know for sure the baby, and therefore Abigail, would be allowed into Eden? At least Cheveyo was right about one thing, Malini would heal her. All of them would care for her, one way or another.

The doors opened and Bonnie scooped an arm under Abigail's, joining Samantha in helping her into the atrium. Cheveyo guarded her back. They ushered her into the foyer, planning to exit the way they'd come in, but as Bonnie glanced up, she saw they were too late. Lucifer, Cord, and Auriel were entering through the front doors.

"Not that way," Ghost appeared in front of them, arms blocking their advance. "Emergency exit." He pointed in the opposite direction.

Bonnie turned on her heel, dragging Abigail along. Only, the older woman's limbs wouldn't obey. Weakness from the pregnancy and months of starvation had taken their toll. She tripped. Bonnie caught her. Still in Cord's larger and stronger body, she decided to use it to their advantage. Sweeping Abigail up into her arms, she jogged toward the glowing red exit sign at the back of the building. Ghost blinked ahead and opened the door, setting off the alarm. Samantha and Cheveyo bolted through first, Bonnie moving slower with Abigail cradled in her arms.

On impulse, she glanced back. The real Cord glared at her, lips peeling back from extended fangs.

Bonnie kicked the door closed behind her, thinking about what the guide had said. Evil would know who she was. "He saw me. We've got to get out of here."

"This way," Ghost said. Racing for the street, he hailed a cab. They all climbed in, just as Cord and Auriel spilled into the alleyway.

"You got too many," the cabbie griped, eyeing the four crammed into the backseat. "Only three seatbelts."

Ghost handed him a hundred from the passenger's side. "Get us out of here."

The cabbie glanced at the advancing suits, shoved the bill into his pocket, and floored it.

Chapter 19
A New Beginning

Abigail repositioned herself on the bench of the boat to Eden. She didn't believe for a moment the baby inside of her was anything but beautiful and innocent, but the cherubim that guarded the gates were a foreboding presence not to be taken lightly.

"Here we go," Bonnie said, red hair still flying from the boat's forward momentum. She stripped out of the coat she'd been wearing in the outside world. As the temperature warmed to a balmy seventy-eight degrees, the others did the same.

The familiar sifting started, cells pulled apart and put back together, and then the rubbery stretch of being forced through a membrane. Just as expected, she popped out on the other side without any permanent damage.

"That was interesting," Samantha said, eyeing Abigail's rounded belly. "I wondered if we'd be able to see the baby's soul, like when Cheveyo was stripped from Dane and judged separately."

"I'm sure my baby has a soul," Abigail said. "Maybe, she's just part of me for now when it comes to the judging. After all, the cherubim are meant to protect, and it's not like she's a threat."

"She?" Ghost laughed. "You already know it's a girl."

"Just a feeling," Abigail said with a knowing smile.

He blinked onto the dock and helped her out of the boat. Abigail appreciated his assistance considering her wasted body wasn't cooperating with her the way it used to. The twins followed, helping her through the jungle and the welcoming doors of the Eden School for Soulkeepers.

Archibald, the head garden gnome, met her at the door, bowing deeply at the waist. "Ms. Abigail, it is my honor to see you again." A fat green tear formed in the corner of his eye.

"Thank you, Archibald."

"The others are gathered in the dining hall. We waited to take down the Christmas decorations, hoping this mission would be the one to find you."

"Merry Christmas," Abigail said, smiling. "And Happy New Year. I haven't missed Valentine's, have I?"

"No." He grinned a mouthful of jagged teeth. "You have a few weeks for that."

She limped toward the dining hall with Bonnie's help, and through the door Ghost held open.

A magnificent fir tree rose at the center of the room, decorated with pinecones, candles, and strung dried fruit. The beauty of the tree was only matched by the people under it. Malini, Jacob, Dane, Ethan, Lillian, Master Lee, and Grace all looked her way when she entered, and a chorus of cheers met her at the door.

And then, Gideon. At first his green eyes locked onto her face as if she were a mirage that would disappear at any moment. His lips pressed together. His pupils dilated. Slowly, centimeter-by-centimeter, the corners of his mouth curled. The reality of her presence seemed to plow into him and knock him from his chair.

He dashed to her, engulfing her in his arms and burying his face in the side of her hair. "Oh thank God. Thank you, Lord," he said.

The tears started then, hers and his. Suddenly, they weren't alone in their hug. The others circled, wrapping arms around them both. Their love was a palpable thing, soaking through her clothes and skin.

After a long moment, one by one the Soulkeepers pulled back. "Welcome home," Malini said.

Gideon's hands rubbed her shoulders. "Malini, she'll need healing. Your arms are so thin. And…" His voice trailed off as he noticed the mound of her belly. Gaping, he stared at the bump under her shirt.

"It's yours," she said. "I suspected I was pregnant before Lucifer took me. I think he was trying to starve the baby from me, but his plan didn't work."

Gideon placed his hands on either side of her belly. "How did you survive?"

"God visited me. She saved me." Abigail looked around the group, eyes pausing on each of their faces. "I'm so sorry I opened myself up to this. I should have waited. I should have asked for help."

Master Lee shook his head. "Any one of us might have done the same."

Lillian nodded. "Now we know. We will be more careful with the stones."

The rest of the Soulkeepers took turns nodding and whispering words of encouragement and forgiveness.

"I think I was captured for a reason," she began. "I believe there were things I was meant to learn and bring back to you. I have news of horrible things to come. I've seen how Lucifer is playing this game." Her voice cracked.

Malini smiled and placed her left hand near Gideon's. "Forever the fighter, Abigail. You amaze me." She frowned slightly, and Abigail felt the healing warmth of her touch under her skin. "I want you to rest and eat. If what you say is true, you'll need your strength."

"But—"

"There's time," Malini said. The golden color of the Healer's eyes held a certainty that transcended her short life, the wisdom of her ancient power surrounded her, an aura that gave everyone in her radius peace.

Abigail lowered her head. "I could use some rest."

Within seconds, four chairs appeared behind her. She chose one and allowed a gnome to bring her a tray of the most scrumptious-looking roasted root vegetables she'd ever seen. She didn't hesitate to dig in.

"Are you all going to watch me eat?" she said between bites. "It looks like you still have presents to open?" She pointed her chin toward the tree.

Jacob cleared his throat. "We opened ours on Christmas."

Ethan smirked, shaking a box wrapped in brown paper. "These are yours, Abigail. I've been dying to know what this is."

"Abigail can open her own gifts, Ethan." Dane smiled and pulled the box from his hand. "I've caught him shaking the box like fifty times."

"You saved presents, for me?" Abigail said, pressing a hand to her chest. A lump formed in her throat.

Gideon grinned, selecting a box from the stack of packages. "Yes, we did. I never gave up hope that we'd find you. Never."

"None of us did," Dane said.

She placed her tray on the floor and accepted the gift, ripping into the paper. She lifted the lid. Inside, a wooden hanger was surrounded by two dozen small bamboo cranes.

She lifted the hanger and listened to the hollow cranes knock together musically. Wind chimes!

From behind her chair, Gideon wrapped his arms around her neck and kissed her on the cheek. "There's a Japanese legend that if you fold one thousand origami cranes, you will be granted one wish. I'm not Japanese, and I don't fold origami, but I have learned something about woodworking. I thought the symbolism was close enough. Must have been, because my wish came true."

Abigail placed the wind chimes back in the box, her arm too tired to hold them up, and rested a hand on his forearm. With stormy vision, she turned in her seat to meet her husband's eyes. "I love you, Gideon. Forever."

She was home. Finally and completely, home.

* * * * *

Days later, Abigail sat on the veranda outside her bedroom, recovering. She'd spent much of the last forty-eight hours sleeping, and she stretched her arms in an effort to shake the groggy feeling that lingered like an unwanted guest. How long would it take to feel like herself again? Or maybe she never would, because she was not the same self.

Beyond the veranda, the lush jungle was alive with tropical birds and small monkeys chattering within the green foliage. Paradise. How she hated to be the one to deliver the message from the guide in the red stone. Malini put her off about it again and again, insisting she get stronger first before explaining her ordeal, but she couldn't wait any longer. The Healer needed to know what they were up against.

On the table beside her, a curl of steam rose from her herbal tea, her own healing recipe brewed by Archibald. Thanks to Malini's daily healing touch, and the gnome's regular meals, Abigail had already gained a few pounds. Still, she took none of it for granted. All of the Soulkeepers lived here on borrowed time.

A knock rang through the room. "Come in, Malini."

The Healer entered with the graceful stride of an old soul. "How are you feeling today?"

"Better. I think our sessions are helping."

"I'm not doing much. My skin doesn't burn anymore when I touch you, which means I'm not exactly healing something that's sick. Instead, I'm just giving you a little extra warmth and love to support your recovery."

Abigail smiled and motioned toward the cushy chair next to her. "We need to talk."

Pausing, Malini sighed deeply. Abigail expected a fight, but after Malini scanned her from head to toe, she resigned herself to the seat on the other side of the small table.

"Okay."

"It's time for me to tell you about what I learned when I was Lucifer's prisoner."

"About the challenge?"

"Yes."

"There will be six curses and six blessings."

"Fatima told me. She said they will go in order, curse then blessing."

"The first curse was pestilence. Lucifer is running Harrington Enterprises. The cure was purposefully made to be addictive."

"We were able to puzzle that one out. We think the first blessing was wisdom. There's an entire anti-Elysium movement now. God had to be behind that."

"The second curse was ignorance. Lucifer used his power to place Auriel in the position of Secretary of Education."

"Like of the United States?"

Abigail nodded. "I'm fairly sure they've disposed of the real Mr. Duncan."

"We assumed he was influenced. Sounds like Lucifer isn't taking any chances." Malini shook her head. "I had to kill a Watcher at PHS the last day of school before winter break."

Abigail raised both eyebrows.

"Said the curriculum was being redesigned. I redesigned her molecules."

"Was there fallout? Who saw? Do we have to cover it up?"

"You know, I thought there might be. When you burn someone in the middle of the hallway, you expect repercussions. But by the time the others came out, she was mostly ash. Dane told them it was experimental theater."

"And they bought that explanation?"

"The weird thing is I don't think the kids who saw really believed our story. They just wanted an explanation. They couldn't process the truth, so they chose to believe the lie."

"Hmm." Abigail lifted her cup to her lips and took a long swallow. "Do you know if the second blessing has happened yet?"

"If it has, I don't know what it is."

Abigail nodded. "Then we may have some time. I've learned the third curse will bring us out of Eden."

"What?" Malini furrowed her brow. "What are you talking about?"

"When I was in the stone—your stone—my guide told me that the third curse will be terror, and even Eden will not be safe. He warned me that we must evacuate. Eden isn't safe any longer."

"The curse makes sense. Lucifer deals in fear and illusion. It was only a matter of time before he used terror to his advantage. But Eden?" Malini shook her head.

"Eden has been our safe house since we found it. I didn't think anything could reach us here. But the guide in the In Between made me promise to warn you. He said, and I quote, 'You must protect the remnant.'"

"The remnant? Eden isn't safe?" Malini searched Abigail's eyes. "Are you certain about this? The guide is a manifestation of my deepest consciousness. I don't have any memory of what he or she says to anyone, but I do know that sometimes the messages can be abstract. Even I have trouble seeing the future."

"I've been human less than a year, Malini, but I've been around much longer. It wasn't just what the guide said." Abigail stared into the jungle, tapping that deep and distant part of herself that used to be a Watcher. "I can feel it in my bones. Something big is coming. Something brutal. Lucifer will stop at nothing to win this challenge. He's not above cheating or trickery."

"Another Trojan horse?" Malini asked absently.

"I don't know for sure, but we must prepare." Abigail turned to meet her young friend's eyes and rubbed a hand over the mound of her belly. "We need to leave Eden."

Chapter 20
The Second Gift

The rubber-coated, foam ball plowed into Tommy Snider's stomach with such force that his young, lanky body toppled backward. He landed with a painful thump on his tailbone. The red ball rolled harmlessly away.

"Snider!" the PE teacher howled, his face turning red with the force of his yell. "Man up and play ball."

Within the body of twelve-year-old Noah Spencer, the angel Gabriel reached down to help God from the floor of St. Andrews Middle School.

"Lord, are you all right?" Gabriel asked.

"Noah! You worry about you," the red-faced teacher yelled.

Another red ball sailed between them.

"You know I am fine, Gabriel. I've suffered much worse humiliations than this," God said through Tommy's mouth.

Smack. A red ball collided with the side of Gabriel's head. He rubbed Noah's aching ear.

"Why must we do this, Lord? Dodgeball? In the bodies of twelve-year-old boys? What good could this possibly accomplish?"

God smacked another red ball aside with Tommy's small-for-his-age hand. It bounced harmlessly between the targets on the other team and was promptly caught. "Tommy Snider has been bullied all year at St. Andrews. For one afternoon, I wanted to lift his burden. There's no better day to do that than dodgeball day."

"But, Lord, we hardly have time for this. Auriel is running the public education system for Lucifer. The things they are teaching the children are horrific. The scales still tip in his favor. We must do something. Perhaps, the next blessing?"

"All in good time, Gabriel."

Gabriel leapt in front of God to block the next barrage of balls. A welt began to form under Noah's right eye.

"Lucifer has gone too far," Gabriel said. "It is time to smite the Watchers with heavenly force. Perhaps another flood? A legion of archangels to reclaim the children?"

God caught a red ball and focused on a particularly snotty-looking boy across the gym. He raised the projectile but did not throw it back.

Gabriel watched as the boy across the gym made eye contact with the Creator and shivered. A dark, wet spot bloomed low on the boy's blue shorts. The perpetually angry PE teacher uttered a curse and blew his whistle. The game stopped.

"There is a time for force and a time to display quiet strength," God said, lowering the ball. He turned piercing brown eyes on Gabriel. "Lucifer never did understand the force of peace. You can never combat ignorance with physical force."

"Then how do we stop this?" Gabriel asked. The boy who'd wet his pants cried openly as the PE teacher ushered him to the locker room with a less-than-compassionate strong-arm. A sea of snickers and pointing fingers followed him.

God sighed. "I hate to do it, but sometimes you have to show a bully for what he is. To combat ignorance, we will impart understanding, specifically discernment of spirits."

"My lord?"

"If any man or woman receives my gift and then looks upon a Watcher in the light of day, the beast's illusion shall fall away and the truth of what they are will be exposed."

"You will remove the power of their illusions? But, Lord, there will be panic. The humans will see them as monsters. Great fear will come to pass. The world will never be the same."

God nodded. "It is too late for the same. Those who choose evil must see the darkness for what it is, and those who choose good must know walking in the light does not come easily. There is a price, a responsibility that comes with knowing the truth and having a heart of peace and love."

Gabriel nodded. "As you wish. How shall I deliver this gift to the world?"

God lifted the red ball toward the ceiling. The rubber skin inflated, thinning and rising from the prepubescent hand of Tommy Snider. Transforming into a giant red balloon, the ball sprouted a string as it floated above their heads. "Take this balloon and guide it in the sky above. See that it drifts for all to see."

"My pleasure." Gabriel gave a small bow and flew for the window, red balloon in hand.

"Prepare yourself, Gabriel," God whispered. "The tide is turning. This means war."

* * * * *

"Shouldn't you kids be in school?" Mrs. McNaulty handed Jacob his Coke but eyed Malini accusingly.

"Senior ditch day," Jacob blurted.

Malini widened her eyes at him, then turned her attention to Mrs. McNaulty. "He's kidding. Of course it's not senior ditch day; it's the beginning of the semester." She smoothed her hands over the table. "Actually, we're doing a project for our sociology class. It's part of the new curriculum. You can call the school." She nodded nervously.

Mrs. McNaulty pursed her lips and drifted off toward the kitchen.

"Do you think she'll call?" Jacob asked. "We can't keep doing this, Malini. Someone is going to catch on that we aren't going to school."

"Bull. Who's going to say anything? Since the Watchers brought in the new curriculum, they haven't exactly taken attendance. If she calls, I bet no one answers the phone." Malini tucked her hair behind her ears.

"It's a small town. I'm willing to bet Mrs. M. tells my uncle." Jacob nodded toward the kitchen.

Nibbling on her lip, Malini took Jacob's hand. "I've been thinking."

"That's never a good sign."

She rolled her eyes. "I've been thinking we should tell our families the truth."

Jacob's mouth fell open. "Are you crazy?"

"No, Jacob, listen to me. They're not safe. The town is crawling with Watchers. Every school is crawling with Watchers. They know who we are. I think the only reason they haven't attacked is they don't want to blow their cover. But it's only a matter of time before they figure out who our families are and come for them."

He shook his head. "So we tell them, and then what? They either think we're insane, or worse, they believe us but can't do anything about it but worry."

"But we can teach them—"

"Oh my God!" Mrs. McNaulty cried from behind the register. She lifted a remote control and turned up the volume on the flat screen hanging on the wall. A local newscaster frowned under a banner that read Special Report. Next to him was a picture of Principal Bailey.

Again, long-beloved principal of Paris High School, John Bailey was found dead today in an apparent animal attack. A memorial service is being planned for the man described as the best educator Paris has ever known. The news of his death was a huge blow to local families, who were trying to have him reinstated after his recent termination. Several families have boycotted the school due to the changes in personnel and curriculum.

Fingers pressed over her lips, Malini's vision swam.

"They killed him," Jacob mumbled, staring at the screen. "It wasn't enough to fire him. They killed him."

Malini squeezed his hand. "I had a feeling..." She didn't finish her sentence.

Dane flew through the door and focused on her. "Have you heard? Did you see?"

"Yes, Principal Bailey. So sad," Malini said.

"No. Not that." Dane rushed to Mrs. McNaulty, who was still watching the news, stiff and crying. Dane yanked the remote control out of her hands and changed the channel.

"Hey!" she yelled, but when the television tuned in to Dane's pick of channel, she paled.

On the screen was a shaky cell phone recording of a Watcher. Not an illusion but a black-skinned, leather-winged beast.

Across the country today, people reported seeing strange winged creatures. Scientists are baffled by the sheer number of pictures, videos, and personal anecdotes but have no rational explanation.

Seventy-six-year-old Hazel Yearly had this to say about her sighting. "My neighbor thinks they're aliens, but I know what they are. They're demons! Mark my words, this is the end of times. Repent now."

The newscaster smirked as the woman's face faded from the screen. *Well, whatever they are, the information coming in indicates they hate the sunlight. All residents are encouraged to lock their doors after dusk.*

"Lock their doors?" Jacob said. "That'll work if your door is soaked in holy water."

"We've got to go." Malini sprang from her seat. Dane handed the remote back to Mrs. McNaulty and followed out the door.

"Where are we going?" Dane asked.

"We've got to warn our families and then evacuate Eden."

"Evacuate?" Jacob pulled up short in the gravel parking lot.

Malini pointed toward the door to McNaulty's. "That, Jacob, was the second gift. They can't hide among us any longer. And if I know Lucifer, when he can't hide, he's going to fight. Now come on. We've got work to do."

"My aunt and uncle are at the flower shop with my mom today," Jacob said.

Malini changed direction, crossing the street to Laudner's Flowers and Gifts. A familiar face stopped her before she reached the door.

"Daddy?"

"Malini," Mr. Gupta said, pulling her into a hug. "Have you heard? Did you see? I was afraid you were at school!" He kissed the side of her head. "Thank God you are safe. There are monsters… great, leathery"—he held his arms out to his sides and shook his head—"winged creatures. I drove to the school after I heard about Bailey and saw one!"

Malini sighed and took his hand. "Come on in. Call Mom. There's something I've got to tell you."

Chapter 21
The Truth

Once her mother and Mary Michaels had arrived, Malini locked the door to the shop and ushered the group into the back, where they couldn't be seen from the street.

Uncle John adjusted his thick-rimmed glasses. "What's this all about? We can't keep the store closed for more than a few minutes."

"Show them, Jake," Malini ordered, brown eyes flashing to a vase of roses on the counter.

Dane crossed the room to put his arm around his mom's shoulders. Always so thoughtful. He gave Malini a nod of encouragement.

Jacob paused, concentrating on the water. A thin geyser erupted, rising from the vase and forming into a rose. The flower turned to ice, then melted back into the vase.

Sarah Gupta squinted, trying to figure out the trick behind it. "How are you doing that?"

Malini raised her eyebrows. "More, Jake."

Holding out his hand, Jacob called the water to him. The liquid shot out of the vase and into his hand, freezing into his favorite broadsword. He twirled it around his body. Malini could feel the cold breeze as the blade sailed past her cheek and hear the sharp intake of breath from the adults.

Aunt Carolyn pressed a hand over her heart. "But how? Is it some kind of a magic trick?"

"Not magic. Genetics," Malini said. "Jacob, Dane, Lillian, and I are Soulkeepers. We've been genetically gifted to kill the creatures some of you saw today."

Mary Michaels whipped her head around to face Lillian, who responded with, "It's true."

Jim Gupta snorted. "Genetically gifted? I know your genetics, Malini."

Malini eyed Jacob. "I need to show him what I can do."

Without hesitation, Jacob drew his blade across his palm, slicing the skin. Blood bubbled up.

"Ah!" Mary Michaels groaned before collapsing in Dane's arms. Thankfully, the other adults were able to keep it together.

Malini reached out and touched Jacob's hand. The cut stitched itself up while Malini's fingers began to smoke. The smell of burning flesh filled the back room. Jacob's cut healed pink, then white, then disappeared altogether.

"Holy mother of God," Jim Gupta said, staring at his daughter's burnt hand.

Jacob commanded some of his sword to melt over her burn, healing the skin before rejoining his weapon.

"How?" John Laudner asked.

"Why?" Sarah Gupta blurted.

"Who else knows?" Aunt Carolyn whispered.

Lillian spoke from the corner of the room. "We kill Watchers. The creature you saw near the school, Jim, and the one you saw on TV, Carolyn, they are fallen angels or you might call them demons. You can see them because we are witnessing war between Heaven and Hell." Lillian pulled up the news segment about the Watcher sightings on YouTube and passed her phone around the group. Conscious again, Mary Michaels insisted on watching the video twice, shaking her head the entire time.

Malini rubbed her palms together in small circles. "We ... the Soulkeepers are gifted by God to kill Watchers. Usually there are only a few on the Earth at any given time, not more than we can handle. But now ... we've been invaded. Lucifer and his army are attempting a takeover. They want Earth."

"The apocalypse," Mary Michaels murmured, clinging to her son.

"But you said you can stop them," Aunt Carolyn said hopefully. Her face was ghostly pale.

Malini nodded. "We're going to try."

Mary Michaels pushed Dane an arm's length away. "Malini said you were one of them. What can you do?"

Dane cleared his throat. "Nothing on my own."

"I don't understand," she said. "You can't go out fighting those things without some way to protect yourself."

"I have a gift," Dane said. "It's just hard to explain."

The adults stared at him blankly.

"I can borrow other Soulkeepers' powers."

He reached out for Jacob's hand. Reluctantly, Jacob channeled his weapon back into the vase, then accepted Dane's palm. A shock ran through both of their bodies, then Dane pulled the water from the vase again, this time forming a Katana in his hand.

John barely caught Mrs. Michaels before she hit the floor. Sarah Gupta fanned her face with a Teleflora pamphlet from the counter. Next to her, Jim Gupta stared at his daughter as if he hadn't noticed Mary pass out at his side.

"Okay, enough," Jacob said. "Give it back."

Dane made a face, but returned the water and reached for Jacob's hand.

Lillian cleared her throat. "I'm sure this all seems overwhelming," she said. "But we needed you to know the truth."

Pale face unreadable, John Laudner shuffled Mary into her son's arms. "So these demons are coming, and there are more than you can stop on your own. How do we help?"

"I'm glad you asked that question," Malini said. At the back of the room, she plugged the sink and turned on the water. "Jacob, your flask."

Jacob passed her his most prized possession, but she had to pry it from his fingers.

"I won't use it all, Jacob." She poured four drops into the filling sink and returned the flask. "Holy water is toxic to Watchers. Everyday weapons won't kill them, but soak them in holy water and they're deadly." She grabbed a floral knife from the basket John kept them in and tossed it into the water.

"How long does it need to soak?" Carolyn asked.

"The effect is immediate," Malini said. "But we don't know how long it lasts. We resoak after every kill." She handed the blessed knife to Carolyn.

John pushed through the other adults to a locked cabinet near the back of the room. Pulling a set of keys from his pocket, he unlocked the metal door and dug through the contents. He pulled out a rifle.

Sarah Gupta gasped; Malini's mother never liked guns.

"If those things are half as terrifying as they look on television, we are going to need a hell of a lot more than a three-inch blade." John dunked the rifle and then a box of ammunition.

Mary Michaels shook her head. Apologizing profusely, she regained her balance, then saw the dripping gun in John's hand and had to steady herself on Dane's arm again.

"Mary, why don't you come stay with us for awhile. Bring the kids," John said. Mary nodded appreciatively.

"What about us, Malini? We have no weapons," her father said.

"We'll bring you some from Eden."

"Eden?" Sarah Gupta glanced around the room as if begging the other adults to make sense of this madness for her.

Malini triggered the trap door in the floor.

John dropped the rifle. Everyone scattered, except for Lillian, who snagged the gun before it hit the floor. She had it safely pointed at the ceiling before anyone could say a word.

"Weapons are my gift," she said, smiling.

Slowly, the adults again turned their attention toward Malini and the trap door. "There's something else we need to tell you."

Chapter 22
The Third Curse

Lucifer paced his high-rise penthouse like an animal in a glass cage. They'd taken her. They'd taken his prize. The stench of Soulkeeper still burned in his nostrils.

"I saw her. It was the redheaded twin again," Cord said. "The one called Bonnie."

"Again she gets the best of you," Lucifer snapped.

Cord physically recoiled. Fortunately, at that moment, Auriel burst through the door, red heels click-clacking on the tile foyer.

"Did I miss it? Have you issued the curse?" she asked breathlessly.

"No, dear. It wouldn't be half as fun without you."

"Good. It's a pain in the ass only traveling at night."

"Yes, the Great Oppressor's last gift is certainly problematic. But since he chose to bring us into the light, let's not disappoint him by hiding under a bushel."

"My lord?" Auriel asked.

"Elysium was successful. We have addicts pounding on our doors for more of the drug. Do you know why it worked, Cord?"

Cord cringed to have Lucifer's attention back on him. He thought quickly and tried to give an intelligent answer. "Because people didn't want to be sick anymore. The humans say the virus causes constant pain. They think they will die without the medicine."

"Exactly, my wretched friend. They fear death. We must make them fear *us*."

"Us?" Auriel questioned.

He slammed his fist into the back of the sofa. "We must bring them death and destruction, and when they loathe us and cringe in our presence, then we will save them."

"Save the humans?" Cord asked.

"Why yes. We must save them to win them. Harrington Enterprises is going into the Watcher eradication business."

"You want to kill our own," Auriel said, appalled.

"Of course not," Lucifer chided. "Don't be an idiot, Auriel. It will all be for show. Amulets, security systems, repellents. We will invent dozens of products and command our Watchers to respond to them. Harrington will make a mint and Milton Blake's face will be on every box."

"Your face." Cord grinned. "Brilliant. They will love you and turn their hearts to you."

"Exactly." Lucifer approached Cord, fire blazing in his pupils. "Do you hate the Soulkeeper that stole your illusion?"

"Beyond hate, my lord. I wish to pull out her teeth one by one before I remove each of her organs by hand," Cord said through his teeth.

"Good. I choose you as my vessel for the third curse."

"My pleasure."

Lucifer strode to the kitchen and procured a pair of scissors from the knife block. "Come here," he said.

Cord obeyed, approaching the counter quickly, although with the shivering limbs of a dead man walking.

Lucifer pointed at the granite. "Rest your head here."

Cord swallowed hard, then lowered his cheek to the cold countertop. Lucifer positioned his hand over Cord's profile, scissors finding the tip of his pinky finger. With a firm grasp, he clipped that piece of flesh, the black stump falling into Cord's ear canal. While his finger healed itself, Lucifer watched his dismembered digit transform into a black worm that worked its way into Cord's skull.

"*Ahhhhhh!*" Cord screeched, banging his head on the counter until his black blood splattered the kitchen. "Get it out! GET IT OUT!"

"It only takes a moment," Auriel said without empathy.

Soon, Cord's thrashing slowed, then stopped. Carefully, he pulled himself to a standing position. "What did you do to me?"

"I simply enhanced your explosive personality, my friend."

Cord smoothed back his black hair and straightened his suit.

"Remember, when you terrorize the humans, you must look like a Watcher." Lucifer lowered his chin. "Milton Blake cannot be associated with the monsters."

"I understand, my lord."

"Now, my gift to you."

Cord cocked his head to the side inquisitively. Lucifer did not give gifts.

"Auriel, can you inform Cord of your latest news."

She nodded. "It seems one of our teachers at Paris High School saw redheaded twins visiting a local flower shop the night Abigail was stolen from us. The two went in but never came out. Seems Paris is a hotbed of Soulkeeper activity."

"Redheaded twins. The one they call Bonnie?"

She laughed. "Oh yes. But be careful. If the shop is the entrance to Eden, your attack must be unexpected and efficient. The Healer is still living there. Remember what she did to you."

"I remember."

Lucifer nodded. "Leave Malini for me. The others you are welcome to kill."

Cord growled and headed for the door. "My pleasure."

* * * * *

"Do you have the weapons packed?" Malini asked Lillian.

"Ethan and I have been packing all day. We have a duffle bag for each Soulkeeper. Everybody carries their own." Lillian yanked the elastic from her hair and reformed her ponytail, tighter, smoother. The Horseman showed no emotion over the task. Her eyes weren't wet with tears, and she didn't look around the dojo mournfully. But Malini knew she felt it, the aching loss. All of them did.

Ethan zipped the last bag and caught Malini's eye. "Are you sure this is necessary? I mean, this place has been here literally since the beginning. Adam and Eve and that whole section of the Bible no one reads that lists their descendants." He slipped his hands into his back pockets. "Seems like a pretty safe place."

"Sorry, Ethan. I know it seems impossible, but Abigail learned Lucifer's third curse would target Eden."

"Maybe it's a trick. Maybe Lucifer planted that knowledge to get us all to leave the only place we'd be safe."

"It wasn't Lucifer who told her," Malini said. "Listen, we don't have time for this. You have to trust me."

He sighed. "You're the boss. Gonna go finish packing." Ethan shouldered past her and headed for the west wing.

"Was it just me or did you sense a little attitude coming off him?"

Lillian grabbed the closest two bags and started lining them up along the hall. "You can't blame him, Malini. This idea seems half-baked. First you and Abigail tell us that the safest place on Earth isn't safe anymore. Then, you fully admit that you have no idea where we will go next. I'm surprised Grace hasn't thrown a full-out hissy fit."

Malini frowned. "It might still be coming. Then again, she's wanted to go back to Nebraska for months. Maybe she hopes this will be her opportunity."

"Look, I know you're the Healer and I trust in that, okay. But even you must realize how crazy this seems."

"I am the Healer," Malini said firmly. "And this isn't easy for me. But it's the right thing to do. We leave in fifteen."

Lillian nodded and reached for another two bags.

"Listen, I don't mean to be rude. This is hard for me too. I…" Malini paused. A knot had formed in the pit of her stomach, and a chill started in her fingertips and coursed to her heart.

A ghost formed in the center of the room. At first she thought it was Jesse, but as the body solidified, she recognized the pink-streaked dark hair and piercings of an old and powerful friend.

"Mara!" Malini said. The immortal, Time, was pale and sweating.

"I can't … stop … it … Malini. Run. RUN!" Mara dissolved.

BOOM! The ground beneath the dojo shook, an earthquake that knocked her into the wall. Malini stared at the air where Mara had been, stunned. Thankfully, Lillian's gift kicked into gear.

"Take these," she said, throwing two insanely heavy duffle bags over her shoulder and pulling Malini toward the foyer. "Jesse!" she yelled. "Archibald!"

Both poofed into existence as another tremor almost knocked Malini on her backside.

"Ghost, bring the rest of the bags. We have to go, now," Lillian said. "Archie, full alert. Tell everyone we must evacuate now." She half dragged Malini by the elbow toward the door.

"Wait!" Malini dug her heels in, but Lillian would have none of the stopping. She hooked an arm around her waist and dragged her on. "Lilly, we need to find Jacob!"

"Jacob can take care of himself, Malini. You need to go now."

"I'm not leaving without him."

In a feat of strength that would have been impossible if she wasn't a Soulkeeper, Lillian hurled Malini and her two bags toward the door. "I will find him, Malini, only if you get to that boat. We need our Healer."

Ghost arrived then, looking like an ant under a huge pile of bags. "I got this," he said to Lillian. He kicked the door open for Malini, just as the place shook so hard the jewels encrusting the walls rained around them.

"Come on!" Ghost ushered her down the hill to the boat. He helped her stow the bags up front and guided her into the seat farthest from the dock. "It's better this way, Malini. The others can load faster."

The worry in his voice wasn't lost on her. She was worried, too.

The twins arrived first, Samantha launching herself into Ghost's arms before she even dropped her bags. Gideon, Grace, Cheveyo, and Abigail came down next, the first two helping Abigail into the boat. Malini thought she looked stronger, but nowhere near ready for this.

The earth shook again, causing Grace, who was still on the dock, to stumble backward. *Crack!* A piece of the shoulder of one of the cherubim crumbled off and splashed into the water.

"You shouldn't have waited for us," Lillian yelled. Jacob, Dane, and Ethan leapt, bags and all, into the boat. Lillian untied the vessel from the dock. "Lee! Come on!"

Looking surprisingly lithe, Lee's feet slapped the dock. With everything he had, he jumped in, simultaneously pushing the boat off.

Malini breathed a sigh of relief that everyone was on board, but the feeling didn't last. *BOOM!* The world shook. The cherubim came apart around them. Huge chunks of gold sailed toward their over-packed ship. Malini covered her head with her arms.

"I've got it," Ethan said.

Malini chanced a glance. Ethan deflected one after another from the boat, pieces splashing into the water around them. By the time they reached the river, his nose was bleeding.

"Almost there," he said. Malini thought it might have been for his own benefit.

Jacob took that as a hint. "Let's not prolong the experience." He held his hand over the water and the boat jerked forward, the water propelling them into the cave. The boat slid to a stop on a heap of white sand as usual. Only the expected serenity of the cave was replaced by madness. The walls were coming apart around them.

"Crap, I got nothing left!" Ethan cried from the center of a storm of rubble.

Malini grabbed as many bags as she could carry and threw herself over the side of the boat. She tripped in the sand. A hand scooped under her arm and pulled her forward. Lee. He kicked a falling stone away from her head then launched her ahead into the passageway.

Bodies crowded the corridor, up the winding staircase. Jacob's hand found hers. And then light. The trap door was open. Too late. The walls were caving in. The shop was on fire!

Suddenly, Uncle John's face was in front of hers. "This way! Out the back!"

Suspended in a sea of shoulders and bags, she spilled into the alleyway and was pushed into a white delivery van. Jacob, Dane, and Ethan piled in before the doors slammed shut. The engine roared to life, Lillian behind the wheel. She reversed into the street and floored the accelerator.

Through the windshield, Malini stared at the burning streets of Paris. A woman bolted in front of the van, forcing

Lillian to slam on the brakes to keep from running her over. She was gone in a flash. Malini didn't even recognize who it was, although she knew everyone in Paris. But she did recognize the Watcher the woman was running from. Surrounded by fire and falling rubble, the snake-skinned beast walked toward the van, wings outstretched, with the unmistakably prideful gait that could only belong to one Watcher.

Cord.

Chapter 23
Race for Cover

Through the windshield, Malini watched Cord pause in front of McNaulty's, the place she'd spent some of the happiest moments of her teenage existence. The restaurant exploded into a pillar of fire. Cord smiled wickedly, delighted with the destruction and still unaware of the delivery van full of Soulkeepers in his path.

"Hey!" Jacob yelled. "Let's kill that son of a bitch." He reached for the flask on his ankle.

"No," Malini said firmly. "That's what he wants. He's trying to draw us out. Get us out of here, Lilly, before he sees who we are. We've got to find a place to regroup."

Lillian agreed and slammed on the gas. Tires screeched as she did a U-turn and raced for the country roads. "We're lucky. Full tank of gas. I'm always complaining that John makes me fill these up every night. Always seemed silly to me. It's not as if Paris has many emergency flower deliveries and certainly not in a neighboring state. But always, always your uncle wanted to be prepared. He's a good man, Jacob."

Jacob rubbed his eyes with his thumb and forefinger. "Did he make it out alive?"

"Are you kidding? He practically threw me into this van. Had his holy-water-soaked rifle over his shoulder and was ready to use it. The Watchers don't know what they're dealing with. Half of Paris has been stockpiling weapons since Obama was elected and the other half had a stash well before that. They have a goddamn NRA club at the high school. The smartest thing you ever did was tell them the truth, Malini. If there's one thing Paris can do, it's guns and holy water."

Dane chuckled. "Yeah, I'm pretty sure my mom carries both of those items in her purse."

"Who? Our Mary?" Ethan said. "The one who could barely remain standing when you told her?"

"Oh, a fainter for sure. But no one with half a brain would live in the country without a gun. You never know when you're going to find yourself on the biting end of something angry and furry. And the holy water … well, I guess you could say Mom's superstitious."

"Did you take care of my parents?" Malini asked Lillian.

"Before I started packing. Jim and Sarah have their very own arsenal now," Lillian said. She checked her side mirror. "The others are behind us."

"Let's put some distance between us and Paris, then stop wherever seems safe," Malini said.

"You got it."

The hum of the road filled the van as they got comfortable between the bags on the floor. Minutes passed in silence.

"What do you think happened to the gnomes?" Ethan asked. Everyone was thinking it, but Dane grimaced to hear it out loud.

Jacob answered, "I've been thinking about this. Cord destroyed the portal. He blew up the connection between the flower shop and Eden. That doesn't mean Eden is gone. My great-great-great-grandfather, Warwick Laudner, built that portal. Who's to say another couldn't be built someday."

"If Eden is still standing," Dane added.

"We have to believe it is," Malini said softly. "I sense that it is."

"Me too," Ethan said. "I think I'd know, I'd feel it in my gut, if Archie was gone."

The three nodded their heads, and eventually Dane seemed to take comfort in their words.

In silence, the miles rolled by, loss and grief seeping in through the cracks like a bad smell. Malini would have cried if she thought it would help, but tears wouldn't win this challenge. She'd known this was coming. Abigail warned her they would lose Eden. But it never seemed real. Well, not until now.

"There's a truck stop ahead," Lillian said, slowing as they merged into congested traffic. "We're just over the border. Indiana. Nothing out here for miles. Should we stop?"

"I don't know about you but I'm starving," Jacob said.

"How can you think about food at a time like this?" Malini asked.

"How long have you known me?"

Lillian exited the highway and pulled into the Dixieland Diner parking area. They weren't alone. The lot was full of vans, RVs, and cars of every shape and size.

"Looks like we're not the only ones running," Lillian said. She found an open spot and turned off the van.

The other delivery van finished parking as Malini jumped down to the asphalt. She stretched. As much as she'd teased Jacob, she could use a cup of coffee and maybe a sandwich.

Grace jumped out of the driver's seat of the other van and walked around to open the back doors. A bloody gash marred the side of her face. Malini would heal that. No problem. The twins hopped down from the cargo area. She couldn't tell who was who without looking them in the face. Oh wait, Bonnie was wearing the stone. They'd both been crying.

"Something's wrong," Ethan said. Malini could feel it too, a generalized sense of dread.

"Abigail?" Jacob said, but Gideon was the next to exit, immediately helping a very pregnant Abigail from the back. She appeared uninjured. Cheveyo climbed down after her.

Grace closed the door.

"Where's Lee?" Dane asked.

Malini froze. She met Grace's weeping eyes and saw the truth.

"He didn't make it out on time," Grace confirmed. "We've lost him."

* * * * *

"Lee stayed behind to hold open the passageway for us. We'd pushed you all through first. The ceiling collapsed. The building came down around him." Grace told the story over her coffee, huddled with the other Soulkeepers around a table too small for their group.

"Is there any chance he might still be alive under the rubble? Maybe if we went back and I used my power to dig him out?" Ethan suggested.

Grace shook her head. "I saw his remains. There is no chance he survived."

Another tear rolled down Malini's cheek. They'd all cried themselves dry over the last hour. The loss was unbearable. Eden. Lee. And worse, more heartache waited in the wings. The diner was brimming with it. People at every table spoke of fleeing the monsters.

"What's next?" Ghost asked.

Malini stared at Abigail, conspicuously quiet since their arrival. She seemed intent on her coffee.

"We could try Nebraska," Grace suggested. Malini had healed the gash on her head but one side of her red hair was still matted with dried blood. "Plenty of rural acreage to get lost in."

"What about LA?" Ethan offered. "It's not rural but I have friends there in low places. We could disappear."

Dane shook his head. "My farm is big enough. We could use the holy water we brought from Eden to enchant a boundary around the property. Plenty of food and well water. We could hole up there for years without having to leave. Not to mention, the Watchers have already blown up Paris. Why would they do it twice?"

Malini blinked at him. "That's a good idea."

Dane's eyebrows shot up. "It is? So we're going back to Paris?"

"Yes, it is, and no we are not. We need to go where the Watchers have already been. Where they *are*. It's what they'll least expect. But we're not going to Paris."

"Then where?" Grace asked.

"Chicago."

Bonnie gasped. "Are you kidding me? We'll be delivering ourselves to Lucifer's front door!"

"And he'll never expect it. We'll find a place, far from any family or friends. We'll slip under his radar." Malini flattened her hands to the table, suddenly sure this was the right thing to do.

"One tiny snafu," Dane said. "How are we going to survive with no bank? I mean, unless we have a bag of cash somewhere, we are in a world of hurt."

Cheveyo agreed. "I don't even know how I'm going to pay for my lunch."

"If we rent or buy a place, we'll need an identity. Lucifer will find us in a heartbeat if I use mine," Lillian said. "We can't take out a loan."

Grace grimaced. "There are twelve of us. A place large enough to house us all in the city is going to cost a mint. Even with the sale of the restaurant, I don't have that kind of cash."

"If it's even possible," Gideon chimed in. "Watchers are walking the streets. We could find a city of boarded-up windows."

Malini folded her hands. In her head, she began to pray. It was a scattered prayer. Nothing she could say aloud. Just phrases really, full of grief for Lee and a whiny and perseverant supplication for help. It had been a long time since she prayed. Seemed silly she didn't stop to do it more often, considering she was a Soulkeeper.

"The important thing is we're safe," Ghost said, squeezing Samantha's hand. "I don't care if we have to live in a cave in the middle of the Andes. I'm thankful we have each other—what's left of us. We've already lost Lee. Let's not lose anyone else."

Samantha rested her head on his shoulder and closed her eyes.

"You're right, Ghost. We have to be thankful for what we have. All we can do is our best," Malini said.

"I have money," Ethan blurted.

Everyone at the table turned to stare at him.

"To be honest, I forgot about it. Maybe I wanted to forget, I don't know."

Abigail smiled. "The money you won in Vegas? When I came for you, you thought I was someone else."

"Uh, yeah." He scratched the back of his head. "I, uh, helped the ball land on certain numbers on the roulette wheel. Won a mint but the casino owner wanted to break my legs for awhile."

"So there's no confusion," Grace said, "how much do you mean by 'a mint'? One thousand? Ten thousand?"

"Two million." Ethan stared at the table as if ashamed. "I kept it in cash so no one could trace it."

"Cash?" Dane's mouth gaped. "Where in the world would you keep that much cash?"

"My apartment. Mattress and box spring are stuffed with it. Closet. Kitchen cabinets. Mostly tens and twenties. They can track large bills. Should still be there. My apartment was paid up for the year."

Malini unfolded her hands. The faces around the table turned to her. The expressions weren't exactly happy. More like they'd just seen a unicycle-riding bear pass behind her.

"It's settled. We'll use the staffs to go to LA to pick up the money. Then we travel to Chicago and buy a residence under a pseudonym. Any objections?"

Gideon cleared his throat. "Is anyone else concerned that we will be using money gained by sinful means? No offense, Ethan, but what you did amounts to stealing. We are soldiers for God, after all. It isn't right, even if we are using it for good."

"I've got no problem with it," Jacob said. Ten pairs of eyes drilled into him. "Oh, for crying out loud. Are we really going to analyze how this ... this ... blessing fell into our laps? The world is freaking populated with Watchers!"

Malini snorted. "I have to agree with Jacob. What's done is done. The world is an evil place. We have to work smarter or we won't survive. We can't overanalyze it."

Around the table, heads nodded. Eventually, Gideon dropped the subject and stared into his coffee.

"Excellent. Ethan will have to go; he's the only one who knows the exact location. Lillian, I'd feel better knowing you were with him for protection. Ghost, you'll be our third. If there's trouble, you can blink out of there and get help."

"Rock on," Ghost said.

Lillian and Ethan bumped knuckles.

"What about the fourth?" Dane asked hopefully.

"We have to keep one staff back here, in case the three don't return. Let's all pray we don't need to use it."

Chapter 24
Mission Los Angeles

Ethan materialized within a wooded area of a small park two blocks from his apartment, Lillian on his right, Ghost on his left. He'd thought the bank of trees would be a secluded place for popping in and out of existence, but he was wrong. He smiled at the bum curled up at the base of the nearest tree. The man smiled back. Ethan didn't explain. The man didn't ask.

"This way," Ethan said, taking off toward the street at a fast clip. "My apartment is a couple of blocks..." He trailed off as he saw the state of his street.

Windows blown out. Homes smoldering. Rubble-filled streets. There was no way you could drive on the road anymore, although people filled it. They wandered aimlessly, a few trying to comfort each other. A woman passed by with a shopping cart. Her shirt was Ralph Lauren—this season. Ethan was pretty sure she hadn't been homeless yesterday.

He hastened to his apartment building, relieved to find it was still standing. One wall was a pile of rubble in the alley, but otherwise the place looked structurally sound. He held the front door open for Ghost and Lillian.

"The elevator is still running," Ghost said, watching the numbers above the metal doors change with each floor. The lights in the ceiling blinked ominously.

"I think I'll take the stairs," Lillian said, moving for the stairwell.

"I'm on the fourth floor," Ethan said.

Lillian smiled at him as she opened the door. It was a dumb thing to do. A ball of fire rolled through the open door, searing her shoulder before narrowly missing Ethan and traveling right through Ghost, who broke apart just in time. Ethan saw a flash of leathery wing and dove out of the way of the door. A second later, black blood sprayed across the foyer. The Watcher fell at Lillian's feet and bubbled black on the linoleum.

"Thank God Malini forced us to take these from Eden," Ghost said, holding up a blessed hatchet. "I thought packing the duffle bags was a pain at the time but…" He motioned toward the body.

Lillian clutched her shoulder and winced painfully. "I've been hit."

Gripping her shirtsleeve, Ethan ripped away the cloth to expose the wound. The injury was festering but shallow. "It's the size of a quarter. You'll need healing."

"It can wait. Painful son of a bitch, but I'll survive. You need my help."

Ethan nodded. "Fourth floor, Ghost."

"I'll pop up there to make sure there aren't more of these hanging around." He broke apart.

Ethan stepped over the body and helped Lillian do the same. "Can you run?"

"Lower body is fine," she said through a tight smile.

He broke into a jog, up one flight, then two, three. Ethan stopped outside the door to the fourth floor. "I don't like this. Ghost is taking too long."

Lillian nodded and flattened herself against the wall next to the door. Ethan unzipped the pocket in his backpack that held his weapons and reached for the knob.

"Come on, you bastards!" Ghost's voice yelled on the other side of the door.

Ethan yanked, entering a hallway of horrors. Hellhounds! The black, oily creatures had Ghost cornered. One crept across the ceiling toward the Soulkeeper, defying gravity. But why didn't Ghost poof out of there?

"Ethan, behind you!" Ghost yelled.

The throwing stars soared from Ethan's backpack, straight into a hellhound. Lillian's kick snapped past his ear, knocking the wounded black beast off its trajectory and saving Ethan's head. It yelped and crumpled to the floor.

"Thanks," Ethan said.

"No problem."

Ghost appeared beside him. "They're guarding every door. The Watchers must know one of these apartments is yours."

Back-to-back, the three Soulkeepers moved into the hallway, Lillian with dagger in hand, Ghost with the hatchet, and Ethan with a backpack full of sharp metal stars. The hellhounds closed in.

"My apartment is 407. Do we run for it or kill these things?"

Ghost shook his head. "Oh, I plan to kill these things, even if we thought we could make it to the door."

"Agreed," Lillian said. "Can't leave them to roam the streets."

"Six," Ghost said. "Two each."

Ethan focused on an extra-large hound growling at him from the corner. The thing opened its mouth and a whiplike tongue made of fire snapped near his nose. The creature lowered itself, ready to pounce.

"If I kill more than two, I win," Ethan said.

Whoosh. The nasty black dog leapt, all claws and flashing teeth. Ethan pushed with one part of his mind and projected a star with another. The thing jerked sideways in midair and yelped as the star collided with its jugular. The metal hissed and smoked, embedded in the dog's flesh.

Where had the second gone? Ethan twirled, searching for his second attacker. *Smack.* A black body landed on his head. He slapped the linoleum face-first, sliding forward with the weight of the creature. Facedown, he couldn't make eye contact to use his telekinesis to push the thing away. The hellhound's claws slashed near his shoulders. Luckily, the backpack he was wearing was taking the brunt of the attack.

The backpack! Turning his head, he concentrated on the corner of a throwing star peeking from the pocket. He propelled it in the direction of the hellhound on his back. The beast howled and reared up. Ethan rolled out from under the thing, scrambled to his feet, and directed another two stars at the creature's head out of panic. The force was enough to decapitate the hound. If that wasn't enough to soak him in black blood, the first hound effectively exploded from his injuries, finishing the job.

Ethan turned to help the others, only to find they were similarly doused in oily black blood. Nothing was left of the hellhounds but a large, dark slick. "Well, that was fun," Ethan deadpanned.

"Dane's gonna love that shiner," Ghost said, pointing to Ethan's left eye. He could already feel it start to swell.

Lillian peeked under the fabric covering her injured shoulder. The sore was now the size of a baseball. "Can we get on with this, boys? I need Malini."

Ghost hugged his chest. "I agree. I'm feeling a little drained myself."

"Right. Let's do this." Ethan fished his keys out of his shredded backpack and unlocked the door to 407. The smell of rotting cheese and sweaty feet smacked them in the face.

"Just as I left it," Ethan said, coughing. He crossed the living room and opened a window. "Of course the food and garbage weren't rotting back then."

Lillian retrieved two folded duffle bags from her pack. "Where do we start?"

* * * * *

By the time Ethan arrived at the truck stop with three of six duffle bags full of cash, Lillian's wound had spread the length of her arm and up to her ear. Malini rushed to her side and worked her healing magic within the privacy of the van. Jacob was ready with a giant Styrofoam cup full of water to help Malini recover. Ghost, relatively unscathed, volunteered to pack the bags of money into the other van while Ethan waited outside the van for his turn to be healed.

"Nice shiner," Bonnie said, sidling up to him around the side of the van. "Do you need some ice while you're waiting?"

"Nah."

"He wants me to see the damage for sympathy," Dane said, grinning. He eyed the black mess still dripping off Ethan. "I'll give you the sympathy, but if you think I'm going to kiss it better, you're sadly mistaken."

Ethan offered a half-hearted pout. Crossing his arms over his chest, he turned his back on Dane for effect, and found himself staring at the side of the van. "Hey, do you think we should cover up the Laudner logo?"

"Oh my God," Bonnie said, hands on her hips. "Can you imagine if we drove into the city in this? How did we not notice before? We have to tell Malini."

"Tell me what?" Malini jumped down from the van and approached Ethan, hand reaching for his eye.

"The vans. We've got to cover up the logo. They know Jacob's last name," Ethan said.

Malini planted a kiss on his cheek, next to his now fully healed eye. "Good catch."

"But what do we do about it?" Dane asked. "We've gotta cover this up."

Jacob and Lillian exited the back of the van and closed the doors. "Cover what up?" they asked in unison.

Bonnie pointed at the side of the van.

Jacob scanned the parking lot, and then squinted toward the restaurant. "I got this."

Chapter 25
New Beginnings

From her place in the passenger's seat of the massive RV, Malini searched deep for a way to comfort Gideon. She came up empty. He had a point, but it wasn't as if any of them had a choice.

"This is wrong. Completely and utterly wrong," Gideon said.

"Relax, Gid," Jacob said from his perch on the counter next to the stove. "We left a note with the keys to the vans. They both have full tanks of gas. This RV is way bigger than that family needed anyway."

Lillian turned the massive wheel to exit onto the interstate. "Think of it as commandeering the vehicle.

Soulkeepers are like Watcher police. We needed it to do our job."

Abigail placed an arm around her husband. "He's lived thousands of years as an angel. Moral gray areas are hard for him."

"We stole an RV!" Gideon said, spreading his hands. "You shall not steal. What part of that is gray?"

"The part where we give it back when we're done saving the world," Jacob said, his head inside the mini-fridge. "Hey, there are sandwiches!"

Ghost, who'd been snuggling with Samantha on the couch, jumped up to join Jacob in his pursuit of an evening meal. Gideon tossed up his hands and retreated to the back bedroom.

Abigail followed. "We're just going to go lie down for a minute."

Malini returned her attention to the hum of the road. It didn't make her happy to have to steal or borrow an RV. But she was beginning to realize Jacob was right. It was a new world, an evil world. She didn't have the luxury of moral absolutes. The Soulkeepers had to survive and doing so meant they must evolve. As the Healer, her job was to choose for the greatest good. Taking the RV provided the greatest good, and that was all there was to it.

As the sun made a slow escape from the winter sky, she thought of Lee, and her eyes misted. When they got where they were going, wherever that was, she'd make sure to hold a proper memorial for him. The Soulkeepers had lost so much.

Too much. She needed to make sure their new home was safe and secure. What would happen when Abigail's baby came? She rubbed her temples. So many questions. So much responsibility.

Leaning back in her chair, she closed her eyes and cleared her mind. She needed help, and there was only one place she could get it, but strong emotion was not a good conduit to the In Between. She crashed into Fatima's villa, metaphysically shredded, as if her soul had traveled through broken glass to get there. She groaned.

"It's about time you visited," Fatima said, pulling her up by her shoulders. "Do you know what's happening down there?"

In the blink of an eye, she was out on the hillside, standing in front of the blindfolded angel statue—the scorekeeper. Henry and Mara materialized beside her.

"I can hardly keep up with the dead," Henry said. "I've never seen such devastation. It's worse than the Holocaust."

"I—" Malini started.

Mara grabbed her arm roughly. "My power over Time won't work. Lucifer's curses are somehow immune from my tampering. I couldn't help Lee, Malini, and I won't be able to help you." She released Malini's arm, looking frustrated and vulnerable.

"I don't know what to say. We are doing the best we can, but none of us knows what will come next or when."

"You've got to do better," Fatima said. Her graceful fingers pointed at the scorekeeper. The scales had shifted, and Lucifer was in the lead by a long shot.

"Oh no," Malini said. "How do we stop it?"

"We don't know," Mara said.

Fatima sighed. "I did find something today. Something that might help. But it's dangerous. It could be a trick."

"Show me."

The landscape folded again, and they were back inside Fatima's villa. "Lucifer has been living on Earth for several months now, running a major corporation. Everything he does impacts people's lives. We know where he lives now, and where he works. We know his closest associates are Auriel and Cord."

"So."

"So yesterday, I wove this." She pulled out a roll of fabric. In truth, Malini had noticed the bolt when she'd arrived. The fabric was black and white, a standout in the infinite warehouse full of colored cloth.

"What is this? Why doesn't it have any color?"

"Think of it as a photo negative. I usually weave the fabric of fate, lives intertwining, people interacting with people. This fabric shows endings. It focuses not on life but on death, on dead ends, on empty souls, darkness."

"You wove the empty space between lives." Malini could see it now. Each thread in this negative was a life but there was a missing thread, an empty space that ran through the entire tapestry like a repeating missed stitch.

"Lucifer has no soul and leaves no thread. But when he's living on Earth, he leaves a hole."

"A hole I can follow. A hole I can project."

Fatima smiled. "This is how Abigail's guide in the red stone, the oldest, wisest part of yourself, knew Eden was compromised. Maybe you *can* foretell what Lucifer will do next, Malini."

Malini ran her hand over the fabric, following the empty thread with her finger. She grinned and straightened her backbone. "Thank you, Fatima. This helps more than you know."

"Don't thank me yet. This is an unproven method. I've never made anything like this before. I'm not sure we can trust it."

"We have to. It's all we've got." Concentrating, Malini focused on the tattered lives that ended at Lucifer's empty space. The safest place was where Lucifer had already been. She found a cluster of rerouted and tangled threads and ran her fingertips over the pattern again and again, until she could see the scene in her head. Quickly, she rewrapped the bolt and returned the fabric to the empty spot.

She hugged Fatima and said her goodbyes before falling back into reality.

"Don't disappoint us," Fate yelled through the ether.

Malini landed with a jolt in the captain's chair of the RV, eyes opening to a dark road leading into a major city. Chicago. The road out of the city was stop-and-go traffic, but going in, there was nothing but road ahead of her.

"Welcome back," Lillian whispered. Sounds of snoring filtered through the cabin.

"I know where we're going to stay," Malini said.

Lillian did a double take. "Really?"

"Absolutely." Malini told her the address.

"You're the boss." Lillian tapped the turn signal and exited to a new beginning.

* * * * *

The front doors to the ornate church were barricaded shut, the lawn scorched, the outer walls crumbling. Only a quarter of the sign was still standing. It read *St. P.* Whatever came after the P was in a pile of rubble on the lawn. Even in the darkness Malini knew this was the place. Her entire body rang with the rightness of it. This church was a historic fixture in Chicago until the Watcher occupation.

She'd seen what the monsters had done to the people here. The church was close to the Harrington building. That meant it had to go. Can't have a congregation of good people around mucking up Lucifer's evil plans. The church was likely the first on Cord's hit list.

What Malini saw when she read the tapestry was that the congregation had gathered here when they began to see the Watchers. What safer place to hide from demons than a church? But it was not safe. Cord attacked. The church burned. People died. Others ran. And while the structure was still standing, the people who made this building a church were gone.

However, Malini could see the place for what it was, underestimated and underutilized. "Pull around back."

Lillian did. When she ran out of road, she simply drove onto the grass behind the church next to a large pile of rubble. The building would provide some cover from the road, but they'd have to do a better job of hiding the RV in the morning.

"Wake up, everyone. We're home," Malini said. She jumped out of the cab and walked to the church's delivery entrance. Boarded shut. Of course it would be. She yanked at the board but it wouldn't budge.

"That building looks like it might be a rectory. Sometimes they're connected to the church." Grace rubbed a hand through her matted red curls and blinked her eyes, trying to wake up. "Looks like an old Irish-Catholic place. We belonged to a church like this back in Nebraska. Not as ornate but just as beautiful."

"Are we staying here? Like to live?" Samantha asked from the door of the RV.

Without answering, Malini followed Grace across the courtyard toward the smaller building. The back door was hanging off its hinges. "Good idea, Grace. I think we can get in." She carefully squeezed through the opening, afraid if she bumped the door it would fall off its frame.

Inside, the thick darkness blinded her. She patted along the wall for a light switch.

"I have a gun pointed at your head," a man's voice said. "If you don't want your brains sprayed across the wall behind you, you will slip out the way you came in."

Malini froze, as did Grace, who was just outside the door and poorly positioned to help. "Please, sir, we need your help."

"No help here. Only death. You want help, you need to leave the city and get as far away from the demons as you can."

"But that's why we're here," Malini said, "to kill the demons. They're called Watchers actually."

"You can't kill those things," the man said. "I've tried."

"We know how. We can teach you."

A click preceded a warm wash of light. Malini stared at the gun in the man's hand. Lillian would have known what kind it was, but Malini was never good with guns. Holding the weapon was an elderly man wearing the black clothing and white collar traditionally associated with priests. Hollow cheeks and a thin frame gave the man a sickly appearance.

"Who are you?"

Tell him the truth. The voice in her head was not her own. God's? She wasn't sure. But she chose to trust the voice.

"I am a Soulkeeper, a human being chosen by God and genetically gifted to protect other humans from fallen angels."

Silence stretched between them, then the man laughed a few times. "I suppose I can't blame you for going a little crazy. The first time I saw one I thought I was."

"You are ill. I can heal you."

He snorted. "Thanks for noticing. No, you can't heal me. No one can. I have cancer." He jiggled the gun. "Anyway, all of us are risking our lives staying around here."

"My name is Malini Gupta. What's yours?"

He considered her for a moment. "Father Jonas Raymond."

"You can see Watchers?"

"Yes. Clear as day. Not everyone can, you know. Half the staff and congregation thought the other half had gone mad." He lowered the gun, set it down on the side of an overturned desk. "They all left. The ones who couldn't see, to flee the bombings; the ones who could, to flee the demons."

"Why did you stay?"

"Dying anyway. Might as well go down fighting."

"I'm glad you stayed. We need your help." Malini stepped closer, reaching tentatively for the man's hand. "You know I'm not a Watcher," she said. "You would see if I was."

Father Raymond softened, and finally, slowly, accepted her handshake. Malini poured her healing power into him. Closing her eyes, her gift curled inside the man, tendrils wrapping around the cancer in his liver, sifting through the organ, healing him.

"What are you doing?" Father Raymond tried to jerk his hand away.

Malini gripped harder, the rancor of her burning flesh filling the room. The burn traveled up her arm.

"Dear Lord, you're on fire!" he yelled.

"I'm fine," Malini said through gritted teeth. "Grace, get Jacob."

She heard Grace retreat from where she'd been waiting outside the door.

"Who is that?" Father Raymond asked, but his words floated away unanswered.

When it was clear to her that her healing was successful, she let go of his hand. His eyes locked onto hers and then trailed to the burn that had spread from her hand to her cheek. At that moment, Jacob ripped the door off its hinges and doused her with water. *Very subtle, Jacob.*

"Who are you?" Jacob asked.

"Father Raymond."

"It's your lucky day, Father Raymond. Whatever it was you had is officially cured. My girlfriend doesn't heal everyone she meets."

"Liver cancer," Malini said. "And yes, you're cured."

Father Raymond rubbed a spot over his heart, his face glowing with the hope that his miracle was real. He swallowed. "Who are you people? Why are you here?"

"We need you, Father Raymond, and we need this place. Will you help us? We can pay you, enough that when this is all over, you can restore your church to what it once was."

The priest looked up at the ceiling and crossed himself. "What do you need from me?"

"We need a place to make camp. A place the Watchers won't expect us to be."

"You need sanctuary."

"Yes."

"How many of you are there?"

"Twelve."

He shook his head. "This isn't a hotel, but if you're looking for a place to make camp, I may have something."

Malini gathered the others. Father Raymond led them through the rectory, down a flight of stairs to a tunnel that led to a massive basement room. "We used to use this for wedding receptions and potluck dinners. There's a kitchen, and if you can dig them out, there are beds in the rectory you can use. Bathroom's over there."

Turning in a circle, Malini pictured the place as a campsite. It wasn't Eden. It wasn't even comfortable. But it would have to do.

The others didn't seem happy about the idea. Samantha leaned on Ghost while Bonnie was openly teary-eyed. Dane and Ethan hovered near the entrance, shoulders slumped. Cheveyo stood in the middle of the room, staring at a blank wall. Abigail rubbed reassuring circles over her swollen belly while Gideon whispered encouraging words in her ear. Ever the practical ones, Grace and Lillian headed straight for the kitchen to take inventory.

Jacob cleared his throat. "I feel…" He shivered. "There's something upstairs." He started for a door at the back of the large room.

"You don't want to go up there, son," Father Raymond said. "It's not safe. Rubble everywhere."

The words fell futilely around Jacob. Malini followed her boyfriend up the stairs into a mess of cracked marble, toppled pews, and broken glass. Statues of Mary, Joseph, and a selection of saints had fallen from their stands and shattered on the floor. Depictions of the Stations of the Cross hung at odd angles from the walls. The marble altar was cracked down the middle. Jacob wove through the mess to the front of the building, the part that must have been the foyer. Malini heard Father Raymond pick his way through the mess behind her.

"There," Jacob said, pointing at a large, square marble fixture the size of a hot tub.

"What is that?" Malini asked.

"Baptismal font," Father Raymond said. "We occasionally performed full immersion on adults. It's filled with holy water."

Jacob clapped his hands together and turned smiling eyes on Malini as he approached the edge and sunk a hand. The water rippled like a long lost friend.

Father Raymond's eyes widened.

"This is the place," Malini said, more certain than ever. "This is our sanctuary."

Chapter 26
Lament

Malini grunted as she carried her end of the twin-sized mattress she and Jacob had recovered from a half-destroyed room in the rectory. Her biceps burned with the weight and angle of the load. If they could get the bulky object past the staircase, things would get easier.

"Why can't we just sleep in the rectory?" Samantha whined from behind her.

"Because the walls could cave in at any moment," Ghost said softly from the other end of the mattress they were carrying. "The building is half burned. It's not structurally safe."

"Father Raymond is staying there."

"Father Raymond is one man in one small room that survived the damage," Ghost said.

Malini was glad Ghost answered her. She was sure her response wouldn't have been half as patient. One by one, the Soulkeepers had moved the beds, chairs, and other homey accouterments they could dig out from the rectory into the multipurpose room under the church. Slowly, the large open space had taken on new life. Lined up as they were, the beds reminded her of antique pictures she'd seen of orphanages or hospitals. No privacy. No amenities. But better than sleeping on the floor.

"One, two, three," Jacob counted, then let the mattress fall on the box spring. As soon as it was in position, Malini flopped on top of it, so tired she barely cared about the poof of dust that rose up from the fabric. Jacob tossed a set of the linens they'd found on top of her. She didn't move.

No one said anything about separating the boys from the girls. Then again, it was a moot point. Exhaustion ensured no one would be doing anything but sleeping.

"I'm going to go make use of the shower," Samantha said, grabbing her bag. Malini cracked an eye, wondering how she had the energy.

"Hey, look what we found!" Dane said. He backed into the room holding one end of a huge flat-screen television. Ethan grinned from the other end.

"So much for believing priests took a vow of poverty," Ethan said. "We found this thing in the living room."

"Excuse me," Father Raymond said from behind them. "It wasn't like we each had one. And it was donated to us."

Dane shrugged and began setting it up. "Let's hope the thing still works."

"And that the cable's not cut," Ethan said.

Abigail, Grace, and Lillian peeked out of the kitchen and took a seat on the side of one of the beds next to Gideon and Cheveyo as the sound of static filled the room. Ethan punched some buttons and plugged something in, and the screen blinked to life.

"Lucifer!" Cheveyo yelled. "What the hell is he doing on television?"

"Shhh." Abigail pressed a finger to her lips.

Exhausted, Malini forced her body into a sitting position and her eyes open. Dressed in a tailored navy suit and standing on a street corner, Lucifer addressed the camera. "Is your home overrun by demons?" He pointed to a suburban home in ruins. The yard was on fire and a Watcher bolted past the picture window. "Is the apocalypse getting in the way of your daily routine?" A mother backed out of her driveway only to have her car swarmed by hellhounds. "You don't have to live this way! I'm Milton Blake, CEO of Harrington Enterprises. Thanks to the best research and development team in the world, we've patented a state-of-the-art security system to keep you safe. Using cutting-edge spiritual and scientific principles, we've developed a foolproof system to repel and eliminate otherworldly beings from you and your property."

Lucifer waved a hand toward a home that seemed impervious to the assault. An octagonal sign in the front yard read PROTECTED BY HARRINGTON and a father, mother, and child stood smiling on the front porch. "See how the demons avoid this home? Our system repels demons from your lawn, house, and even from yourself." The camera zoomed in to the black amulet around each family member's neck. "What are you waiting for? Let the apocalypse happen to somebody else. Sign up today and join the growing number of survivors." A URL blinked on the screen.

Ghost jabbed at his phone. "The URL leads to a website for the Harrington Demon Eradication System. In order to buy one you have to sign a contract swearing allegiance to Milton Blake, any of his identities, and related associates."

"Does it really say that?" Grace said. "The allegiance and identities part."

Ghost held up his phone.

"Why are you surprised, Grace? Lucifer makes a virus in order to cure it, takes control of the education system to ensure nobody learns anything, and now brings about the apocalypse in order to pretend to protect people from it." Malini bounded out of bed and paced in front of the television, which was now playing a Hooters commercial. "This is Lucifer at his best, or worst depending on your perspective. The Lord of Illusions never stops misrepresenting himself. He will cheat and lie and mislead until we are all his damned slaves!" Her voice echoed in the large room.

All eyes rested on her, widening at her tone.

It was Father Raymond who piped up first from his place near the door. "I thought you people killed the demons? What's the plan? What are you going to do about this?"

Malini was all charged up to tell him she had no flipping idea what they were going to do when she was distracted by a series of urgent, demanding tones issuing from the television. The words SPECIAL REPORT scrolled across the screen.

"The White House pressroom," Bonnie said. "Looks like the President is going to make an announcement."

The President approached the lectern. "Good evening. Today, our great country came under attack by true, unadulterated evil. Men and women, of all walks of life, confronted massive winged creatures intent on consuming human flesh. Some people say these monsters are demons from Hell. Others claim to see only other human beings. Our government experts are not certain where the creatures came from, what they want, or why they've come now. One thing we can all agree on is this: they are due justice. This is terrorism. Human or not, these beasts are attacking our homes and our very way of life. That is why, in response, I am forming a new group of experts to determine our best course of action against the invasion.

"The Council for the Eradication of the Unholy will unite the brightest political, scientific, and corporate minds to find a way to end this invasion. The devastation our country is experiencing at the hands of these demon terrorists is unforgivable and requires immediate action."

"Immediate? It's been going on for over a day?" Jacob griped. "I guess it's good they're doing something."

"The new council will be headed by Senator Bakewell," the President said.

"Bakewell?" Malini said, alarmed. Bakewell was the one politician they knew for sure was under long-term Watcher influence.

"Harrington Enterprises, the leading supplier of demon-eradicating products, will work closely with government experts and comprise an important part of the team," the President said. "CEO Milton Blake has agreed to donate unlimited company resources to the problem and will be working closely with Mr. Bakewell."

"Ugh!" Samantha groaned. "He's everywhere."

"Turn it off. I can't listen to this. Has he already won? How can we possibly recover from this?" Bonnie said. The panic in her voice rattled through the room.

Malini shook her head and spread her hands. "It's not over. There are three more curses and four more gifts to go. He hasn't won yet."

"But what can we do? He's got the ear of the President. People think he's going to *save* them." Gideon pointed a hand toward the screen. Abigail shook her head and whispered something in his ear.

Malini glared at the image of the President. The room seemed to tilt and sway as she tried to process the implications. The President finished his speech and began taking questions from reporters, but Malini couldn't hear anything. Her ears were ringing.

Gideon had asked what they should do. Malini had no idea. She'd just been to the In Between. She should have seen this coming, but she hadn't. Everything was out of control.

Eventually, Lillian crossed the room and turned off the television. She gave Malini a long, hard look before addressing the others. "I'll tell you what we're going to do. We are going to get some sleep. Tomorrow, Malini, Grace, Abigail, Gideon, and I will convene as we would in Eden. We'll discuss what we've learned and form a plan."

Malini nodded and mouthed *thank you* to Lillian. The older woman gave her an almost imperceptible nod. Malini plopped back down on the bed Jacob had thoughtfully made up while she was panicking.

Father Raymond said goodnight. He'd decided to stay in his room in the rectory despite the obvious risks. Lillian turned off the lights. After a period of squeaking hinges, rustling covers, and whispered "good nights," the room quieted. Malini wasn't sure how much time passed before a deep snore came from Dane's direction.

"You look tired," Jacob whispered from the pillow next to her. He was still wearing his muddy sneakers but Malini didn't have the energy to tell him to kick them off.

She glanced at her watch. "It's four in the morning, and we haven't slept yet. Of course I'm tired."

He rubbed a knuckle under his nose. "I don't mean that kind of tired. You look tired to your bones, to your soul."

She stared up at the ceiling, her thoughts swirling with the gold Celtic design. She'd wanted to bury this, but like always, she couldn't keep her real feelings from Jacob. Nor could she deny that those feelings compromised her ability to lead. She turned on her side.

"We're not going to graduate," she said.

"No." Jacob tucked his hands between his head and the pillow. "But nobody else will either. Are they even holding classes anymore?"

"I don't know."

"Anyone who can see the Watchers will pull their kids out of class faster than you can say 'homeschool.' Those who can't might attend classes, but if the Watchers are teaching them, they won't be learning anything. They'll have to repeat the year when God wins the challenge." Jacob shrugged his shoulder.

"*If* God wins," Malini murmured.

"Malini Gupta, as Healer you of all people cannot lose faith."

"Optimism is my job, eh?" She frowned, sighing deeply through her nose.

Jacob stared at her for a few minutes, eyebrows pinched over his nose. He examined her face as if he was seeing her for the first time. "I know you're disappointed, Malini. You've done everything right academically and sleeping in the basement of a church is not what you planned for yourself. You climbed on a bus to California and ended up in New York. But you know what? New York needs you more."

She smiled. "I thought I was in Chicago?"

He swallowed and licked his lips. "I'm speaking figuratively. Life didn't turn out the way you planned. You've told me like a million times that you want to be a journalist. A citizen of the world you called it. You wanted to help people by providing honest reporting around the globe."

Malini nodded.

"Your life is here, Mal. You don't need a degree to help people. You're already here, in your future, helping people. You are going to heal the world."

"But—"

"No buts. Maybe you need a good cry. Maybe you need to grieve the future you lost. That's okay. I'll support you. I'll even wipe your tears. But what good is a degree in a world ruled and ravaged by Watchers. Whatever you expected for your life, this is the most important thing you will ever do. Look around this room. Every life here is in your hands. You are seventeen years old and the leader of the best chance this world has of surviving the apocalypse."

Malini pressed a finger over his lips. "Enough. I get it. I'll straighten up and focus."

"Not because you have to, Mal, because you believe it."

She pursed her lips.

"Seriously. Your job is to tell the future by what has happened in the past. Can't you see that God always wins? Good always triumphs over evil."

"You don't know that for sure."

"Yes, I do. Because Lucifer's promises aren't real. Everything on that commercial tonight was a lie. The amulets don't work and whatever security system Harrington is selling is a complete scam. They won't be able to keep up that illusion forever. Eventually truth bleeds out into the open."

Malini grabbed his head and kissed him, hard, only releasing him when his body softened on the bed next to her.

"What was that for?" Jacob asked, grinning.

"For shutting you up."

Jacob scowled.

"Thank you, Jake, for reminding me why I'm here." She placed a palm on his cheek.

He covered her hand with his. "Good night, Malini."

"Good night, Jacob."

She closed her eyes and drifted off to racing images of Watchers, hellhounds, exploding churches, and finally Master Lee. Even in her dreams, she cried.

Chapter 27
The Third Gift

Gabriel checked out his reflection in the giant bean sculpture, turning his face this way and that, watching the old man's head in the shiny metal narrow and stretch with his movement. Millennium Park was empty aside from the rare jogger with a Harrington medallion keen on overcoming the early morning chill. Next to him, crowded on the small bench in the dark, an aged and corpulent black woman tossed birdseed to a group of wiry pigeons—God.

"It's freezing out here, Lord," Gabriel complained. "Couldn't we talk inside somewhere?"

"The only places still open are those who've sworn allegiance to Lucifer." God gave a tired sigh. "Everyone else has boarded up their windows and is in hiding from the Watchers."

Gabriel hugged himself and rubbed his shoulders. "No one is brave enough to fight? Where are the Soulkeepers?"

"They're here, in the city. They just need some time to get up to speed." Another handful of seed scattered across the pavement.

"Time they don't have," Gabriel said.

God grunted, bobbing her frosted-gray curls.

"May I suggest, Lord, that you provide courage as the third gift? People need to stand up and be brave, or the evil will walk all over them." Gabriel leaned back on the bench, looking smug.

"Can't blame people for being afraid. Human brains are hardwired to fear the Watchers."

"Soulless fallen angels who eat human flesh—what's not to fear?" Gabriel rubbed his hands together briskly.

The Lord crumpled up the empty seed bag and tossed it east. The brown paper soared through the air, cut through the oncoming wind, and landed in a garbage can across the park. "They fear the Watchers because some part of them knows the fallen angels represent a future without God. They see the darkness within the beasts, and think how easy it would be to become like them, but at the same time fear the separation from me. Why do you think more people haven't signed up for Harrington's offer? They must be terrified. But some part of every human heart is stamped with my name. Man will not come easily to Lucifer's table."

"Then courage. Courage to fight," Gabriel repeated.

"Courage is useless in the absence of anything to be courageous about. What we need to do is give them hope. We need to show them that there is a reason to fight. If evil is the only choice, the best a person can do is not to choose. But if we give them hope, hope that there is something on the other side of the struggle, then they will see the value of the fight."

Gabriel smiled. "Hope is a powerful gift. One that forever changes the one who lets it into their heart."

"You are correct, dear angel."

A jogger crossed between them and the giant metal bean sculpture. A Harrington talisman bounced on her chest to the same rhythm as her brown ponytail.

"Already so pervasive. How did he reach so many so fast?"

"Social media." God stood. "Walk with me."

Gabriel fell into step beside her. "What vessel will bring hope into the world? Can I deliver it?"

"No need. I've already arranged for its arrival."

Gabriel frowned. "You mean, it is already here, on Earth?"

"Yes. It has been for some time."

Looking right then left, Gabriel noticed a group of Watchers walking up the middle of the street. "What are we waiting for?" he asked. "Why not unleash it now?"

"The vessel isn't quite ready. There is a time for everything and a season for every purpose under the heavens."

"A time to be born and a time to die?" Gabriel said, smiling.

"You know this one?"

"I've heard it somewhere before."

The two walked toward the lake, noting the Watchers they'd seen earlier duck inside as a silvery glow began over the water, the first hints of sunrise. "They hate sunlight. Always have."

"Lord, if the vessel is already here, why did you want to meet with me? What can I do to help if you do not need a messenger?"

"This time, Gabriel, it is not what I need you to do, but what I need you not to do."

"I don't understand."

"What will happen today, I allow to happen. It *must* happen or hope will not come on time."

"And this is something I will want to stop but must not?"

"Correct."

"So, do nothing? That doesn't sound difficult."

God stopped and faced him. "It will be." A chill wind rushed Gabriel's neck. "Now, one more thing before we go home." The Lord leaned in and whispered in Gabriel's ear. He had a job to do after all, and this day *would* be difficult, perhaps the most difficult of all of his days.

* * * * *

Abigail tried to roll over without waking Gideon, but it was almost impossible with a stomach the size of Texas. She wasn't sleeping well anymore. The baby kicked her in the ribs every time she lay down, and no position was comfortable for sleeping. On her back, there was too much weight on her spine. It was physically impossible to sleep on her stomach. And there was only so long she could rest on her side before her hip started to hurt.

As quietly as possible, she lifted herself from the mattress and crept toward the kitchen for a glass of water and maybe a snack, if there was anything left to eat from the RV. The kitchen was the industrial sort with stainless steel counters and a massive refrigerator, sadly empty. All the way in the back, crisscrossed steel bars jailed a walk-in pantry. Abigail looked at the massive lock on the door and wondered why the high security was needed in a church.

"High theft area, and the church is often open to the public," Gideon said. "I asked Father Raymond last night."

Abigail turned on her heel to face her beloved. "I didn't mean to wake you."

He shrugged. "It's a twin bed. Besides, I think I was ready to be up. Soon enough we'll be taking turns with early-morning feedings." A smile crept across his stubbled face. "Might as well get used to it."

"More of a reason for you to have your sleep now," she said. She turned the lock and rummaged through the pantry. Plates, napkins, plastic silverware, cups. Nothing edible. *Damn.*

Gideon cleared his throat and played with a stray twist tie he found on one of the shelves. "Abigail, how long do you think we have before the baby comes?"

She stopped and placed her hands on her belly. "I've never been to a doctor. Never had an ultrasound. Malini says the baby is healthy, but we have no idea the effect Lucifer's prison had on her development."

"You must have a feeling. You said you knew you were pregnant before you left Eden."

"Yes."

"How pregnant?"

"My clothes were tight."

"So it could be…"

"It could be soon. Very soon. We might have a month. Six weeks, maybe?"

Gideon's face paled.

"It will all work out, Gideon. We will make do."

He opened his mouth to say something, then closed it again and blew out a giant breath. Moving in closer, he placed his hands on the sides of her belly. The baby kicked him in his right palm. "Oh!"

"She knows your voice already."

"She? You keep calling the baby a girl. Do you know something I don't?"

Abigail hesitated. "Just a gut feeling." She sputtered a laugh at the unintended pun, and Gideon joined in. He ended by kissing her on the forehead. Wanting more, she tilted her face to partake in a proper kiss. He obliged, then held her in his arms until she was sure everything was going to be okay.

"I'm starving," she said finally. "Let's go check if there's food left in the RV." Abigail threaded her fingers with his and led him from the kitchen. She climbed the stairs and passed through the tunnel to the rectory. The sun hadn't broke the horizon yet but the sky glowed a soft winter's gray behind the dormant trees in the courtyard. Gideon stopped her at the door, looking both ways to make sure the courtyard was safe before taking Abigail's hand and leading her toward the RV.

He paused halfway across. "Did you see that?"

Abigail shook her head, looking in the direction he was facing.

"I thought I saw someone."

"Is that Gabriel?" Abigail asked, squinting, but her human vision was too dull to make out the figure standing in the distance. Still, she knew an angel when she saw one. She could practically feel the warm glow of his presence all the way across the yard. She took a step toward him. "Do you think he has a message for us?"

Gideon scowled. "Look where he is, how he's standing. When I was an angel, that's not how I would deliver a message. It's how I would deliver a—"

"Warning," Abigail finished. She launched her leaden body back toward the door pulling Gideon behind her, but it was too late. The Watcher swooped down from the sky, talons ripping through her right side and knocking her from

Gideon's grip. She landed on her hip on the frozen ground, her body rotating on instinct to protect her young. As soon as she could catch her breath, she screamed as loud and as long as she could manage.

Gideon found a metal rod in the rubble and positioned himself between her and the Watcher, who seemed almost entertained by the display. Gideon thrust at the creature's heart. The thing laughed, then broke apart in a ripple of darkness, forming behind Gideon. Before he could react, the beast's wing swept him into the air.

"No!" Abigail cried. But a word couldn't stop the scene in front of her. Gideon rose ten, twenty feet, and then dropped onto the rubble near the rectory. His leg snapped, bending at an unnatural angle, before his body rolled off the broken brick, over wood beams and jagged stones. Abigail watched in horror as his head smacked a sharp piece of rubble and red blood sprayed. The Watcher licked its lips and moved in for the kill. Gideon moaned but did not get up.

Abigail scrambled to her feet, grasping the nearest object she could lift, a chunk of concrete the size of a bowling ball. "Hey!" she yelled. The Watcher turned, and she hurled her weapon with everything she had.

The chunk bounced harmlessly off the Watcher's chest. Two yellow snake eyes locked onto her. The beast sniffed the air, smelling her fear. Licking its lips, it continued toward Gideon, cloven hooves crunching on the frozen grass.

Helplessly, Abigail screamed as the beast reached Gideon, lifting his limp body. His head was bleeding and one of his legs dangled in the wrong direction. Eyes fluttering, his hand clenched as if he was trying to fight, but he was too injured.

"No! No!" she cried. The Watcher's teeth clamped down on Gideon's neck. Blood sprayed from the wound, showering the courtyard.

The world tilted. Abigail's butt hit the ground, black spots swirling in her vision. Then, a miracle. A knife flew from the door of the rectory into the Watcher's neck. The thing howled, the blessed knife steaming. Gideon's body hit the ground as the Watcher reared. Lillian and Jacob sped from the door, racing for the beast with weapons drawn.

The Watcher made a hasty retreat, barreling toward Abigail in the process of dodging Jacob's blade. The beast wasn't fast enough. Jacob's holy water sword sliced through its chest, causing the black flesh to bubble and sizzle. Still, the creature reached for her. Then the unthinkable. As the Watcher came apart piece by infected piece, it looked straight at her and hurled.

Fiery vomit heralded the fallen angel's end. The beast came apart like a popped balloon full of oil. But that last breath, that last spew of magic, hit Abigail from bottom rib to neck. She dropped as the pain moved in, gasping for breath. Her body seized. The pain didn't stop at her torso, it wrapped around her abdomen and squeezed. Warm and wet flowed down her leg.

"Oh my God, Jacob, help. We've got to get her to Malini." Lillian's arm was under her shoulder, lifting.

"Gid…" Abigail cried, but her mouth filled with blood.

"Don't speak. Dane and Ethan are helping Gideon. We need to get you to Malini."

Whisked through the rectory door, she closed her eyes against the pain. The next time she opened them, Malini was hovering over her, forehead wrinkled and jaw tight.

"We have to deliver the baby, Abigail. You have to push."

Grace was there too, holding one of her hands, and Lillian the other. Both women wore matching grimaces. They sat her up. She was on the island in the kitchen, covered in a sheet and nestled in pillows. Malini was holding her knees apart, one of her hands noticeably burnt. She'd been trying to heal her, but Abigail didn't understand. She wasn't healed. In fact, her entire body screamed in pain.

"Now push!" Grace cried.

Abigail did, with everything she had. Her eyes rolled back in her head.

"Her blood pressure is dropping," Lillian said frantically. "Can't you do something?"

"I tried!" Malini said. "All of my healing energy is taken by the baby. It's as if her body is feeding it to her abdomen. I can't heal her until we deliver this baby."

Digging deep, Abigail tried to stay conscious. Human women had babies every day. She needed to do this. Another contraction gripped her, a massive snake constricting her middle.

"Push!" Grace said.

Abigail obeyed.

"I see hair," Malini said excitedly.

Another contraction came and then another and another. They piled on top of each other until Abigail screamed. The pain was so great, she was only vaguely aware of the women around her shouting with excitement. Over the sheet, her daughter appeared. She'd been right! A girl.

There was a bustle of activity. Something was wrong. The baby was the wrong color. Lillian rushed to Malini's side.

"Hope!" Abigail rasped.

"Hope?" Grace asked.

"Her name is Hope," Abigail said more clearly.

Grace patted her shoulder. "A perfect name. Try to relax, Abigail. She's in good hands. You did a good job." Grace lowered her to the pillows. "Just rest for a minute. Hope will be in your arms before you know it." The woman brushed her hair back from her face.

The most beautiful sound cut through the kitchen, a baby's cry. Malini and Lillian cheered. Grace squealed with joy.

Abigail's eyes locked on her baby girl, her mouth bending into a painful smile. Her entire body began to shake. Grace grabbed her shoulders. Lillian shouted something and Malini's hand reached for her, but the few feet between her and the girl might as well have been an ocean. Pain rocked her chest, and then...

Darkness. Silence.

A blink later, she was standing next to the table, staring at a door. It was a beautiful door, white with gray scrollwork. A familiar face waited beside it.

"Henry?"

"It's time, Abigail."

"Time?" Abigail looked over her shoulder. The scene was frozen. Lillian pressed two hands over Abigail's heart. Grace was attempting to give her body air, pinching her nose and covering her mouth with her own. Malini held Hope with one arm while she tried her best to heal with the other. But you couldn't heal the dead.

"I'm dead?" Abigail whispered.

"Yes."

"But Hope? Gideon?"

"Hope has a purpose here, and Gideon is waiting for you."

"Waiting?"

Henry held out his hand. Abigail placed her fingers in his and stepped forward. He opened the door for her. Light and warmth washed through the opening, the sound of children's laughter drawing her forward into the beyond. Cherry blossoms floated in the air, welcoming her in like a ticker tape parade. And there he was.

"Gideon?"

He held open his arms and smiled. She ran into them, joy flooding her as he swept her into his embrace. For a moment, she could still see the kitchen through the crack in the door. She threaded her fingers with his. "We have a daughter, Gideon."

"I know. You named her Hope," he said.

The door closed, and then there was nothing but joy, warmth, and light. And Gideon. Forever.

Chapter 28
The Watcher

Earlier that day…

Cord was late for work. Again. Lucifer would tie his entrails in a bow if he wasn't careful. Harrington Enterprises needed leadership, and Auriel would use his lateness as an excuse to cover up her own laziness if she had the opportunity. The days of lounging around Nod, feeding on captured humans, were over. And, while he believed that if Lucifer won this challenge things would be infinitely better for him, he hated the present, hated the expectations and responsibilities.

The new Harrington Demon Eradication Systems required constant monitoring. Oh, the systems themselves were never intended to work. It was the Watchers who needed monitoring. Cord's job was to keep his brethren from attacking anyone with an HDES sign or talisman. But Watchers weren't keen on denying themselves an easy meal. Cord's work was difficult and constant. Living this way, he might as well have remained an angel.

He should go now. He should finish his morning walk to the Harrington building and get started. The glow on the horizon meant his illusion would break soon. A few blocks more and he'd be safely inside his dark office.

The problem was a deep and unused instinct kept him riveted to a particularly mundane square of sidewalk in front of a boarded-up church. A strange scent had drawn him here, the long-forgotten essence of sunrise, citrus, and ocean, the indescribable musk of Heaven. There was an angel nearby. He'd bet his life on it. While staying here a moment longer might cost him, he couldn't pass up a battle with an angel. So, he stayed, using his senses to narrow in on the smell.

A delicious scream pierced the predawn. Cord took to the air, landing in the upper branches of a tree with the best view of the church courtyard. He'd destroyed this place days ago. Rubble peppered the yard where a Watcher hunted a pregnant woman and her mate. He couldn't make out who the Watcher was, nor did he care. No HDES sign here. The Watcher could eat whom he pleased. The quarry, however, ignited his interest. Cord licked his lips. A pre-work snack might be nice. He leaned out from the tree, prepared to swoop down to join the feeding.

The Watcher swept the man into the air. His body landed with a tenderizing *thunk* on the rubble. The woman screamed again, the air perfumed with her fear, then moved from her position to toss a chunk of concrete at her attacker's chest. When she advanced, Cord got a good look at her face.

Abigail! Oh, the praise he'd receive if he brought her back alive. Now that he looked more closely, the man was Gideon. If the two of them were here, and she was with young, it was almost certain there were other Soulkeepers nearby. A perfect opportunity to slaughter them all!

Then again, the scene seemed too convenient. Perhaps the entire fight was a trap. The Soulkeepers had so many tricks up their sleeves. He must not rush in. He prized himself too much to risk injury.

Cord made himself comfortable in the branches, waiting to see how things played out below. He would attack when it would cause the most damage with the least consequences.

Stealthily, he watched, and he was rewarded when two Soulkeepers came to Abigail's aid. She was still alive. Lucifer would want her that way if Cord could manage it. Gideon, on the other hand, was dead. The redheaded twin Soulkeepers emerged to retrieve his body. Cord growled. That one—the one with the mole on the right instead of the left—she was the Soulkeeper who had impersonated him. He gritted his teeth. If nothing else, he would enjoy killing her. She'd cost him dearly.

He waited until all of the Soulkeepers were inside, and then flew to the ground next to the bubbling black remains of the Watcher who'd failed in his attempt at a meal. Cord followed through the door he'd seen the Soulkeepers take the bodies. The room was pleasantly dark, and he slipped into shadow, folding from one corner to another until he found their hiding place.

"Lillian, hold her up," Malini commanded.

What luck! Abigail was delivering. Cord blended into a dark corner to watch. He'd wait until the spawn was born, then slaughter the Soulkeepers one by one. He had a grand daydream of capturing Abigail, and then forcing her to watch while he ate her baby for breakfast. Lucifer would be pleased. The challenge would be as good as won.

He waited in the shadows through the moaning and the pushing. So much blood. His mouth salivated. *Patience*, he said to himself. *Soon enough.*

The young arrived, and the woman, Lillian, raced to Malini's side. He couldn't see what the two were doing to the infant from the safety of his shadow. The Healer and the Horseman worked over the babe, blocking his view with their bodies while the Helper, Grace, stayed back to tend to Abigail. The former Watcher had taken on the stink of death. Cord wondered if there would be anything left to return to Lucifer.

A sharp cry filled the space. Death stood at Abigail's bedside. *Crap.* Lucifer would not be happy to learn she'd passed on. There was nothing he could do. The death was done.

He watched her pass through her door into the beyond. When he looked back, the baby was wrapped in a blanket like a burrito. He licked his lips, thinking of the sweet blood and tender flesh. Oh, how he was going to enjoy this, with or without the audience of her mother.

The three women blubbered over Abigail's body. He'd kill them all now if not for the Healer. She posed a problem and required caution. No, he'd wait for the perfect opportunity. He'd pick them off when they least expected.

The Healer walked into the main room and announced Abigail and Gideon's death to the other Soulkeepers. Pitiful sobs filled the space. Cord rolled his eyes.

Malini handed the baby to the redheaded girl named Bonnie. He slipped through the shadows to get a closer look, baring his fangs.

"Please take her, Bonnie. I just ... can't." Malini wiped under her eyes. "I need to find Father Raymond. We'll have to find a place to bury the bodies."

More blubbering. *Sick.*

"Dane?"

"Ye-ah." The boy's voice cracked.

"Can you and Ethan go with Grace and Jacob to try to find some formula for Hope?"

He nodded, and the three climbed the stairs.

"Ghost, Cheveyo, Samantha, please go to the RV and bring back everything that's not nailed down. When you are done, we need to hide that thing. We can't have a rerun of today."

Ghost blinked out of sight, and Samantha and Cheveyo followed up the stairs.

"Lillian is coming with me. You'll be okay here by yourself?" Malini asked.

The one named Bonnie nodded her head, cradling the babe against her chest. The Healer left with the Horseman named Lillian.

Cord couldn't have imagined a more advantageous scenario. He waited a moment to ensure the girl was truly alone. Then, he crept closer. The girl cooed to the baby, totally enthralled by the tiny human on her shoulder, while Cord gathered himself from shadow only inches behind her. How should he do it? Decapitation? Or maybe he should reach through her ribcage and tear out her heart?

No, he would taste her. He would taste each of them like a human box of chocolates. Cord opened his mouth to bite.

"Let's see you," Bonnie said, peeling back the blanket around the baby's head.

As Cord lowered his fangs, Bonnie turned. His eyes locked with hers, then on the red stone around her neck, and then on the baby's round, pink face pressed next to the gem. He couldn't help it. Drawn into their gravitational pull, his entire body stiffened. He gagged. His fangs retracted, and he snapped his lips closed. Paralyzing pain gripped him like a vice. Cord's limbs fell limp to his sides. His mind blanked.

Collapsing to his knees, his skin began to twitch with tiny shocks of electricity. The physical discomfort paled in comparison to the ancient feeling that crept into his body—

warmth, and *empathy*. No longer did he want to eat the baby. He wanted to hold her. He wanted to *protect* her. A blooming heat started behind his breastbone and radiated out, through his arms and legs, all the way to the tips of his fingers and toes.

Glancing down at his hands, his skin changed, pinked and then took on a slight glow. Before he could process what was happening, a heavy chain lassoed his neck and constricted. He saw a flash of red hair, and then the end of the chain smacked into his temple.

Chapter 29
Bonnie's Prisoner

The baby was crying. Bonnie instinctively bounced Hope on her shoulder while she stared at her captive. At the end of the chain in her free hand was the Watcher called Cord. Her understanding ended there. Everything about the situation was weird. Wrong. Unexpected.

First, there was the way he remained on his knees in front of her. He didn't struggle. He didn't pull against the chain. Eyes wide, he gawked at her, arms limp, hands palm up on his thighs. She was prepared for more. Cord's hand could shoot out at any moment and grab her ankle. He could snap poisonous fangs at the baby. Watchers could normally break apart into black mist, although the blessed chain should have prevented that particular scenario.

Which reminded Bonnie of an even stranger revelation. The chain around his neck, flush against his skin, should have burned. This chain was from Eden, soaked in holy water. She'd never used it before, and she didn't think the effect wore off with use anyway. The blessed steel should have steamed against his Watcher flesh, but Cord seemed ambivalent to the chain, almost resolved to his capture.

"What are you?" Bonnie murmured.

Cord looked down at his open hands as if he didn't know how to answer that question. If his actions and his immunity to holy water weren't enough to set off her equilibrium, the smell did the trick. Citrus and fresh air, not the usual sulfur and saccharine stench of the fallen. Plus, his skin carried a faint glow.

"I was here to kill you," Cord mumbled.

Bonnie yanked the chain, causing him to gag. "You did not succeed."

"I no longer wish you dead. Please forgive me." He lowered his head toward her feet.

Attached to his back, two fluffy white wings stretched to the floor. *Damn, those look real.*

The baby stopped crying. Hope had fallen asleep on her shoulder and now made cute sighing sounds next to her ear.

"Are you the Watcher named Cord?" Bonnie asked. Watchers borrowed images from others. They could look any way they wanted. This could all be a careful illusion.

"I am."

"And you came here to kill us?"

"I did."

She kicked him in the shoulder, hard. He grunted but did not attack.

"What's changed?"

Bonnie heard a noise flow up from the carpeted floor. Weeping. The Watcher was weeping.

"What changed?" she yelled.

He moaned and shifted, rising slowly on his knees to meet her eyes. She was surprised at the depth of feeling in them. "I think *I* did. I looked at you, at the baby, and at the stone around your neck, and *I* ... changed."

Bonnie frowned. "I don't believe you." But a part of her did. She'd imitated this Watcher's appearance twice. She'd paid attention to every detail of his former illusion. His eyes had been navy blue, almost purple, and held an element of menace that made her so uncomfortable she could barely look in the mirror when she was acting as him. Now his eyes were a normal shade of blue. If anything, they appeared lit from within. When she looked at him, she didn't feel menace or fear or dread. She felt pity.

"What should I do with you?" she asked herself.

"Kill me," he said immediately. Tears had formed in his eyes. "I've done terrible things. Horrific things. I could change again and hurt you or the baby. You must kill me now while you have the chance."

Bonnie gripped the chain tighter. The duffle bag she'd retrieved the weapon from was only steps away and held a variety of implements she could use to kill the Watcher. She could decapitate him with one slice of a sword, or gouge out his heart with a dagger. She wished Malini would come back and help her decide what to do. But they were alone here. She needed to handle this.

Kill him or not, that was the question. She'd already waited longer than she should. She needed to act before he changed his mind. Why not kill him? What good did it do to keep him alive? Then again, she had a baby on her shoulder. Setting Hope down wasn't an option. Too risky. Killing him with one hand seemed optimistic. No, she needed to save him for Malini. She'd know what to do.

"Follow me."

Cord rose and followed behind Bonnie like a dog. Flabbergasted by his docility, she led him with one hand through the kitchen, cradling Hope on her shoulder with the other. Abigail's body was still on the table, covered with a sheet, an ominous bloodstain soaked through the lower half. Cord gasped and wept at the sight of her.

Holding back her own reaction, Bonnie turned the lock to the pantry. "Inside," she ordered.

Without hesitation, he did as he was told. She dropped the chain, slamming and locking the crisscrossed steel bars of the pantry door as quickly as she could. Cord did not struggle. He did not fight. Eyes locked on hers, he backed away, deep within the pantry. The chain around his neck rattled against the tile as he lowered himself to the floor. Those white, fluffy wings stretched out and wrapped around his body, encasing him in a cocoon of feathers.

Bonnie backed away, bumping the stainless steel island in the process. She turned then to look at the human-shaped mound that was Abigail. On impulse, she peeled back the sheet to see her face, but the body barely looked human. Her skin held the gray hue of death.

"Goodbye, Abigail. I hope you and Gideon are happy in Heaven." Tears slipped from her eyes. On her shoulder, Hope stirred, erupting into a high-pitched wail as if she sensed her mother's lifeless body.

Bonnie seethed at the Watcher in the pantry. "You did this! You killed her."

Cord flinched under the force of her words.

She checked again that the pantry door was locked, and then left the kitchen, hoping she'd done the right thing.

* * * * *

"What is this place?" Malini asked. She followed Father Raymond into a small garden with weatherworn stone markers surrounded by a decorative iron fence. Holly bushes and small pine trees fought back the winter chill while other smaller plants and flowers hibernated under crispy brown remains.

"A retired cemetery," Father Raymond said. "It hasn't been used in over a hundred years. This church used to be an orphanage. The monks and nuns who lived on this property cared for the children. The few who died while it was open, and had no other family plot, were buried here."

Tucked beside the rectory, the south-facing exposure meant the graveyard would get maximum light. Malini approved. Abigail and Gideon deserved to rest in the light.

"Is there room for two full graves and a third marker?"

"Third?"

"We lost a friend to the Watchers before coming here."

"Oh, my condolences. So much loss. So much destruction. It is difficult to bear."

Malini's eyes filled with tears.

"I think there's enough space here." He pointed to a grassy patch against the far border. "Especially considering we don't need room for traditional coffins."

Tears flowed unhindered now.

Father Raymond took her gloved hand and led her to a bench near the center of the cemetery. She sat down and sobbed properly, her shoulders bobbing with the effort.

"Would it be okay if I told you a story? Maybe it will take your mind off the grief."

She nodded between sobs.

"To become a priest, I had to go to seminary school. I went when I was twenty-two, just after completing a degree in theology from Notre Dame. Theology. Seminary. You would think that I of anyone would be firm in my faith, right?"

Malini nodded.

"I thought so. I thought my faith was unshakable. Then, something happened. I was home for Thanksgiving, sharing the holiday with my family and friends. My brother and I shared a bottle of wine; everyone in our family loved wine. I was staying at my parents' house, but my brother had his own place by then. He left for home after the festivities. He never made it."

"What happened?"

"Car accident. He drove into a tree. Blood alcohol level was over the legal limit."

Malini placed a hand on his. "I'm so sorry."

"Oh, I am too. I'm sorry I let him leave the house knowing he'd been drinking. I'm sorry for a lot of things." Father Raymond looked at his toes. "See, after that, I hated God for a while, and I couldn't bring myself to pray. I said the words when I was supposed to, but my heart wasn't in it. What kind of God allows that to happen? It didn't make any sense to me. You might say I stopped believing."

"Did your faith ever return?" Malini whispered.

"Eventually. But it was never the same."

Malini grimaced.

"It was never the same," he continued, "and that was a good thing. See before my brother's death, I thought religion was my personal magical toolbox that could solve everything. It's not. Those of us who do God's work know it is a thankless job. Faith doesn't always make our lives easier or protect us from our circumstances."

"No. It doesn't."

"None of us live forever, whether we believe or not."

Malini winced. How could Father Raymond know he was talking to the one person who could not die until she was replaced? "Some would say living forever would be a curse, not a blessing," she said.

"Oh, I agree."

"If you don't mind me asking, why did you become a priest if you were so angry with God?"

Father Raymond smiled all the way to his eyes. "Because, Malini, I realized that in this tragic, fleeting life, all we have is love. Religion, when it's done right, is an organized expression of unconditional love and acceptance. What power we have as a group to serve each other! I wanted to be part of that. I wanted to make a statement that the tragedy of my brother's death wasn't going to stop me from living the life I wanted to live. A life full of love and giving and compassion."

Malini swallowed the lump in her throat. "I think Abigail and Gideon would have liked your story. I'm sure they would have loved getting to know you. Our friend Master Lee, too. He would have said you were centered."

"Master Lee? What was he master of?"

"Mixed practice martial arts. We always called him Master Lee. I found out last year his real first name was Confucius."

"Confucius?" Father Raymond chuckled behind his hand. "Sorry. My old ears aren't used to hearing that name."

"No, he thought it was hilarious. Called his parents Chinese hippies. That's why he never told anyone what it was. We always called him Master Lee or just Lee. The man was an amazing warrior though."

She leaned back on the bench, staring at the patch of earth where the Soulkeepers would have to dig their friends' graves. From the gray winter sky, snow began to fall, white fluffy flakes that gathered quickly over the graveyard, covering the dirt in sparkling white.

"I hope the ground isn't too frozen."

"It won't be a problem."

Father Raymond looked at her quizzically.

"Soulkeepers, like me, have above-average strength and other talents."

"Like the one you used to heal me."

"Yes."

"So your friends will dig the graves. Would you like me to officiate the funeral?"

Malini turned to look at him head on. There was nothing extraordinary about Father Raymond's appearance. He was balding with gray patches over his ears, had a plain face, and a reedy body. But at that moment he seemed to glow. His kindness radiated from within.

"My friends and I would be honored if you would help us give Abigail and Gideon a proper burial, and Lee a proper memorial service."

"Come," he said, offering his hand. "We have work to do. Better to act before the sun goes down."

Malini couldn't agree more.

Chapter 30
Confrontation

Malini returned to Sanctuary, as she'd come to call the room under the church, to find Bonnie pacing with Hope. The baby's cries reverberated off the walls at a brain-splitting decibel. Bonnie's face was pinched and Malini reached for the baby to relieve her.

"Don't worry. Ghost and crew should be back with formula and diapers any time now."

Bonnie stepped backward so that Malini couldn't reach the baby. "I'm not worried about Hope. Something happened while you were outside."

"What? What's going on?"

"Check the pantry."

Malini charged into the kitchen, trying not to look at the sheet that covered Abigail's body. Behind the bars of the pantry, an angel huddled on the floor. She smelled him first, citrus and ocean, and saw the white feathers of his wings twitch with his breath.

"Who are you?" Malini asked. Had God sent them an angel for protection?

The wings lowered, and the angel's face came into view.

"Cord," Malini said through her teeth. A blood-red rage washed through her. She did not hesitate but readied her left hand, her healing hand, unlocked the door, and reached for him. He did not attack. He did not resist. Her hand connected with the skin of his throat. Nothing happened. As a Healer, the skin contact should have burned Watcher flesh. Cord's eyes flicked to hers. Clear blue eyes. Not purple. Not navy. His eyes did not hold the threat of evil but the promise of innocence.

"What sorcery is this? Who are you?" Malini shook him by the neck.

"I am Cord, the fallen."

"You admit you are a Watcher."

"I was."

"You *were*? As in past tense?" She laughed through her nose.

"I don't blame you for doubting me. I don't understand it myself. I came here to kill you, and now I am this." He held out his hands palms up.

Malini noticed the glint of gold. She grabbed his fingers and flipped his hand over. Cord's lion's head ring. She eyed his tailored suit with distaste. She'd seen him in this before at Harrington.

Infuriated, she yelled for Bonnie. "Bring me a dagger."

The twin responded immediately, handing her Eden's finest. She pressed the tip to Cord's neck, noting the blessed blade did not react against his skin. She fisted the chain around his neck. "Come with me." Dragging him through the kitchen, she ascended the stairs. Truth be told, he was much larger than she was, and if he had wanted to, Malini was sure he could break away. She hoped that he'd try. That would make sense. This, whatever he was doing, did not.

She led him out into the sunlight and snow. The midmorning light hit his skin. Nothing. He tilted his head to smile at the sun, fluttering his eyelashes against the snowflakes.

"It's a beautiful day," he said, tears filling his eyes.

"Oh, spare me." Malini tapped her foot. He should have changed in the sunlight. If his appearance was an illusion, the sun should have cut through it. Why wasn't this working? There was one last test. She remembered something about Gideon when he was an angel, something she'd found surprising.

"Hold out your hand," she commanded. He obeyed. With the dagger, she sliced across his palm.

"Ow," he cried, but he did not pull his hand away. Blood bubbled from the wound, not black or even red but sparkling white, almost silver. The sun glinted off the blood and the angel scent grew stronger.

Malini cursed.

"I am sorry this is troubling to you. I do not understand it myself," he murmured.

Both turned at the sound of running footsteps. Jacob, a box of diapers under one arm, held a hand to the sky, crossing the courtyard at a full out run. The snow swirled toward his palm and formed into his favorite broadsword. Before Malini could take her next breath, the blade was flush against Cord's neck. Ghost appeared next to Jacob, and Lillian flipped down from the top of a pile of rubble to Cord's other side.

"What's going on, Malini?" Jacob said. "This looks like Cord but everything else about him is wrong. He smells like Gideon."

"I was just trying to figure that out," she said.

Lillian grabbed his wing and yanked. Cord winced but did not fight back. Feathers came off in her hand and floated to the dirt. When they landed near her toes, they did not dissolve into black tar but blew, light and fluffy, across the frozen ground. "Feathers! This is not an illusion. What does it mean?" Lillian asked.

"I don't know." Malini lowered her dagger, placing her fists on her hips. "Maybe this is the third gift. Do you think God changed them all?"

"Is that within the rules?" Ghost asked. "Seems like Lucifer would just change them back."

"Maybe this is Lucifer's work," Lillian said. "A plant, a spy. That seems more likely."

Jacob nodded. "I agree with Mom. Lucifer changes his right hand man into an angel and sends him to us. Once we trust him, he reports back all of our secrets."

"That's not what happened," Cord said.

"Then what did happen?" Malini asked.

Cord opened his mouth but Malini raised her hand. "Wait. Let's get those supplies to Bonnie. Hope is starving and it's too cold and too dangerous for us to be having this conversation here."

Just then, Dane, Ethan, Grace, and Cheveyo crossed the courtyard and joined the group. "It's done," Cheveyo said. "RV is disposed of."

"Shit!" Dane said when he noticed Cord. He jumped behind Lillian. Cord's body flew through the air and slammed into the side of the church, a shower of feathers releasing on impact. His body flopped to the rubble like a beanbag animal.

Ethan put an arm around Dane. "I took care of it."

"Nice, Ethan," Ghost said. "Blast first and ask questions later."

"Didn't you notice we were all standing right here and nobody was fighting?" Lillian asked.

"What? What's going on?"

Malini waved a hand in the air. "You know what? Who the hell cares? It's Cord. I'm not shedding one tear at seeing his head smash into a wall. Let's get him back into the cage. When he wakes up, we'll see if we can use him."

"Can the cage hold him?" Lillian asked. "Watchers can travel through shadows."

"I'm not entirely sure he's a Watcher anymore, but to be safe, let's douse the bars with holy water," Malini said.

Ethan gawked at Dane then turned toward Malini. "What did I miss?"

Chapter 31
The Milk Carton

Lucifer, otherwise known as Milton Blake, leaned back in his executive chair and looked out over the city that had become his new home with a smile. The last curse had been wildly successful. Over two hundred thousand souls had signed the contract of allegiance and paid a huge sum to have their house protected from demons. In exchange, Harrington Enterprises had supplied a box of useless crap. Milton Blake's face smiled from the back of every item.

With an annoying buzz, Lucifer's phone vibrated on his desk. His private number; the call must be important. "Speak," he barked upon answering.

"Mr. Blake? This is Ted Jameson in public relations. We've g-got a situation."

"What kind of situation?" Lucifer growled.

"The Harrington Demon Eradication System kits ar-aren't working. Twenty registered users were, um, eaten last night. The call centers are flooded with reports."

Lucifer stiffened. Cord was assigned to enforce his edict that Watchers avoid humans with HDES trinkets. Cord was responsible for keeping the Watchers in line. *Crack!* Lucifer's phone screen shattered in his tightening grip. He forced his hand to loosen. "Have a plan on my desk in an hour. We need a spin on this to explain the defective kits and avoid the blame. Find out the habits of the twenty who died. There has to be a scapegoat. The same hand lotion. Church attendance. Something."

Mr. Jameson responded with a high-pitched wheeze.

"Are you still there, Jameson?" Lucifer yelled.

"Yes, Mr. Blake. One hour."

Lucifer ended the call and slammed the unfortunate piece of technology down on his desk. He'd have Cord's head for this and the heads of the Watchers responsible. As much as he'd miss the numbers, he would not tolerate dissension in the ranks.

"You called, my lord?" Auriel entered the room and took her place in front of his desk. In his anger, Lucifer had sent out a metaphysical ping to his first- and second-in-command. Auriel had responded as expected, but she was alone.

"Where is Cord?"

"He hasn't come in today," Auriel said smugly.

"No? Did you send a car to his penthouse? Bastard probably slept late and couldn't risk the sun."

"I did. The man said his home is vacant." Auriel frowned. "Do you think he's been captured? Or slain?"

Lucifer snorted. "Cord? Impossible. I will call him to me through shadow."

Concentrating, Lucifer focused on the imprint of Cord's being, the black stuff he'd become the day he'd followed him from Heaven. Lucifer had an intimate knowledge of each and every fallen angel. He owned their very cells and could demand their presence at any time. He searched the cosmos for the being called Cord, but Lucifer could not find the Watcher. Perhaps he was slain, and there was only one person who could do it.

Growling, he continued his search, this time focusing on the Healer. He'd called Malini's soul to him before; it should be a simple thing now that Paris was destroyed and with it the presumed entrance to Eden. He sifted through souls until his head throbbed. Nothing. Was it possible that they were wrong about Eden? No. There was something else. Dane's soul was similarly blocked.

"I sense a change. The tide has shifted," Lucifer murmured.

"My lord?"

"I cannot find Cord. Perhaps he is dead or captured." He kept his other revelation to himself. It would not do to have his second in command know he could not track the

Soulkeepers. "The Great Oppressor has cheated me again. You will have to take over his duties."

Auriel hissed.

"Do you have a problem with that Auriel?"

"No, my lord, it is a pleasure to serve you." Auriel smoothed her gray suit. "However, running the education system and the pharmaceutical division leaves me little time for managing Watchers."

"If he remains missing, we will replace him," Lucifer murmured.

"Yes, my lord."

He stood and paced around the table to her, eyes shifting back and forth across the room. "Have you heard if the Great Oppressor has given the third gift?"

"If the gift has been given, none of us know of it."

Lucifer paced, paced, paced until even Auriel seemed dizzy with the motion. "This is wrong. This is not how it is supposed to be. The Great Oppressor has done something to Cord for a reason." He narrowed his eyes. "God is the cause of this mess with the kits."

"Would you like me to look for Cord?" Auriel asked, sounding bored.

"No. We have a public relations nightmare on our hands with this Harrington security thing. I want you to kill the Watchers who did this, then spread the word that any Watcher caught eating a human with an HDES kit will have to answer to me."

Auriel pouted. "I'll have to wait until sunset, unless you want half the world to see me in a snakeskin onesie. Besides, I have a meeting at two. I can only be in one place at a time."

Lucifer slammed his hand on the desk, causing Auriel to jump back in fear. The wood splintered beneath his palm.

"I know what you can and cannot do. I too can only be in one place at a time. Do it as quickly as possible. Call some of the Watchers in from the field to help. Do *something*, Auriel."

She nodded and backed toward the door.

Lucifer walked around the desk and picked up his phone. Time to call Senator Bakewell. He had to get ahead of this thing.

Chapter 32
Saying Goodbye

While the others changed into the best clothes they'd brought, and prepared in their own way to say goodbye, Jacob crept into the kitchen and pulled up a stool next to Abigail's body. His only audience was Cord, who was still passed out behind the bars of the pantry. Jacob guessed he'd be out for a while. Half his head was bashed in, although the bleeding had stopped and the bones showed signs of healing.

Reaching under the sheet, he felt for Abigail's hand. Ice cold and stiff. He let go. With a heavy heart, he peeled back the sheet from her face. Dead. Gray. His eyes focused on the cross she still wore, the one he and Malini had given to her on her wedding day. She never took it off when she was alive, and now she never would. He returned the sheet to its place and then rested his hands on his thighs. She wasn't in there anymore. This was an empty shell.

"Abigail," he whispered, "wherever you are, I want to say something to you." Jacob clasped his hands together. "I am completely pissed at you and Gideon for getting yourselves killed. I mean, what the hell? All you had to do was ask me to get whatever you needed. Why did you go out there alone? What were you thinking? That's what pisses me off the most. You never explained. You just left. And now we have two less Helpers and two more bodies to bury. You suck, Dr. Silva." Fat, wet, drops fell like rain between his elbows. Tears. Arms shaking, he didn't bother wiping them away.

"You suck for leaving us," Jacob said again. "But I forgive you. Because even though I know you were invincible and could stop a train with that look of yours, I know there must have been a reason you allowed that Watcher to hurt you. You would have never left your baby if you had a choice.

"I've been thinking that maybe you wanted us to have Hope. She must have meant everything to you. You and Gideon died protecting her. That must've been the reason. Somehow, you ended up in that position and gave your lives for the greater good. That's the only way this makes sense. Just like last summer, when you died on Lucifer's altar. You didn't have to do that either."

Jacob sat up and wiped under his eyes. Now for the hard part. The thing he wanted to say the most but would hurt the most. "Thank you for being there for me. I was just an angry little runt when you took me under your wing. And yeah, we hurt each other and stuff a few times. I think I still have bruises on my neck from when you thought I left the gate open. But I always knew I could count on you. You saved me. More than once.

"I'm not sure how to make it up to you now that you're gone except to live the life you wanted me to live, being the best Soulkeeper I can be. Oh, and taking care of Hope. We all will. Don't you worry."

He sat up and straightened his shirt. "And I guess this isn't really goodbye, is it? It's more like see you later. Some days I think it might be sooner than later the way this battle is going. Enjoy Heaven, Abigail. You've earned it."

Jacob stood from the stool, took one last look at the sheet, and let her go. He walked into the main room with the slightest feeling of peace in his heart.

It lasted less than sixty seconds.

"Oh, good," Malini said, heading for him. "Hold Hope so I can get ready." She placed the baby in his arms and handed him a bottle of formula.

"Wait, I don't know how—" Yeah, she was gone, and he was left holding the baby in the crook of his arm. He repositioned her and took a better look. She had a thin layer of light brown hair, more like Gideon's than Abigail's. But Hope's eyes were her mother's. Jacob smiled at the ice blue color, remembering the first time he'd seen it, hovering outside his bedroom window. That color had scared the bejesus out of him back then and was doing a good job of it now.

Hope's tiny face bunched up and turned red. Her rose petal mouth opened. "Waa. Waa. Waaaaa!" Short bursts of angry protest.

"I think she's hungry, Jacob," Grace said, pointing at the bottle.

Jacob looked at the older woman, slack-jawed, and gestured for her to take the baby. Grace shook her head and walked away. The crying continued until he plugged Hope's pink, bow-shaped lips with the nipple. She sucked greedily.

"You have a good appetite," he whispered, smiling at the way she closed her eyes and wrinkled her nose while she drank.

Lillian appeared by his side, placing her hand under his elbow and lifting. "Keep her head up or she'll get a tummy ache from gas."

Jacob adjusted Hope's position and raised his eyebrows.

"And you need to burp her every few minutes." His mom made cooing sounds at Hope. "I can take her if you want."

Jacob removed the nipple from Hope's mouth and repositioned her on his shoulder, patting her back like he'd seen Bonnie do. "No. I think I've got it under control, Mom."

She grinned. "Yes, I believe you do."

* * * * *

Just before noon, Ghost, Dane, and Ethan brought down two slabs of wood from the old church, the seats of broken pews. Lillian and Malini loaded Abigail's body onto one and the other was taken to the rectory to accommodate Gideon. Bonnie took Hope, now fully fed and sleeping peacefully, so that Jacob, Dane, Malini, and Lillian could serve as pallbearers. The four lifted Abigail's body onto their shoulders and carried her to the graveyard. Ethan, Ghost, Grace, and Samantha met them at the gravesite, Gideon's body on their shoulders. Cheveyo brought up the rear of the processional, carrying a dagger wrapped in silk that had belonged to Master Lee.

Ethan used his power to lower Abigail, then Gideon into the holes he and Dane had dug. Once the bodies were settled, Cheveyo laid the dagger in the smaller hole next to Gideon.

Three carved pieces of wood served as markers. They did not bear the Soulkeepers' names. To do so would be inviting desecration. Instead, Lillian had used her knife skills to carve ornate patterns into the oak. Abigail's marker depicted a mighty tree with twisted branches that bore strange but weighty fruit. The focal point of Gideon's was the sun with beams of light over a set of outstretched wings. Lee's was a twisting dragon around the Chinese symbol for warrior.

Father Raymond stepped forward to the edges of the grave. "Let us commend Abigail and Gideon Newman, and Confucius Lee to the mercy of God."

Jacob turned to Lillian as Father Raymond continued to speak. "Was that his real name? Confucius?"

"He always thought it was too formal," Lillian whispered. "He once told me and the other student in the dojo to call him Bob."

"You guys were close. How are you doing with all of this?" Jacob asked.

Lillian pressed her lips together before answering. "Before I was taken, we celebrated Lee's eighty-fifth birthday. I guess I always knew he was on borrowed time. This is how he would have wanted to go. He held the passageway open so that all of us could get out. He died a hero and a warrior. No better way to go, if you ask me."

Jacob nodded and refocused on Father Raymond.

"We therefore commit Abigail, Gideon, and Master Lee's bodies to the ground; earth to earth, ashes to ashes, dust to dust; in the sure and certain hope of the resurrection to eternal life." Father Raymond motioned to Ethan who filled in the holes over the bodies and Master Lee's weapon. "Would anyone like to say a few words?"

Malini walked to the front of the graves and unfolded a piece of paper from her pocket. With a deep breath, she began to read.

"Today, the birds fall silent
and the sun refuses to shine.
The grass below lies dormant.
Lost these friends of mine.

Every head does bow

and darkness presses in,
the water slows and stills
a new phase does begin.

They say the world is turning.
I'm not sure I can agree.
The sadness of your leaving
seems its own eternity.

In time we will move on
with the work you have begun.
We'll recover from this loss
and ignite the fading sun.

But today the rain does fall,
and creeps in the chill of night.
The loss of you reigns on
Goodbye ...
my friends
my warriors
my confidants
until we meet again."

Malini returned to her place by Jacob's side while the
other Soulkeepers shifted uneasily, wiping icy tears and
sniffing cold noses.

"That was beautiful. Did you write that yourself?" Jacob
asked.

"Shhh."

"And now, Bonnie and Samantha Guillian have offered to sing." Father Raymond moved aside and the twins took their spot at the front of the group. The snow picked up again, creating a mystical backdrop to the twins' red hair. The two shrugged out of their coats and handed them to Ghost.

The two girls wore identical purple dresses with silver ballet flats, their fiery red hair cascading in loose waves across their shoulders. Gracefully, they began to circle each other, dancing in mirror image, a lyrical, sweeping ballet. Within the wave of pointed toes, arched backs, and swirling arms, Bonnie began to sing in a low and hollow voice that seemed to come from somewhere other than her petite frame. "When peace like a river, attendeth my way."

Samantha followed with, "When sorrow like sea billows roll."

"Whatever my lot, thou has taught me to know." Bonnie twirled and reached for her sister.

"It is well, it is well, with my soul," they both sang together.

Even Jacob knew this song. *It Is Well With My Soul* by Horatio Spafford. They sang it often at the Laudners' church. The meaning wasn't lost on him. He'd heard that the author had written the hymn after losing everything.

As the twins continued the hymn, Jacob caught himself drifting. He listened with his Soulkeeper ears, expecting the Watchers to attack at any moment. With Cord locked up downstairs, how long until they attacked? For all he knew, they could be tracking the Watcher right now.

Reality hit him like a blunt fist. They'd lost Eden! Lucifer could sense any of their souls if he wanted to, or demand their astral-projected presence as he had Malini's. Why hadn't he? Suddenly, the thought that they hadn't been discovered seemed impossible. Were they all on borrowed time?

He squeezed his eyes shut. He couldn't think that way. He needed to trust that God led them here for a reason and that everything was unfolding as it should, a tall order considering. With a sigh, he opened his eyes.

The twins finished the hymn and joined hands, using their power to form first into the image of Master Lee, then Gideon, and then Abigail. The waterworks started again when he saw Abigail. He wasn't embarrassed though. There wasn't a dry eye in the crowd. Even Hope, snuggled on Grace's shoulder, began to fuss.

Bonnie and Samantha ended their tribute, transforming into themselves again and returned to their places among the other Soulkeepers. Father Raymond, in a state of amazement after watching the twins, shook off his awestruck stupor to say one final prayer before dismissing them. In silence, the group trudged toward the rectory, shoulders slumped and faces drawn.

Malini stopped Jacob as they reached the threshold, allowing the others to go on ahead. "I don't think I can stand to lose anyone else, Jacob."

He wrapped his arms around her. "Then let's do our best to make sure this never happens again. Lucifer doesn't know what he's started here. When you push the Soulkeepers, they push back."

In the circle of his arms, Malini stiffened. Tipping her face up, she gritted her teeth. "You are right about that, Jacob. We will fight back, and Lucifer has no idea what he's in for."

Chapter 33
New Rules

Bonnie needed to clean the kitchen. Everyone grieved in his or her own way and hers was sanitation. A quick exploration of the kitchen rewarded her with powdered scrub and a scouring pad. Cleaning-therapy tools.

The island seemed like the logical place to begin. Even though Grace and Lillian placed bedding under Abigail before the birth, the thought of someone delivering a baby and then passing away in the same place they might have to prepare food grossed her out. She couldn't blame her mother though. No other place in the church was as clean, safe, or private. Malini and the others did the best with what they had.

As she scrubbed the stainless steel, she thought the counter looked a lot like a surgical table. She closed her eyes against a barrage of images of how else they might have to use the island in the future. This was war. Would they be setting broken bones here? Digging out shrapnel?

"I heard you singing," Cord said from the pantry.

Bonnie jumped back, heart hammering in her chest. "Oh, you're awake."

"Yes. I have been." He pointed at the mat of black hair at the back of his head. "All healed."

Cautiously, Bonnie glanced down to make sure the barred door to the pantry was locked, then turned back toward the sink to ring out her wet rag. She rinsed off the counter she'd just scrubbed, the scent of bleach burning in her nostrils.

"I heard you singing," Cord said again. "You have a beautiful voice."

Bonnie paused for a moment, then continued her scrubbing.

"Your sister was singing too, but I could tell when it was you."

Face tightening in annoyance, Bonnie rinsed the rag out again. "We're identical twins. We look, sound, and act exactly alike. There's no way you could tell our voices apart from a distance."

"You don't look exactly alike."

"No?" she asked, placing a fist on her hip.

"Not to me."

Bonnie threw the rag into the sink and turned the full force of her stare on him, crossing her arms over her chest. "Tell me what you think is different about us," she snapped. She leaned back against the sink. She couldn't wait to hear what kind of bullshit he came up with next.

He snaked his fingers through the steel grate and blinked at her. "There's the obvious. The mole. Yours is on the right and hers is on the left."

Observant. Bonnie frowned.

"Then there's the less obvious. You make larger gestures when you speak, and you speak louder. It's almost as if you want people to know you are different from your sister. Samantha, on the other hand, speaks softly, if ever, and pins her elbows to her sides. She's happy to blend in and go along. Nothing like you, Bonnie."

Bonnie's mouth dropped open slightly. She closed it.

"And your voice today, when you sang, held more pain than hers. You've been through more. Even if you've experienced the same losses, for some reason you felt them more fully."

She laughed incredulously. "Really. Which verse did I sing?"

He shook his head. "You alternated. You sang the first line and Samantha sang the second, and so on. You both sang the refrain."

Now her mouth really did fall open. Cord was locked in the pantry during their performance. He couldn't have seen her sing, which meant he'd actually differentiated her voice.

"Am I wrong?" he asked.

She took a deep breath and blew it out before answering. "No."

"You are beautiful," he murmured. "Almost magical. I changed when I saw you. Everything about me changed."

Seething, she placed her hands on her hips. "*You* are not beautiful, Cord," she stated clearly. "You are a killer. You came here to kill me, and you've killed before. How dare you come here and try to what? Ply me with flattery? I hate you. I hate everything about you. You and Lucifer and the rest of the Watchers, are liars and cheaters. Just because we haven't figured out your game yet, don't think for a second I don't know you are playing one."

Cord's eyes widened, and he backed away from the door. He sank to the floor at the back of the pantry and wrapped his wings around himself.

Skin hot and heart pounding, Bonnie resumed her cleaning. With clenched teeth, she threw her back into it, until the scrubbing became an aerobic activity, and her mind blanked with the effort. When the counters were done, she moved to the floors. When the floors were done, she moved to the walls. For hours, she worked, until her hands and knees were raw from the effort.

She jumped when the door swung open and Samantha poked her head in. "Bonnie, we need you. Malini's called a meeting." Her sister looked around the spotless kitchen and raised an eyebrow. "Good job. Sparkly."

"Thanks." Bonnie watched Samantha's retreat, noticing as the door swung closed how her sister kept her elbows close to her sides and her soft words had floated into the room barely above a whisper. She hated that Cord was right. Violently, she rinsed out her supplies and stored them under the sink before pausing in the doorway. Against her better judgment, she glanced toward the pantry. He was staring at her, looking hungry and vulnerable. She scowled and let the door close behind her.

A circle of chairs waited for Bonnie in the main room. She took a seat between Samantha and Dane, apologizing for being the last one there. Malini was quick to dismiss her apology. Her small brown hands circled nervously, palms rubbing in front of her body. Bonnie noticed she'd trimmed her hair again. Her bangs had grown out to chin length, and she'd had someone cut the back shorter than the front. The effect was badass. Tonight, Malini didn't look the part of nurturing Healer. She looked like someone who was about to lay down the law.

"Today, we lost two friends, Helpers and Soulkeepers. We've said our goodbyes. Now we've got to move on," Malini began.

Bonnie heard her mother gasp at the blunt words.

"We are at war. Earth is occupied by Watchers. Lucifer has found a way to protect the humans who align themselves to him and kill the ones who don't. And he has probably sent Cord"—she pointed at the kitchen—"to spy on our operation."

Malini shifted her weight from foot to foot. "We can't lose anyone else. I can't lose any of you, not personally or otherwise. We have to protect each other."

Ethan coughed. "Sorry, but isn't that what we've been doing? We've always protected each other."

Malini shook her head. "We need to be more careful. More deliberate."

Bonnie straightened in her seat. "You mean we need to be like...an army. More organized."

Malini nodded. "Exactly, Bonnie. A mission-by-mission approach was fine before, when Watchers rarely appeared above ground and tried to hide the people they killed. But the world has changed. Now Lucifer *wants* his Watchers to be seen. We are soldiers for God. If the Watchers fight every day, we have to fight every day. And that means rules, a schedule, expectations."

"Rules," Ghost said. "What kind of rules are you thinking?"

"First, no one goes out alone. We go out in threes or not at all."

"Why three?" Samantha asked.

"If one of you is attacked, another can attempt a rescue while the third calls for backup."

Heads nodded in agreement.

Malini continued, "We'll create a rotation. Dane, when it's your turn to fight, you will borrow a power from the last team on rotation."

Cheveyo shifted in his seat. "We're sending Dane out regularly? What if he dies in the field? We'll lose two Soulkeepers instead of one."

Malini glared at him. "Then I guess he can't die. Stay alive, Dane."

Grinning, Dane bobbed his head, but Ethan's jaw tightened. He wasn't the only Soulkeeper looking uncomfortable. Ghost fidgeted with a torn section of upholstery on the bottom of his chair, Jacob's pale face froze like a mask, and Grace looked like she might be sick.

"What about the expectations? You said we'd have expectations," Bonnie said.

Malini nodded her head. "Each team will have a quota." A murmur rose up from the group. "We are not simply defending ourselves. We are waging a counterattack. Lucifer cannot make more Watchers, which means that every one we kill is one less out there to harm a human. We will start with three per night and adjust from there based on our experiences."

Bonnie noticed Samantha mouth *three* to Ghost, looking quite shaken. Whispers floated up around her. Shock, worry, and even distrust played across the other Soulkeepers faces. Well, they all had something to lose. She didn't.

"When do we start? I want to go first," Bonnie said. Samantha's glare cut her like stabbing daggers.

Malini smiled. "We start tonight, Bonnie, and I'll take your volunteering under consideration." She looked at Samantha pointedly.

"One more thing," Bonnie said, regaining Malini's attention. "Can we kill Cord? If we think he's a spy, we're better off with him dead. I volunteer to do it."

"Yeah," Cheveyo said. "I'm completely freaked out having that thing in the next room."

As Malini pondered the question, she paced the space inside the circle of chairs, seeming to go somewhere else for a moment. Her eyes took on the spacey sheen of a daydreamer, and her stare seemed to favor the wall. "I need to think about that."

Didn't she know how important this was? Bonnie stood up, knocking her chair over. "What's to think about? We have a ticking time bomb locked up in the pantry," she yelled. "He came here to kill us. He was going to start with me and Hope." Bonnie pointed an open hand toward Lillian, who bounced the baby on her shoulder.

"He bleeds like an angel," Malini said softly.

"Yeah, he does. So what does that mean? You're the Healer. Can a fallen angel unfall? Can a Watcher become an angel again? Did God do it? Did I?" She began to tremble. "It doesn't make sense. It's a trap. I know it."

"My decision is to keep him alive, for now," Malini said firmly.

Bonnie turned her face away, scowling. "I should have killed him when I had the chance."

Malini crossed the circle and pulled Bonnie into a hug. Warmth flowed through her causing the tension to bleed from her neck and shoulders. When the Healer backed away,

Bonnie expected her to agree to kill the Watcher in disguise, that the hug was a peace offering.

Instead, Malini turned to the others. "For now, we will keep Cord alive and imprisoned. My instincts tell me he could serve a purpose for us in the future."

"What?" Bonnie said, hands slapping her sides. "Are you kidding me?"

Malini raised a finger, pointing at Bonnie's face. "Stand down, Bonnie. If Cord truly has changed, he'll help us. He'll tell us about Lucifer's plans. If he hasn't changed, we may be able to use him to get false information back to Lucifer. One thing I know for sure, he's useless dead."

Bonnie felt violated. How could Malini not see that keeping either an angel or a Watcher locked up in a pantry was a recipe for disaster?

Malini didn't argue the point but moved on to the next one. "Watcher activity is greater at night. That's when we'll patrol. During the day, we'll obtain food and supplies. We'll take turns watching Hope." She turned a circle, making eye contact with each of the Soulkeepers.

Bonnie wasn't sure what the Healer was looking for. Everyone was antsy and restless, even the adults. If she wanted reassurance, she wasn't going to get it.

"Lillian, Jacob, and I will take the first patrol tonight."

When Bonnie began to protest, Malini held up her hand. "I know you volunteered, Bonnie, but I need to get the lay of the land."

Bonnie shifted sideways and rolled her eyes.

Malini stepped in front of her, a hard look on her face. "There *is* something I need your help with."

"What?" Bonnie asked defensively.

"I need you to feed the angel," Malini said.

Bonnie kicked her fallen chair and stormed off toward the bathroom.

Chapter 34
The Scorekeeper

Malini arrived in the In Between gracefully, a ballet dancer landing a giant leap. She'd been shredded her last several times coming over, distracted by Lucifer, the war, problems with the Soulkeepers. But today, she had a singular focus. The apocalypse had toughened her. No longer the meek teenager who jumped at her own reflection, the power and responsibility that used to scare her, now motivated her. When she watched Abigail die, something inside of her shifted. A holy rage blossomed, a contained wildfire for truth and justice. With a tight grip, she held the feeling, strengthening it in the kiln of her resolve. The hot ember fueled her hurried steps.

"Welcome, Malini," Fate said.

On the veranda of her stucco villa, Fate sat at a table with Time and Death. Malini gave them a tight smile. Mara and Henry would always be more human to her than Fatima. Maybe because she could clearly picture them dancing at prom. That night seemed so far away now. It was hard to believe it was less than a year ago. A year since she could almost call her life normal. Now, what was normal?

"Am I in time for tea?" Malini said, staring at the pot and cups on the table.

"A celebration of life, Gideon and Abigail's," Fatima said. From her abdomen, she produced a brightly colored cloth made of raspberry, turquoise, green, and black thread.

Mara gave a little wave of her hand in lieu of a hello. "Lucifer stole Abigail's thread, but Fatima wove a tapestry from all of the lives she helped. Gideon's thread is part of the green."

"I got the idea after we followed Lucifer's missing thread." Fatima held out the tapestry to her.

Malini ran her fingers over the glinting material. "Gorgeous. A masterpiece."

Henry nodded. "We thought so too. We loved both of them."

For a moment, Malini wondered why they had excluded Master Lee, but then they'd never really known him, not like Gideon and Abigail. As former angels, the immortals had known the two for thousands of years. Immortal before mortal. No two people had ever lived a life like Abigail and Gideon.

A brown face popped up beyond the stucco border of the veranda. "Hi, Wisnu," Malini said to the mongoose. The animal gave a high-pitched bark and returned to playing in the yard, trotting out to the edge of the forest beyond.

"Would you like a cup?" Fatima pointed to the teapot.

"I'm not here for the tea," Malini said. "Sorry, I don't mean to be rude, but I can't partake in the pleasantries while my team is fighting for their lives against the apocalypse."

"The apocalypse?" Mara asked. "You're calling the challenge the apocalypse?"

Malini's hands balled into fists. "How dare you sit up here drinking tea and ask me that question?" She glared at Mara, not even flinching at the girl's black eyes or the way the universe revolved inside of them. "Don't you think it's fitting? The veil has lifted. The Watchers occupy Earth openly. They kill openly. Everything has changed, Mara. This is the end, the final battle between good and evil, and we're losing. Everything. You must know how desperate it is down there."

Mara glanced away, but Henry angrily stood from the table. "It's hard for her, Malini. She sees the past, present, and future all at the same time. Mara doesn't mean to be harsh. She has to concentrate to focus on the pinpoint that is your existence."

"I understand but—"

"You're not losing," Mara blurted. Her eyes waxed vacant, staring off into the distance, toward the hill with the scorekeeper.

"What do you mean? We just lost two of the most important people in the fight."

"The Lord has given the third gift. You just don't realize you have it yet. A weapon, a Helper, is in your presence with the power to change everything. The fate of many is tied to the fates of few. Only one can cure the many, but many will deliver the cure to all."

Malini scowled. "I have no idea what you just said."

Mara turned to face her, looking as strange and otherworldly as Malini had ever seen her.

"Wait, do you mean Cord? Is he the answer?"

"Cord?" Fatima spat in disgust. "The Watcher?"

"We've captured him. He came to kill us and now bleeds white, smells like an angel, and has feathers that stay feathers when they fall off. He says he was transformed."

"Impossible!" Fatima shook her head.

Malini shrugged. "It is what it is. We haven't been able to figure him out."

"Cord is not the gift. Cord is your key to understanding the gift. The gift is not a thing or a person. It isn't material. It can't die or be used up."

"What is it, Mara?" Malini asked.

"Hope."

"The baby, Hope?"

Mara stared off into the distance, squinting and then closing her eyes with the effort. "Hope is the bringer of the virtue she is named for. The baby is a symbol, but the gift is so much more. The gift is hope. The gift is knowledge that God is far from finished. Believe it, Malini."

Henry shivered. "She has the gene."

"Huh?" Malini placed her hands on her hips. Talking to immortals could be so frustrating.

"Hope. Gideon and Abigail drank the water. They lived in Eden for months. Recreated human by God, their bodies carried the recessive gene. Their daughter, Hope, now carries the Soulkeeper gene. I can feel her soul right now. She's special."

"Special how?"

"No way to tell. Like all Soulkeepers, she must be challenged, and she must make the choice, but all of the potential is there," Fatima said.

Mara squinted. "I can't sort out her future. I'm blind to it."

Fatima cleared her throat. "Of course you are blind. The challenge is changing the fabric of our power. The thread I use is shifty between my fingers. Colors change in the midst of my weaving. None of us can see the outcome. The closer we are to the destination, the less we can see the path."

"And what about Cord? Can we trust him?" Malini asked.

Fatima lowered her eyes. "No human soul, no thread. We could follow him, as we did Lucifer, by the emptiness he's left behind. However, if he has changed by some miracle, what would be the point? We would only see the future of the Watcher named Cord, not the angel he claims he's become."

"Great." Malini tossed her clasped hands over her head and squeezed her ears with the insides of her arms. "Ugh. It's so frustrating."

Mara stood and tugged Henry to his feet. "Come, Malini, you need to see the results of your effort."

Malini followed her and Henry onto the lawn, Fatima joining them at the base of the hill. The horizon folded, and without taking another step, Malini found herself at the feet of the scorekeeper. The blindfolded angel loomed over her, frozen in her marble shell, wings outstretched.

Disbelieving, Malini stared at the scales in her hand. One tray was white, the good side; the other was black, Lucifer's. At the start of this challenge, before any temptations or gifts were cast, the scales were tipped in Lucifer's favor. The evil inherent in human hearts seemed to weigh the darker side down unfairly. Now, somehow, the tide had shifted. God was *winning*. It wasn't by much. The dark side was only slightly higher than the light, hardly noticeable, but it was true.

"For the first time since the beginning of the challenge," Henry said. "We can't explain it. Circumstances on Earth seem at their worst, but the scales say otherwise."

Malini tipped her head. "I think you are onto something. Human hearts rise to the occasion. Maybe we are at our best when things are at their worst?"

Fatima crossed her arms. "I've seen humans at their worst when things were at their worst. Do you want me to show you?"

Malini held up both hands. "No. I want you to let me bask in the hope that today things are different. Today, people everywhere are changing. They are helping each other. They are asking questions and rejecting the devil's false gifts." She stared into the orb, watching black and white lights dance through the crystal.

"Very well," Fatima said.

A breeze swept over the hill, causing the scales to knock together. "Are you doing that?" Malini asked the three immortals. The In Between was constructed of consciousness. Ordinarily, everything here was Fatima's doing as this was her realm. But Fate shook her head.

The breeze turned into a gale-force wind. Malini grabbed the scorekeeper to keep her feet planted on the ground. But the grass under her was as untrustworthy as the air around her. The ground shook. Fatima's eight arms flailed at her sides in an effort to keep her balance. Henry's skin peeled back from his face and hands, exposing the skeleton within. And Mara floated above the ground, stars spinning around her as if she were the nucleus of a human atom, the center of a revolving universe.

Dark clouds rolled in overhead, through the usually cloudless sky. Malini followed their path until the dark gray turned black and funneled to the grass. *Lucifer.* He stood in the eye of the hurricane, his black suit and blond curls flapping in the wind.

"Did you think I would go quietly?" he spat toward the sky. Lightning struck a tree in the distance behind him, its branches bursting into flame. "What was your third gift? You cheat! You've blocked my power to demand souls! You've changed the humans and forced the scales to tip."

A crack of thunder rocked through Malini's body.

"Your accusations are false, Lucifer," came a booming voice. "The scorekeeper cannot lie. And as for my gift, you know the rules of the challenge. The die is cast."

Lucifer howled, skin glowing red. He pointed a finger at Malini. "What have you done with Cord?"

She didn't answer, even when a painful tug in her chest tried to coax the words from her. Fate, Time, and Death closed ranks, placing themselves between her and devil and blocking her view of Lucifer. She adjusted her grip on the scorekeeper.

"Oh, hell!" Henry said.

All three immortals turned their backs to Lucifer and covered their heads with their arms. Malini took the hint and turned her face away. Eyes closed tight, a gust of heat blasted into her back, blowing her hair into her face. For a solid minute, she wondered if her skin would peel off from the force. Then the storm quieted. The wind died down. She dared to open her eyes.

Fatima's villa and the forest beyond were gone, replaced by a barren wasteland. The house was nothing but an empty shell with blown out windows.

"He nuked the place," Mara whispered.

Fatima took a deep breath. "No worries. He's gone. This is mine again."

From left to right, Fatima knit her world back to the way it was. Burnt trees regrew, the lawn sprouted green, and the house returned to its former glory. The ambient light of the In Between's sky brightened.

Malini headed down the hill toward Fate's villa.

"Where are you going?" Fatima asked.

"To pull out Lucifer's tapestry," Malini said. "If he thinks that little stunt is going to scare me away, he is vastly mistaken. I'm going to predict his next move, and then I'm going to return to Sanctuary and help my team rid the world of that bastard."

The Soulkeepers had come a long way in this battle. Malini was done grieving the loss of the future she'd dreamt for herself. She could see a new future. A new hope. And no one, not even the devil, was going to keep her from it.

The Last Soulkeeper (Excerpt)

Book 6 in The Soulkeepers Series

Chapter 1

The Replacement

Auriel needed to feed. The torturous ache in her gut was only made worse by the scent of six humans, bloated with blood and sitting just a talon's strike away, hunkered over the conference room table at Harrington Enterprises. If it weren't for Lucifer's looming presence, she'd have stripped the flesh off any one of them before her victim had time to scream. But Lucifer, otherwise known as CEO Milton Blake, was running a tight ship these days, galvanized by Cord's continued absence. She'd witnessed his wrath enough times to know she would not willingly be on the receiving end of it, and at the moment, she could sense his fury brewing.

The dark one drummed his fingers at the head of the table, obviously annoyed. The heat of his soulless interior, the part of him connected to Hell, had passed the barrier of his skin and raised the temperature in the room several degrees. Even Auriel was uncomfortably hot. The human participants sported red faces and wet spots under the pits of their arms.

While Auriel hated the business world, she'd learned a few things about Harrington's operation. The purpose of this meeting was for the Harrington department heads to update Lucifer on the progress of their respective divisions. It was also their only chance to request more personnel or funding. Lucifer had come to rely on these meetings in Cord's absence. The human employees outnumbered the Watchers and were far more motivated to achieve success in their petty, limited lives. Unfortunately, the news today wasn't improving Lucifer's mood.

This was war. God had challenged Lucifer for human hearts. Six temptations versus six gifts, winner takes Earth for one thousand years. Lucifer had already cast three temptations: affliction, ignorance, and terror. In response, the Great Oppressive Deity had gifted wisdom, understanding, and a third gift she hadn't been able to interpret yet. Lucifer had been in the lead since the inception of the challenge ... that is, until that last, mysterious gift. Somehow, God had taken Cord—at least Lucifer thought He had—and with him Lucifer's control over his army of Watchers. The last gift was more than Cord's undoing though. She could feel it in the air. The humans changed in a way she couldn't put her finger on that day. Now, for the first time, the scorekeeper's scales tilted slightly in God's favor.

Auriel had worked hard to fill Cord's shoes. Too hard. But just like Lucifer, she couldn't be in more than one place at a time, and the Watchers were growing too used to eating whomever they pleased whenever they pleased. If she and Lucifer couldn't get control of the Watchers, they would be at risk of losing this challenge. Auriel didn't want to think about what might become of her then.

"The problem isn't with demand, Mr. Blake," Mr. Adams said, loosening his tie against the heat. "We are moving more Elysium than ever. The problem is with the financials. We've given away too many pills. People are hoarding them and selling them on the black market. Meanwhile, my department is on the verge of bankruptcy."

A tooth-baring frown contorted Lucifer's mouth. "Why would people buy them on the black market and not from Harrington?"

Adams dabbed his temple with a tissue. "The distribution channels." He paused as if he thought the reasons were obvious. "Since the, er, anti-Elysium movement and the demon invasion, many of the doctors and hospitals we've worked with in the past won't sell the drug anymore for reasons of conscience."

Auriel inconspicuously wheeled her chair away from Lucifer under the guise of adjusting her boot. This wasn't going to be pretty.

"Reasons of conscience?" His voice, barely a whisper, held the promise of menace. "What business are you in, Adams?"

"The pharmaceutical business, sir," Adams said.

"Ah yes, we sell drugs for profit." Lucifer nodded his head. "I don't recall hanging out a shingle promoting our social consciousness. Who should take Elysium?"

"Elysium is prescribed for the treatment and management of the latest strain of bird flu," Adams recited.

"Blah, blah, blah." Lucifer made a duck face with his hand, opening and closing his fingers to mock Adams. "Everyone should take Elysium. Every man, woman, and child should be popping the stuff three times per day. I don't care if they need it. I don't care if it helps or hurts them. But I do care that they pay. They must all pay."

"But the doctors—"

Lucifer slammed a fist on the table and leaned forward until his nose was centimeters from Adams's. "Are you mentally impaired?"

"No—"

"Sell it on the street, you idiot. If the money is flowing on the black market, then *you* control the black market. And if doctors and hospitals won't sell Elysium, perhaps you could make things more difficult for them. Deny them Harrington Security. Let the demons eat them."

Auriel had to stop herself from cheering. This was the Lucifer she knew and loved, all-powerful and merciless.

"Yeah, about dat," Ted Kowalski interrupted in his thick Chicagoan accent. The man's corpulent body stressed the fabric of his white dress shirt, brown tie askew and bald head beading with sweat. "I'm not sure dat's the best strategy at this juncture. I think we oughta scrap the Demon Eradication System."

"What did you say?" Lucifer asked.

Sweat rolled from Kowalski's hairline to the round hump of his cheek. "I think it's time we phased out Harrington's Demon Eradication Systems. The things don't work. I been puttin' out fires for weeks. People are dying 'cause they trust in this product, and it's a lemon. Harrington's getting a black eye over this one. We'll be lucky to get out before the lawsuits hit."

Lucifer glared, lips peeling back from his teeth in an expression that couldn't be confused for a smile. "What department do you run, Kowalski?"

The man shifted in his chair, eyes darting around the room like a drowning man searching for a saving branch. None were offered. "Er, public relations."

"Public relations." Lucifer stood, leaning forward to plant his fingertips on the table. "I seem to recall the function of your department is to manipulate the public perception of our product."

Kowalski's jaw dropped. "We don't manipulate folks. We just manage the spread of information to the public."

"And why aren't you spreading the news that the eradication systems work?" Lucifer hissed. Auriel straightened in her chair at the foreboding sound.

The man rubbed his scruffy chin with his thumb and forefinger. "'Cause. They. Don't."

Silence. The other department heads froze in their seats. Lucifer strode around the table until he was standing next to Kowalski, the hip of his khaki trousers leaning against the table. "I am not paying you to be honest, Kowalski."

Kowalski's mouth bent into a frown, and his breath began to whistle in his throat. The nervous wheeze crept through his pseudo-confident exterior. He swallowed. "I ain't your patsy, Mr. Blake. I know what you're doing. I ain't gonna take the blame when the law comes down on us for this."

"You're not the man for the job, eh?" Lucifer said, eyes narrowing.

"I guess not."

Lucifer glared and leaned forward. Auriel knew what he was doing but suppressed her laugh. It wouldn't do to distract him. The dark one was allowing the man to glimpse who he really was, to see Hell through the window of his pupils. The wheezing grew louder. Kowalski coughed, his face turning the color of borscht before his hands began to flail at his sides.

"I think he's choking," Lucifer said calmly.

Kowalski slapped the table, airless, throaty grunts coming from his head.

Mrs. Anderson, vice president of human resources, looked up from her page of notes and slowly processed what was happening. "Maybe try the Heimlich?" she said slowly. She did not move from her chair.

"I think he has asthma," Marketing chimed in. "Maybe we should call 911."

Lucifer did not respond. No one reached for the phone.

Kowalski scratched at his ruby throat, eyes bugging and tongue extending from his mouth. A dying fish. He flopped to the floor, tipping over his chair in the process, and twitched on the low pile carpeting.

"Ms. Grimswald," Lucifer said to the mousy-haired secretary taking notes in the corner.

"Yes?"

"Please make a note that there is a position open in public relations, effective immediately."

"Yes, s-sir," the woman stuttered.

Lucifer spread his hands and addressed the room. "Meeting dismissed." He winked at Auriel. "Ms. Thomson, can you stay and help me deliver Mr. Kowalski to the nearest hospital?"

"Of course, Mr. Blake," Auriel said, grinning at the piece of meat now unconscious on the floor. The others rose from the table and filed from the room. No one even looked back to see what had become of Ted Kowalski.

As soon as the conference room door closed, Auriel begged Lucifer with her eyes.

"My gift to you." Lucifer motioned toward Kowalski.

"Thank you, my lord," she said, before pouncing on the body and using a talon to strip a bit of flesh from his neck. "His heart is still beating."

"You deserve the best my pet. You've served me well these weeks."

She nodded, slurping in the next strip.

"I fear we may never recover Cord," Lucifer said, "and we can no longer afford to wait for him to return."

Auriel nodded. Finally. She thought he would never admit they'd lost him for good. "Then he *is* dead."

"It appears so."

She wiped the back of her hand across her bloody lips. "The Soulkeepers are behind this. Call Malini's soul to you and rip the truth from her filthy mouth." Auriel bared her fangs.

Lucifer scowled, turning his back to her as if he had a secret to keep. But then, Lucifer always had secrets. It was not her place to know or ask about his reasons, and she was smart enough not to press the issue.

"It is done, Auriel. He is dead. We must name another."

"Who shall we call? If only Mordechai or Turrel were still with us, what an awesome power we would make." She licked her lips.

Lucifer growled. "But they are not. No, the one we call forth must be supreme in his depravity. Intelligent and ruthless."

Auriel stopped eating and pointed a bloody talon in his direction. "You have someone in mind."

"More than one someone."

"Who?"

"The Wicked Brethren."

"I have not seen or heard of the Wicked Brethren in decades. They've gone their own way. Haven't lived in Nod in millennia. Never followed the quotas. What makes you think you can rein them in?"

"Because I hold their dark hearts in my fist," Lucifer snapped, balling his hand in front of her face.

Touchy, touchy. Auriel backed off immediately. The Wicked Brethren were a family group of six brothers, angels that fell with Lucifer and killed brutally in the early days. Made Watchers like the others, the brethren claimed one critical difference; they paid allegiance to each other and no one else, not even Lucifer. Each had come to serve a particular vice in the human world. Over the centuries, three had met their end, victims of the urges that drove them. The other three had stayed rogue, the last she'd heard, living and feeding on villagers in rural Romania. Lucifer had allowed it to this point, Auriel supposed, because the brethren had a nasty habit of impulsivity that made them poor candidates for close living.

Perhaps desperate times called for desperate measures. Lucifer needed a monster. Cord's replacement must both wreak destruction on the humans and control the legions of Watchers on Earth. If he could enlist the brethren for those duties, he'd be more powerful than ever.

Auriel held up a disembodied finger between her own. "I miss Cord," she murmured, then popped the digit between her teeth.

"There is only one way to gain the allegiance of the brethren," Lucifer continued. "We must get Damien to agree to help us. He has always been their leader."

"Yes, my lord, although I found Asher quite entertaining for a number of years." Asher was the pretty one. Always had a thing for the ladies, even the human ones. She supposed with the elimination of the compact between God and the Devil, he was exercising that particular vice again. Since Noah, human sexuality had been off limits. Not anymore.

"Asher is too easily distracted. I will call Damien to me, and we shall enlist him in our cause. He will bring the others."

Auriel nodded. She finished her meal and wiped what remained of Mr. Kowalski off her face with a tissue from her pocket. "I am ready, my lord."

Eagerly, Lucifer closed his eyes, and Auriel understood he was sending his call through shadow, a talent he alone possessed. The Devil owned the stuff Watchers were made of. Once he connected with the thumbprint of Damien's black heart, he would pull his essence into his presence. The call could not be refused.

Auriel wasn't at all surprised when three funnels of darkness channeled into the conference room. The brothers always stuck together. She surveyed the brood as one by one they fully formed. Their massive shoulders seemed to fill the open space around the table, despite this being the largest conference room in the building. She'd forgotten how formidable the Wicked Brethren could be.

Damien's gray-green eyes narrowed with suspicion. Dressed in a business suit the color of money and Italian loafers, he looked like the typical executive. Auriel's eyebrow arched when she noticed his dark hair was peppered with gray. His appearance, like all of the Watchers, was an illusion. He didn't *have* to have gray hair or slight wrinkles around his eyes if he didn't want them. But why would he want them? Upon further thought, she remembered Damien's particular vice was greed. Perhaps his appearance facilitated his priorities, this illusion serving him well in the business world. Rumor had it he was exceedingly rich and even owned a castle in Romania.

Next to him, the lustful Asher turned his bright smile her way, his movie star good looks giving Auriel a warm, melty feeling. His sandy blond coif, wild on top and short on the sides, made his aqua eyes dazzle. She knew it was an illusion, but somehow Asher wore it better than the rest.

Near the back of the room, the silk-shirt wearing Levi checked his jeweled rings to ensure he hadn't lost any in his travels. He was wearing a decidedly Greek illusion these days, with longer dark waves and olive skin. Levi's vice was envy and thus he was the least predictable. The only certainty was his desire to obtain whatever anyone else had, whatever that might be.

"You called," Damien said, straightening his suit and adjusting the shiny watch on his wrist.

"Yes, I did. I am in need of your services."

"The brethren are very busy, my lord. We cannot offer you our assistance at this time."

"I'm not asking, Damien. I'm enlisting you," Lucifer said in a deadly quiet voice.

Damien stepped back. "Now is not a good time. I respectfully decline."

"I respectfully do not accept your decision," Lucifer growled.

"Why us? Why now?"

"The apocalypse needs you. If I am to win this challenge—and if I win, you win, Damien—I require your assistance."

Levi groaned, throwing his head back and spinning in the swivel chair where he'd taken up residence. He'd hooked one tall boot over the arm of his seat and looked decidedly pirate-like. "Sounds like a lot of work. Why should you get to call the shots after all these years, Lucifer? The Wicked Brethren have done splendidly on our own for centuries. Find someone else to help you." He waved a hand in the air.

With a growl, Lucifer extended one hand and clenched it into a fist. Levi stopped spinning. The demon writhed in pain, face reddening as his hands gripped his neck.

"You have done fine on your own, Levi, because I have allowed it," Lucifer said. "Do not forget that I own the very stuff you are made of, down to your black heart." He flicked his hand open, and the demon flew out of the chair and smashed against the back wall, his overdeveloped muscles leaving a dent before he slumped to the floor.

Damien's eyes shifted from his brothers to Lucifer. "What is in it for us?"

It always came down to greed with Damien. The sin was both his greatest strength and weakness. This was good. Lucifer had taught Auriel that a servant with no desires couldn't be properly motivated. One thing about the Wicked Brethren, their desires were as strong as their physiques.

"If you help me, and I win the challenge, you will become Earth's princes. Each of you will be given your own domain to rule as you will, and all of the riches of that domain will be yours."

Sprawled on the floor where he'd fallen, Levi started to snore. Asher, who had strutted across the room to Auriel's side, turned toward the brother and laughed. "Seems Levi could do without ruling anything."

"Levi," Damien said. The brother stopped snoring and got to his feet, brushing himself off.

"This conversation bores me," Levi said.

Auriel could sense Damien fighting with himself as his eyes darted between Levi and Asher. Was freedom such a strong motivator?

"Nothing compares to serving Lucifer, Damien. It is its own reward," she said.

Lucifer grinned at her comment. "Come, my pet," he said to her. He wrapped one arm around Damien's shoulders, and then took Auriel's hand. At the moment her fingers touched his, smoke swallowed the three of them, wicking them from Harrington to a rooftop in the sky. Auriel gasped at the grandeur of the panoramic view.

"Where are we?" Damien asked.

"The roof of the Empire State Building."

"Why?" Damien stared across New York City, pursing his lips as if this side trip was highly inconvenient.

"Only to show you all that could be yours." Lucifer motioned toward the city with his open hand.

Auriel stiffened. She'd been promised the world. Was not New York part of the world?

"The city of New York?" Damien clarified.

"And every other major city. You will be my second. The world and all the riches in it will be yours. When I win, you can bathe in the jewels of the humans you eat for lunch."

His second? Auriel was his second. She clenched her fists at her sides.

Damien's battleship-green eyes reflected the city. He licked his lips. "The world economy, all the money in all the world, will be mine to rule autonomously," Damien said, not a question but a demand.

"Of course. But all or nothing. You must convince your brothers to join me as well or no deal."

Damien clasped his hands behind his back, his face growing stony with thought. Auriel found herself wishing he'd say no, suddenly threatened by the Wicked Brethren's presence. Her wishing was futile.

"Consider it done," Damien said.

Lucifer's self-satisfied grin said it all. He reached out a hand and sealed the deal with a firm handshake.

A strange foreboding made Auriel's insides itch as she watched the arrangement, but there was no going back. Cord had been replaced.

About the Author

G.P. Ching is the bestselling author of The Soulkeepers Series and Grounded. She specializes in cross-genre YA novels with paranormal elements and surprising twists. The Soulkeepers was named a 2013 iBookstore Breakout Book.

G.P. lives in central Illinois with her husband, two children, and a Brittany spaniel named Riptide Jack. Learn more about G.P. at www.gpching.com and more about The Soulkeepers Series at www.thesoulkeepersseries.com.

Follow G.P. on:
    Twitter: @gpching
    Facebook: G.P. Ching
    Facebook: The Soulkeepers Series

Sign up for her exclusive newsletter at www.gpching.com to be the first to know about new releases!

The greatest compliment you can give an author is a positive review. If you've enjoyed this title, please consider reviewing it at your place of purchase.

Acknowledgements

Once again, this book is only possible due to the help of a number of dedicated individuals. Big literary hugs go out to authors Karly Kirkpatrick and Angela Carlie, who have come on this journey with me from the very beginning and catch little things about Paris and the Soulkeepers that even I forget sometimes. I could not do what I do without you guys. Also, thanks to Elizabeth Kasper for her fresh eyes.

Heather Crabtree, thank you for being an amazing editor. Thank you to Steven Novak of Novak Illustration for filling in on short notice when my regular cover artist became ill. I think the cover embodies the spirit of the Soulkeepers series.

And finally, thank you to my husband and family for helping me carve out the time necessary to make this novel happen.

Book Club Discussion Questions

1. There were several ways God could have dealt with Lucifer's tirade over Fatima's role in Dane's transformation. Why do you think God issued the challenge?

2. If the scorekeeper were real, how do you think the scales would look right now?

3. Are there things in your life that remind you of Elysium? Discuss.

4. Lucifer does great evil by disguising it as good. Which do you think is worse, someone who does wrong publicly and gets away with it or someone who disguises their wrongdoing? Why?

5. After everything she'd been through, why do you think it was so difficult for Katrina to admit she was addicted to Elysium? Do you see a comparison to the Soulkeepers' resistance to leave Eden?

6. If you were imprisoned by Lucifer in the way Abigail was, what would be the hardest part for you?

7. Both Lucifer and God use illusion when appearing before humans. How are their illusions the same or different? Why?

8. On a couple of occasions, the Soulkeepers use items gained by sinful means (Dane, the RV, Ethan's money). Gideon calls the group out on it, but Malini thinks their actions are for the greater good. What do you think?

9. Do you think the Soulkeepers did the right thing telling their families the truth? Do you think they should have done so earlier?

10. At the end of the book, Malini says that sometimes humans are at their best when things are at their worst. Do you believe this? Why or why not?

Made in the USA
Middletown, DE
29 July 2015